Sam's Boy

Geoffrey Finch

To Natalie,

With very best wishes,

Geoff,

January 2020

geoffrey.finch@ntlworld.com

ISBN: 978-1-7178-3898-8

For Marian

'Everyman's Life may be best written by himself.'

Samuel Johnson

Acknowledgements: thank you to members of my family and my good friend Pat McHugh for their invaluable help in the writing and production of this book

1

London

1772

Johnson's Court: - perched on the edge of roaring Fleet street like a beetle on a mound of dung.

'I have reached my apotheosis Frank,' he joked. 'I shall end my days here.'

Though it was not to be yet and not here. I watched him, swathed in sheets against the nightly cramps which plagued him, a monstrous sickly infant, and remembered a story from my childhood of a peasant who had caught a strange sea beast in his net and feared to set it free. Even so, he cared not for my solicitude.

'I am not helpless Frank. I thank God I can still attend to my own backside,' he said after his usual fashion.

'I thank God for it too master,' I replied and heard his customary snort.

'There are worse duties than wiping a man's arse Frank. Be thankful you will not be required to dissect my carcass when I die. Anatomy may be necessary to the advancement of science but I have known none of that trade who would not just as happily have been employed in the slaughterhouse.'

This was ever his way. He cared little for the opinions of others or indeed for those distinctions by which men set most store. I have known him ride outside on the chaise to the disgust of many who were his inferiors and it was often his custom to walk the streets late at night in despite of the rain. The welsh shrew would remonstrate in vain.

'You have a position in society Sam. Leave night wandering to thieves and whores. If there are errands to be run there's Frank with younger legs than yours and a £300 education which has at least put a tongue in his head.'

Her head quivered on its stalk, lidless eyes staring in permanent surprise like the Gorgon which master told me of. She was of legendary fierceness, dressed mostly in black, in mourning for her sight some said. Her room, on the ground floor had its door always ajar to catch the slightest movement of the household and I fancied its opening like those wondrous ear trumpets used by elderly women.

'Frank's youth ma'am is not in dispute, neither is his education, which I consider well worth the expense,' master replied. 'But you must consider that I am a man, and a man does not take kindly to interference.'

I was glad of his rebuke. She never loved me, nor I her. She had been the first of those 'adopted' by my master and thought to rule over us all. When master's wife died she cast her eyes that way for a time but he was not such a fool to be caught by an old maid's tongue. Her voice was like the screech owl's which I have sometimes heard, in the still of the night, high above the streets. Men say they are the spirits of those who died without confessing their sins, and I do well believe it. But I am not accustomed to complain. There was latterly too much of that, and in any event my life was generally easy, though some were bent on rendering it not so. But it was true enough. Master cared not for his position. Nor mine. He would not let me dress him as other servants did, though I was called his 'valet'. Ill-fitting gaiters, loose, heavily stained frock coat, and battered wig were his customary apparel. The Colonel, at his lowest ebb, would never have appeared so before a servant. And for Johnson's Court, it was but cramped and meanly furnished in the manner of a cheap lodging house. This put me to much loss of face particularly before those who enjoyed my discomfiture. Soubise, could not believe such meanness when first he visited me.

'This is low indeed Francis. Your master lives like a dog. I wonder that you bear it.'

He traced his finger in the dust along the arm of a chair. Powdered wig, polished shoe buckles. Of late he had taken to wearing a sword, which much became him.

'He holds such things in scorn,' I replied.

'It must be the duty of a good servant to persuade him otherwise. How else can you hold up your head. When I joined my Lord of Queensberry's household it was his practice to change his linen too infrequently. I observed to my Lady that men were talking. Since then he is as delicate in his person as any courtesan.'

'Lord Queensberry cares what others think of him.'

'So does any man of sense.'

I shook my head.

'Take my word your master is as vain as any,' said Soubise. 'He thinks to subdue men by his learning. But what care they for that. I have heard my Lord speak mightily of his Dictionary yet has he never opened so much as a page and thinks too high a price is set on it.'

Soubise took a kerchief from his sleeve. 'He is laughed at Francis and so are you. They say only a black could dress a man so.'

He tossed the term casually towards me as if it had been a plaything and despite myself I flinched, as he knew I would. My colour was a constant reproach, his was not. Soubise had been taken into the household of the Queensberry's as a small child, and had been fortunate in becoming the favourite of his mistress, the Duchess. It was rumoured she could deny him nothing and, though a servant, he lived the life of a gentleman. Things were not so with me, as the shrew was constantly at pains to make clear.

'That boy has ideas above his station,' she said. 'If you had not taken him in he would have been shipped back. What need have you of a servant? We are all ready to serve you here.'

She was right, as always. Besides herself there was Agnes, her maid, a Scottish girl of eighteen whom she scolded night and day and who answered her in a tongue thick with obscurities, like the lumps in cook's porridge. And there was Dr Levet besides, a thin, middle-sized man with a corrugated face who my master liked I believe because he was as ill-dressed as he and whose profession as a physician involved a deal of walking from which he would often return drunk. All could do as much for him, and more, than I.

'You forget Anna that Frank is a free man. The Colonel provided for that in his will. He cannot be shipped back as you say,' replied my master.

3

'Man indeed. He's no more than a boy. And you spoil him. There's Hodge in need of oysters for his meal and Frank is too high and mighty to be sent.'

'Frank is employed to wait on me not on my cat.'

'He is not employed in anything Sam. He spends his days in idleness, gossiping with that worthless blackamoor, who fancies himself one of the nobility.'

'Frank has one great virtue, ma'am,' said my master with feeling. 'He knows when to hold his tongue.'

So it continued. The household was seldom free from wrangling and turmoil. My recourse at such times was to fancy how things might have been in my native country among those of my own kind. But such indulgences were weak and profitless. I had no memories that I cared to recall. Others could remember something, a parent's voice, a snatch of song. But my mind was veiled. I was not ungrateful for this. The tales though fond to the teller were often tedious to the listener. I knew not why I had been spared their sickly power. I asked my master about this.

'Memory is a treacherous ally Frank. It seldom recalls those things which give us pleasure. Be thankful for its absence.'

I had slave memories of course. Those we all had. The life of sprawling compounds, of heat, hunger, and fever. But of my parents, nothing. The Colonel told me my mother died on the voyage to Jamaica. A common enough fate. She left me a chain of silver, fashioned after the manner, so I am told, of her tribe. Of my father I knew nothing.

'Colonel Bathurst became a father to you Frank,' said my master. 'You were fortunate. Slave orphans are not a valuable commodity.'

He spoke true. There was little advantage to a captain from a slave with child and I have heard that many an infant was thrown overboard. But the Colonel, for whose plantation my mother had been destined, would not have countenanced such brutality. He was my first master. His plantation stretched as far as a man could ride in a day and seemed to me the limit of the earth itself. My early years I spent fostered by a black woman of gargantuan size who left me in perpetual fear of being trodden underfoot. She would take me to the plantation at first daylight imprisoned on her back like a lizard skewered on a stick. From which I am convinced I first developed that infirmity of the lungs which has plagued me ever since. But of these days I remember little except that she was of a kindly disposition and shed tears when at last I left her. For at about five years old I was taken into the Colonel's household to learn the trade of a houseboy. It was he who gave me my European name. Of my native name I knew nothing.

We were five in number. In addition to myself and Soubise, there was Famistan, a young black in service to the Earl of Dornwood and Obadiah, a man of sixty with a skin that seemed aged in oak. Obadiah had been servant to a wealthy merchant who set him up in trade. He owned a grocer's shop in the Strand and his independence gave him straightway an advantage over us. At first, Soubise and Famistan affected to look down on his manner and address which lacked the briskness of the modern fashion. But the courtliness of his demeanour was not to be trifled with. He seemed to us like one of the ancients, dressed in a heavy serge, with worsted stockings and his flowing hair tied back in the manner of a seafaring man. The last of our group was Costano. He had been a prince in his own country and his bearing, except when darkened with much ale, could not disguise his elevation. He had been taken during a war with a neighbouring tribe and sold to a merchant when his father could not raise the ransom. The merchant brought him to England and made much of him. But by degrees he grew bitter at his situation. In London he saw other blacks, sons of wealthy princes, who had come to England as free men to be educated.

'They are free by reason of their wealth,' Obadiah said to him. 'Their fathers trade with the English.'

'My father is also wealthy' protested Costano. He had fine, pencil-sharp tribal marks which thickened when he grew angry and obscured his face. Soubise told me they were the marks of a warrior and meant to spread fear among his enemies.

'Then he did not care to buy your freedom,' replied Obadiah. 'You must have displeased him greatly for him to abandon you.'

Despite his superior birth, I was the better educated, which he never quite forgave.

'Hail the scholar,' he would greet me, rising from his chair. 'Recite for us. Something in Latin.'

Costano, who still could speak his native tongue.

'No nigger language, not that savage babble. Give us Caesar at the gates of Rome.' He would grin and push a pewter mug towards me whilst I made ready to perform.

Costano was our leader. 'Slavery exists in the mind. I am as free as those I serve,' he would tell us. We believed it, or attempted to do so.

I repeated it to my master who said, 'A noble thought, but Costano would be wise not to advertise such sentiments. All men may have their freedom though not all enjoy their liberty. There are worse situations than valet to his master.' I relayed this and for my pains saw Costano smart at this rebuff. He was quick to take offence, haughty by nature and could boast a royal lineage longer than his majesty's. Yet he ended in chains at the last. But it was because of him that I first began my quest.

It was Costano who suggested we form a club, such forms of social gathering becoming increasingly fashionable of late. My master had long boasted of his membership of the Literary club where, Mr Boswell said, if nothing else, it was possible for a man to get drunk in good company.

'Men consider us ignorant heathens,' Costano said. 'We will show them that we think as other men, and our thoughts are not the less because we are black.'

The following day I saw, with some surprise, that he had wasted no time in acting upon his idea. There, in that day's edition of *The Morning Post*, was the following notice:

The fraternity of Christian Negroes

We, who are engaged in serving the most noble citizens in the land, being of foreign, yet not ungenteel blood, having learnt the merits of living in a Christian country, wish to disperse the same more liberally by meeting to converse weekly on any topic which may enlarge understanding.
The Dog and Partridge, Fleet Street, Thursday.

The notice drew some favour and much derision, the latter particularly from the landlord of the Dog and Partridge, a sprawling, ill-favoured man, not given to libertarian sentiments, whom Costano with difficulty prevailed on to allow us the use of a back room.

'Mind there's no nigger fuss, no hollering and shrieking,' he said on the first evening. 'Don't you disturb my dogs.' He pointed a thick discoloured object at us which with surprise I saw was a finger.

Costano took the chair at our first meeting and we cast about for subjects to converse on. Captain Cook having recently embarked on his circumnavigation our talk turned to that.

'So the Royal Society has sent the good captain in search of their will-o'-the wisp again', said Costano.

'You do not believe in the existence of the southern continent?' Obadiah asked in surprise.

'Terra Australis? Travellers tales, no more. What does your master think?' Costano turned to me.

'He has little faith in the accounts of travellers. I heard him say that few books disappoint their readers more than the narrations of travellers.'

'Yet it is rumoured he intends travelling himself to the scottish islands,' said Obadiah.

'Mr. Boswell has spent many hours persuading him but the shrew is against it,' I replied.

'She would rather he journeyed to Wales I suppose,' said Soubise.

'She is against all travel. What need is there to see Scotland when there is Mr Boswell to tell you of it? she said.'

'Some truth in that,' replied Soubise. 'Boswell is a fine gentleman with a pleasing address.'

'If whoring and gaming are considered pleasing.' put in Obadiah.

'They are delightful occupations,' replied Soubise. 'And the only ones for a gentleman.'

Famistan laughed, the pink interior of his mouth opening suddenly like a cat's. Since joining the service of the Earl it had been his ambition to be as Soubise. But there was little likelihood of that. Soubise's mistress showered her favours on him. He had learnt to ride, fence, and speak French whilst his duties consisted almost wholly in attending on her as a confidante. It was never his misfortune to empty chamber pots. I remarked on this once to him and saw his face tighten into a grimace. 'You should not complain,' he said. 'Your dirty work is such as any honest man might do.'

'If your master does not care for Scotland why does he intend going there?' Famistan asked. 'Why not Italy or France?'

'He is a philosopher,' replied Costano. 'Such men journey to acquire knowledge not to amuse themselves.'

'He goes to escape the shrew and because the expense of Scotland is not so great as the Continent,' I said.

Obadiah stirred again and cleared his throat as if preparing an announcement of some consequence.

'Until I was fifteen I had not journeyed anywhere beyond my village. Then my father took me into a neighbouring country. He said I had become a man and must learn to live until the next new moon on my own. I had to hunt and fish as my forefathers had done. At the end of the time he said he would come and take me home. I waited till two new moons had passed but he did not come. So I travelled back. I found the village was deserted, except for the elderly. The slavers had taken everyone else. Shortly after that I was taken too.'

Obadiah's words fell heavily among us. It was always so. We began with gossip and ended by fetching up this dark sediment.

'We need not have gone to the trouble of hiring a room,' said Soubise angrily, 'to remind ourselves of that.'

'I fear that may be the least of our concerns,' Obadiah said.

From the outer taproom came the noise of shouting accompanied by much swearing.

'Did you not notice the landlord's manner just now?'

'The fellow's a ruffian. So are all innkeepers,' said Soubise loftily.

Obadiah ignored this. He was a sober and industrious man to whom Soubise appeared frivolous and light. We had all been drinking steadily except for him. 'I saw him earlier in the day down by the quay. I went to view a cargo. He was there talking to an officer, a lieutenant. They were discussing an action purposed in the Americas for which men will be needed.'

'Why did you say nothing of this before?' said Costano.

'I was not sure at first. When he brought in the ale just now I observed him more closely. He was counting us.'

I looked at Famistan. Alarm was written in his eyes. Being the youngest he would be pressed first.

'We cannot be taken,' said Soubise, 'our masters are known. It would occasion too much offence.'

'Soubise is right. No press would seize the servant of a gentleman.' added Costano. 'Besides we are too many.'

'Nevertheless it would be wise not to depart singly tonight,' said Obadiah.

'You at least are safe,' put in Soubise. 'They will be wanting young bucks not old stags.'

After a short while the noise in the taproom died down, but Obadiah's information had cast a gloom over us which could only be dispelled by more ale. A remedy we resorted to freely. As the evening deepened and our tongues thickened we eventually resumed our good spirits and the threat of the press assumed a greater degree of impossibility. But any pretence at enlarging our understandings was gone. The old bitterness had been loosed and it swirled in our veins like the pestilence.

'Rank and fortune are all the world cares about,' said Soubise, emptying his tankard. 'All else is cant.'

Costano nodded heavily, 'We suffer the caprices of rank and fortune, but more so because we are black. We are beneath even the servants.'

'Though our colour is not hateful to all, so I have heard', put in Famistan suddenly.

Costano looked disconcerted. 'What is this?'

Famistan smiled. His hair still had the softness of youth and had been curled in tongs giving him the appearance of a startled lamb.

'They say Soubise has enjoyed the favours of the Duchess.'

'If I have, what of that?' said Soubise. 'You will find that women do not like their white husbands. Their Lords are weak in bed and think to govern them by force. But they are subtle and know where to find pleasure. Ask Francis he will tell you.'

'An adventure Francis? Tell us,' demanded Famistan. His gaze rested lightly on me and I sensed the echo of a taunt.

'It is nothing,' I replied. 'At least it must remain so to you and anyone else.'

I was annoyed at Soubise. I wondered how he could know of the episode. But there was little of which he was ignorant. It was one of those incidents, trivial in themselves, by which I first became aware how I was regarded among women. I cut a poor figure and had determined never to speak of it. But the company were of a different mind and would not let the matter rest. The general feeling was in favour of some entertainment even if at my expense and, as for me, so careless had I grown of public report that despite myself I yielded. I was to perform again

The incident had occurred some years before, about the time of haymaking, in mid-summer, when the evenings were long and fine. Master had taken me with him into Lincolnshire to visit an old friend who owned an estate with several farms. One day some of the labourers fell sick and master said, 'Frank will assist. He can do the work of a dozen of your men'. This was not a proposal I rejoiced in, but I concluded that my master had business to conduct which did not require my presence. He had of late seemed more anxious and burdened than I had known him to be.

The day was exceeding hot and when I joined the labourers in the field many had discarded their shirts. Some, to my consternation, were women. Though they had not gone so far as to offend modesty by disrobing, a few of the younger sort had tucked up their skirts, even to their waists and their upper garments hung loose about them. They looked on with merriment as I took off my shirt and began binding the corn. All about me men and women were working familiarly, like companionable beasts and I thought of drawings I had seen of feeding herds on the plains of my parents' country. After a short time my skin burned with moisture and its sour smell reeked in my nostrils. I drew a kerchief from my pocket and began wiping my face and neck. It was then I saw one of the younger women look over at me, most particularly. She was of middle stature, with long brown hair held up by a pin on the crown of her head which as she worked swayed like a wave. I had noticed her earlier and fancied to myself what would happen should her hair break free, but though it swelled and rose continually it stayed bound by its restraint.

About noon-time we rested for a while and the women passed round loaves of bread and portions of a hard, thick-rinded cheese. I was hungry and ate eagerly. Absorbed thus, I did not notice her standing above me till a hand brushed my shoulder. I turned and met her gaze. It was frank and free, like that of street-walkers in London. She was bending towards me holding in her hand a small cask full of dark liquid. The other women looked on, a few paces distant, pretending to eat, whilst the men smiled and swilled back the liquor. I drank thirstily as a drowning man gulps at air and felt the liquid at first cool and sweet but afterwards like fire in my veins. Through the long afternoon we toiled and on, into the evening, until my limbs grew heavy and my tongue swelled from the dust. When we stopped at last, I was parched more than before and drank yet more liberally. I remember little of what followed except waking from a deep slumber some hours hence with the chill wind of sunset on my skin, and a face close to mine. I started up in consternation and saw it was her, lying crumpled like a child, her hair loose to the waist and, more disquieting, my lower garments all undone, my manhood exposed to common view.

Master was much merry with me about this circumstance and spared me not before the company.

'What is this Frank? Cannot poor country females perform their rural duties in peace but you must be debauching them in the fields?' He turned to Bennet Langton, for it was he. 'I apologise for pressing Frank into your service sir. Had I known he should prove a scandal to public decency I would have kept him quietly within doors.'

'I believe no harm was done,' replied Langton, smiling at me. 'The women, so I am informed, were to blame. They were curious about his person and wished to see if the colour was uniform in other parts.'

'Parts,' roared my master. 'Observe what danger comes from having parts Frank.'

'They did not attempt possession it appears' said Langton. 'Frank has his virtue still. Matters could have fared worse. They forebore whitening.'

Master observed him with an air of interrogation. He had a deal of curiosity. I have heard him say on more than one occasion that to a man of sense everything is information. Langton well knew this weakness.

'What foolery is this Sir? Whitening?

'No foolery I assure you. It was a belief among the rurality until very recently that a blackamoor's colour is only superficial. A few years ago an experiment was tried upon a poor fellow, the servant of a gentleman of the sugar trade. He had the misfortune to be the first negro seen in these parts. By some means he was persuaded his skin should be whitened. The experiment was encouraged by his owner, a man of inveterate malice, who told the villagers he had seen a blackamoor's skin blistered with boiling sugar in the Indies whence it had returned to its native white. Needless to say, on this occasion the trial was not successful and the man was left deprived of his wits and a generous amount of his skin. The perpetrators narrowly avoided the law and only escaped because the blackamoor had been willing.'

'They were not entirely at fault,' replied my master. 'Many advances in scientific knowledge have proceeded from experiments no less the consequence of ignorance. This cannot excuse the gentleman, however, who well knew the uselessness of the attempt and was willing to cause pain merely for amusement. But it does not surprise me. I have long held plantation owners to be among the most depraved of our species.'

This incident persuaded me that I must be a person of very little consequence even to the children of toil but my comfort was that even Soubise would have been treated in like manner. The following morning, however, a strange occurrence cast me in yet greater confusion. We were embarking on the coach for Leamington when I observed a girl appear in the press of people alongside. To my mortification she was the same brown haired girl who had disrobed me. I was instantly alarmed, but as she did not look in my direction I began to think her attention was engaged elsewhere. Our company consisted of a couple in middle years, who I judged to be in trade, two young well-favoured ladies accompanied by their brother, and a stiff featured man with the sorrowful air of a parson. Shortly after noon the coach set off and I concluded I had been mistaken in assigning any untoward motive to the girl's presence. But as the horses rounded the first bend there came a shout from the coachman to clear the way. I looked out and saw her stepping forward into the path of the moving carriage, her hand raised. The coachman uttered a violent oath and then a small bundle fell into my lap. My fellow passengers were at first fearful. It had been but two days since an attempt was made to halt the stage at Stoke by a man who ignited some cloths under the horses' feet. Their fears were assuaged, however, on discovering the article to be a sheaf of corn fashioned in the shape of a man.

The parson, for such indeed he was, took it upon himself to address the company and let fall an observation about country manners, whereupon master who had been steadfastly perusing a book the while looked up. He was ever poor sighted and not seeing at first the figure thought himself the object of unwonted attention.

'Do you address yourself to me sir?'

'I was remarking to the company,' the man began gravely, 'on the stubbornness of country superstitions.'

Master followed the man's gaze and saw the figure lying in my lap, for I had not dared disturb it. Soubise had told me of those in his home village who possessed great power and could injure others through such figures. I wondered how I could have offended the girl that she should wish me harm.

'Outside London and the great cities sir,' he continued, 'the land is heathen. I fancy your servant knows more of their ways than do we.'

'You flatter his understanding,' replied my master. 'Frank knows no more of heathen customs than by all accounts do you, else you would know that cities are their chief resort. A man is safer on the plains of Africa than in the alleys of Whitechapel.'

The parson, seemingly unused to opposition, looked at master as one opening a parcel and discovering a venomous occupant.

'I am amazed you maintain that sir. A man may be physically safer, but what of his soul?'

'A man's soul is more in peril in London than anywhere else on earth, excepting perhaps the Americas.'

The parson stung to the quick attempted to pass off the rebuff. Addressing the young ladies most particularly he said with heavy good humour, 'We are sharing our carriage with a follower of Rousseau I fear.'

Master glared. 'We need not Rousseau to inform us that cultivated nations are no more advanced in moral sentiment than their savage relations.'

The parson paused briefly, and then made a cursory bow.

'I fear it is idle to argue further. I give way to you sir on this occasion.'

'You abandon your cause too easily,' master replied. 'I could give you several good reasons to the contrary.'

'I have no doubt of it, but I owe it to my cloth to shun fruitless contention.'

'A jade's trick,' murmured master taking up his book again in much bad humour.

I journeyed to Leicester in great trepidation after this not daring to touch the figure, lest it should occasion more attention. By degrees, however, I fancied a sensation of heat in my groin. This was at first not unpleasant but after a few miles turned to burning. I thought the company must notice my discomfort and attempted to stretch my legs so that it would fall to the carriage floor. But the corn was of such newness that it clung fast to the fabric and I began to fear lest it should take fire with the heat. I saw the young ladies fix their gaze on me and their eyes seemed to inflame it further. Matters came to such a pitch that I could not help calling out, at which my master raised his head from his book and straightway divining the cause of my distress took hold of the figure and flung it from the coach.

'T'is nought but a love token Frank', he said.

On an instant the burning ceased, of which I was most heartily glad. From this occurrence arose that unfortunate story that I had somehow bewitched a country maiden who had pursued me to the metropolis.

Raised voices, much louder than before, and the sound of tables being overturned, greeted the end of my narrative.

'Someone has taken too much liquor,' said Costano. 'It need not concern us.'

Prolonged banging on the door interrupted him. And then what we feared most to hear. The shrill cry of 'press' repeated like the holla which greets the sighting of a fox. For a moment we remained immobile unconcerned almost about our fate. And then pandemonium broke loose. The door burst open and a surge of faces slack-jawed with drink fell into the room and quickly surrounded us. Borne aloft by this tidal wave we were tossed like flotsam towards the taproom from where the heaviest sounds of violence proceeded. And then, as we were driven towards its centre, the crowd parted and became silent. I felt a fist push me firmly from behind and half stumbling I emerged into a ring of faces illuminated with merriment. In the middle was the landlord. I turned and saw beside me Soubise, Costano and the others, confused and shaken.

'What trick is this?' demanded Costano, the first of us to collect himself.

'A 'flush,' jeered the landlord. 'A flush of niggers. There are gentlemen from The King's Navy who wish to talk with you.'

'You are surrendering us to the press?'

'Aye. Niggers have no business pretending to be gentlefolk. The lieutenant asked whether there were any here who would do their duty. I told him the fraternity of Christian niggers would oblige.'

Upon that there was a burst of clapping followed by laughter and we found ourselves thrust through the doors of the tavern. Outside we were seized on by four thick-set men armed with clubs who manacled us to each other. I looked in the eyes of Obadiah and saw resignation and despair. Even Costano hung his head. As for Soubise he flounced and paraded until struck from behind and stripped of his wig and sword. We were taken at a trot down to the docks until suddenly the troupe halted and the senior of the men came forward. In the starlight I could make out the insignia of a lieutenant.

'You are not for us tonight,' he said suddenly and bending down he undid our shackles.

Famistan began to weep softly, thinking some greater evil was in store. Costano stared blankly forward smarting with shame.

'What then, are we free?' I asked in disbelief.

The lieutenant looked briefly at me as if some nuisance had attached to his shoe.

'Go home and keep to your station. Your masters have not deserved that you should play the fool.'

He signalled to his men and they disappeared silently into the gloom. We stood for a moment in complete silence like guests left standing at a party and then turned dejectedly towards home.

'Why did he let us go?' asked Famistan.

'We have been the sport of some private amusement. These men were paid to do this,' I said.

'The landlord shall be whipped for his part in it,' said Soubise.

Obadiah shook his head.

'We shall seem more foolish. Let us say nothing.'

We had come to the parting of our ways. I stopped and gazed up Fleet street. It was a chill morning. From the ditch a light winked mercilessly. Towards St Paul's the night-soil men were finishing their loathsome business. I was seized by a desperate loneliness. It wrapped itself around me like the knowledge of death.

'We are as ticks which live on the hides of cattle,' I said.

Obadiah grunted, 'But it is the ticks which survive.'

We made our farewells and I was already on my way up the street when Costano came after me and drew me aside. He put his face close to mine and I felt the sour breath of ale fan my cheek.

'You have better fortune than you know.'

I looked at him in some surprise.

'Ask your master about the Colonel.'

'To what purpose?'

'Just ask,' he said and then was violently sick.

2

*S*ummoned to master's bedchamber.

'Frank, you are to assist Levet here. He has not enough blood. He wishes to take mine'

He spoke feebly, scarcely above a whisper, as if from a great distance. He had been ill for days. His breathing laboured and harsh like an old bellows. The shrew scolded him on his return from Mrs Thrale's.

'You are a fool to yourself Sam. Why do you stay so long at that house?'

'Because they do not fuss ma'am.'

'You prefer the attention of servants and maids. That's the truth of it. But they will not nurse you properly.'

'You are scarce in a condition to nurse yourself ma'am let alone others.'

This was true. She had of late become a sickly thing. Far into the night her dry, goat-like coughs, would echo through the house. Agnes shared her room and complained bitterly.

'A body canna sleep. Tis naything but coff coff all night.'

Agnes had the worst of it, peevishness and bad temper as well, though none escaped absolutely. Master let her govern in his absence, a task she undertook as dutifully as they say Hercules did his labours. Every weekend when he returned to us from Streatham she would render an exact account of household affairs.

'You must hold your master's arm Frank whilst I draw off the excess blood.'

I edged further into the room and observed a kerchief tied tightly around his forearm which made the vein bulge out like the lining of his flesh.

'Must you lose more blood master?'

'There is nought to be frightened of. This will steady my nerves, from which I have suffered much. After which my breathing should return to its normal regularity.'

'Yes master,' I replied, and took his arm.

His nerves, if such they were, had been excessive of late. His face contorting itself in a strange chewing motion and his arms jerking violently as if warding off an assailant.

'The Thrales were concerned for me. I fancy their guests thought they were dining with an inhabitant from Bedlam,' he wheezed.

'Rich food is not advisable in your condition. It thickens the blood and excites the nerves,' said Levet.

'A circumstance of which Henry Thrale is singularly unaware. He consumed enough for a battalion of Guards and exhibited less excitement afterwards than a dead cat.'

'I would be happier sir, if you exhibited less yourself at this moment,' replied Levet, opening a lancet.

Streatham was master's retreat. I had on earlier occasions been allowed to accompany him but he had latterly obliged me to stay at Johnson's Court.

'I have no need of your services there Frank,' he said. 'And besides I fear you are falling into idle company. Mrs Thrale's servants consider themselves fine fellows but I cannot keep you in the style to which they are accustomed.'

'I have heard it said, master, that a servant's duty is to maintain the honour of the house in his dress and manner.'

'Mere cant. Popinjays all of them Frank. As you would be if I let you strut about in satin breeches and a powdered wig.'

'Powder is sometimes necessary master when the wig has seen much service.'

'You young dog. You would smoke me would you. That is a privilege reserved for Bozzy. Come sir would you see an old friend provoked in this manner?'

Mr Boswell stirred from where he sat legs apart, head hanging like a wilted flower on his chest. He lifted his eyes and blew out his cheeks in a huge sigh.

'Francis is in the right of it sir. Your wig is commonly thought a disgrace as you yourself know. Mrs Thrale tells me she has resorted to handing you a decent one before you enter the company.'

'It pleases her to do so,' replied master.

'And I have never been one to interfere with the pleasures of others provided they are innocent, as I can see by your present demeanour that yours have not been.' '

I have already received admonishment from Mrs Williams. She has much in common with my father and thinks to cure me by nagging.'

'You see Frank the consequences of idleness. I wish only to keep you from temptation.'

I knew, of course, what he meant. Mr and Mrs Thrale had female servants. And not crabbed and unkempt as ours. But ladies' maids, serving girls, with fair skins and sweet-smelling clothing. They made much of me on my first visit there and I amused them with tales of my Master's household. Their curiosity was greatest over Poll, our latest. A tongue shrill as cockcrow and foul as the Fleet ditch. Master had brought her back one evening slumped over his shoulder at which Dr Levet protested in his own careless way.

'You are undertaking my work as well as your own now?' he said eyebrows raised.

'She requires nothing that a night's sleep will not provide. The wench is drunk Levet.'

Dr. Levet lifted her head and surveyed the vacant features. She had been pretty once. '

Smallpox. Spoilt her trade I fancy. Throw her back sir. A gaudy tulip sprung from dung.' He grimaced in disgust.

'You were not always so fastidious Levet.'

I recognised her as did Dr. Levet. She was one of those who frequented the alley close to the Benbow, an inn of low repute. On occasions when my errands took me that way I had to run the gauntlet of their attentions. But she always hung back, whether through natural reserve, or disinterest in my person, I could not tell.

'A poor unfortunate,' I heard him say to the shrew. 'It is us or the Bridewell.'

'Sam,' she replied, in a low tone, 'Is this wise? The girl is a slut.'

'It is merely for one night ma'am, possibly two.'

But of course it wasn't. It never was. And in time master learnt to rue his benevolence.

'Support the arm over the bowl Frank and be so good as to close your mouth. I have no wish to alarm the patient. It is a simple enough procedure.'

Dr. Levet flourished the lancet briefly and then drew it lightly, like a painter making a brushstroke, across master's forearm. A thin line of blood bubbled to the surface and began to course down the cheeks of his elbow. I remembered Costano telling me how as a boy he had been taken into a hut by the elders and held while the marks of the tribe were cut into his face. I glanced further up master's arm and saw several scars, many of them recent.

'Does it not seem strange to you Levet that you have the power should you wish it to end my life with a single stroke.'

'Nothing would be easier my dear sir. There lies your life. Frank holds it in his hand.'

We looked at the bowl filling slowly, and growing darker, like a bruise.

'If we do not stanch the flow then I shall indeed have killed you.'

'You confirm my belief Levet that medicine is wrongly termed an art. The same service performed on animals is called butchery.'

Mr Boswell who all this time had seemed bored by the proceedings rose to his feet and went over to the small fire burning in the grate. It was not a cold day but the shrew had insisted on a fire: 'Streatham Place is very fine, but its corridors are draughty. Frank can stir himself and make a fire.'

So I did, which caused us to sweat and cough uncomfortably. Mr Boswell stretched out his hands even so.

'Does not the thought of death fill you with horror?' he asked suddenly.

'How's this Bozzy? Are the effects of your debauch receding?'

'You will never take me seriously. You join with my father in thinking me frivolous.'

'There's little I join with your father in. He considers me an evil influence. Come sir let's have no more of this hang-doggery. You know I love you to excess. As to your question, no rational man can die without uneasy apprehension. But I think on this occasion Levet may strive to save me.'

'You are patched up for a while longer,' said Levet, 'and may toss and gore a few more people.'

I watched him wipe the lancet on a cloth and place it in a leathern wallet. Despite his advancing years and fondness for the bottle he was most careful of his instruments. Once, when I had but newly entered master's house, he caught me touching his crucible. I had seen tongues of fire escaping from it in a strange and magical fashion. Green and blue flashes, like a rainbow on fire. He took me by the ear and thrusting my face close to the opening said,

'I have a nostrum here which calls for the skin of a young nigger. Perhaps you will oblige me Frank?'

He was the first in the house to use that term, though I never resented it of him. But I avoided his room afterwards and he would amuse himself by affecting to study my skin closely.

Dr Levet was a gaunt and withered man. I fancied him like a twig and expected when he bent down to hear him snap. Mr. Boswell jested that dining with him was like dining with a corpse, though a corpse was better company. But master would not hear a word against him. It was impossible to think he could inspire passion in the fair sex, but some years before he had been briefly married. She was a pretty woman, though not handsome like my Betsy, and much younger than him. Many men looked admiringly at her, even my master. Levet said she was heiress to a fortune though why such a one should be homeless I could never understand. One day the shrew came home in a fury, having come upon the lovers in a coal shed off Fetter Lane

'You must speak to him Sam. It's a disgrace. In common view.'

Later that evening, when Dr Levet came home, I heard them, their voices sharp and sour. Master had been intent on remonstrating with him, but the doctor was before him and announced roundly that he would marry the woman. The bellow which followed startled the cat I had been comforting so that she scratched my face.

'She's a whore Levet. A streetwalker. If you must use her, do so as Mr.Boswell does her kind. A man does not marry such a woman.'

'A man may not, but I shall. She is no street walker but a woman who has fixed her unfortunate affections on me. Does that surprise you sir?'

'As little as does the certainty that she seeks to profit by the alliance. Does she know you are without means?'

'If I recollect aright you were in the self-same position when you married Mrs Johnson.'

'Mrs Johnson did not get a good bargain with me, it is true. A man generally wrongs a woman by marrying her. You will be the exception Levet. Your wife's creditors will be knocking at the door e're long. With Mrs Johnson they were mine.'

I knew master would be stung by Levet's talking of his wife. Her death hung ever about him like a sentence over a condemned man. It was but two weeks after she was buried that I entered the household. I thought then that I had been sent to an asylum. The house was in continual darkness, the shutters down and but three candles burning. Master kept to his room and scarce could look at me. The shrew, haunted everywhere, like a harpy. She asked me if I knew why I was there. I answered that I was to serve my new master as I had my old. She nodded and said my master was distraught with the loss of a perfect wife, and if he should say anything in the transport of grief I was to ignore it.

Dr. Levet knew better. I heard him say to Mrs Thrale on one occasion that she was drunk and killed herself by taking opium. As for his own wife, master was right, of course. Within four months the doctor was in hiding, and his wife, discovering his poverty, had left him. He was spared further embarrassment by her being taken up for picking pockets and transported.

Once master was comfortable Dr. Levet left the chamber and Mr Boswell, sobered by the operation we had witnessed, returned to the subject he had started.

'I have heard it said sir, that a wise man does not fear death because death is nothing, and how can we fear nothing?'

'You will find those who profess to believe that are deceiving themselves,' replied my master, 'They confound annihilation, which is certainly nothing, with the apprehension of it, which is truly dreadful. For a man would rather exist than not.'

'But we can surely hope for salvation?'

'Indeed but salvation is founded on repentance and obedience and no man can be sure he has performed either of these duties sufficiently to obtain it.'

'So there is no benefit in being a king rather than a peasant.'

'There lies the great wonder of it. A king may derive some comfort from his pleasures but he must face the same end and is no better equipped for it by his wealth. Indeed the scriptures teach us the reverse. You and I are not better than Frank here. He is our equal. As indeed is the lowest criminal. '

'If that is so then should we not open the prisons and abolish all rank and distinction?'

'We must live with our imperfections Jamie as best we can and hope for mercy. You are troubled by the excesses of the night. They sit heavily upon you. Be thankful you do not have weightier sins to trouble you. If I could exchange my conscience for yours I would do so willingly.'

'You are kind, as ever, sir.'

Master grunted then looked over at me. I was still holding the bowl and a small towel, heavily stained.

'There is no need to stay Frank. You have performed an invaluable service.'

I left the room and made my way downstairs. On the first landing the door of a bedroom stood open. Inside I saw the figure of a woman. Her back was toward me, but I recognised her as Poll. Her skirt was slightly raised and she was straightening a petticoat. She heard me on the stair and turned her head.

'D' you like what you see blackie?'

She had taken to calling me that having heard Agnes use it in sport once.

'I can show you a bit more if you want.' She turned round and raised her skirt higher. I saw a flash of thigh and felt the bowl shake a little.

'You'll be thrown out Polly if Mrs Williams sees you.' I said, keeping my voice low.

'I couldn't give a fart. That welsh bitch would've jumped your master long ago if he'd have had her.'

From below stairs I heard a noise. It was almost the hour at which master took his afternoon tea with her.

'He is too religious to think such things.' I said.

Her lips curled slightly and she seemed about to say something. Then her gaze fell on the bowl I was carrying.

'If you're collecting those you can take mine.'

She bent down quickly and withdrew a chamber pot from under the bed.

'Empty your own pisspot.' I said and carried on downstairs.

At the bottom the shrew caught me. I felt her eyes settle on me like black beetles. She could tell from the slightest sound what was going on in the house.

'What are you doing Frank?

'Assisting my master madam.'

'Very well but I will not have you idling. You have work to do.'

I saw her nose quivering as she smelt the blood and I fancied for a moment that she would seize and drink it. 'You may think you are clever Frank, but I am sharper than you. No good will come of hussies like that.'

'Master has said we should show her charity.'

'You're a fool. Go and throw that away. Then you are to help Agnes set out the tea things.'

Her room was larger than those upstairs. Even so, it appeared more cramped and confined. Inside were two beds, a small one, like a cot, in which she slept and a made-up bed consisting of a mattress lying loosely on the floor, for Agnes. Between the two was draped a thin curtain which afforded a meagre privacy. In one corner of the room was a dressing table with but two objects on it. The first a heavily ornamented bible which lay open at a different page each day, and the second a portrait of a bearded sea-faring man who looked out on the room as if on a foreign shore on which he had been marooned. Most of the space was taken up by piles of books, from floor to ceiling. The shrew was a hoarder of literature. In her youth she had thought to be an author and wrote some poems but finding they did not take abandoned the project. Master said she had a fine mind but spoiled by narrow circumstances and disappointment.

Agnes and I laid out the cups, saucers, jugs of milk and hot water on a small table in front of the hearth.

'I canna mind the deal of tea they drink,' she said. 'It wadna dee in Scotland.'

Agnes had small fierce eyes which misted over at the mention of her own home. When first she joined the house no one could understand her, though Mr. Boswell professed to.

'Bozzy will translate for us,' said master. 'He has lived long enough among the barbarians to know their language.'

'I was reminded by a clergyman,' replied Mr. Boswell heatedly, 'that God made Scotland.'

'Indeed so sir, but he also made hell. And we must remember that he made it for scotsmen to live in.'

This proved too much for Agnes who could contain herself no longer.

'It wasna hell until the sassenach came. The duke of Cumberland an' his butchers. Ma faither forced to sel' and leave his ain hame. It wasna right.'

'The lassie has the truth of it Jamie, and she has answered me home. I think she will suit us fine. All we are wanting now is an Irish cook and we shall be a miniature kingdom.'

'Though scarce united sir,' said Mr. Boswell.

He spoke true, though it was some time before matters came to a head. By that time Agnes had been persuaded to continue as a maid only by master adding secretly to the meagre amount given her by the shrew. At tea I remained with master in case he should be taken with a fit after the loss of such a quantity of blood. They were indeed both so enfeebled that I fancied neither could wish to prolong the visit. But in that I misjudged master's appetite for company. For her part, the shrew showed such an attachment to his person that I wondered how things might have been had the intimacy between them been of a different kind.

'We are both wearing out ma'am,' said master, 'it will be a race between us I fancy.'

'I shall win it Sam. And I am glad of that. I think I have seen enough of life to know it will not improve.'

'I am sorry for it ma'am. I would not lose you.'

'Then you are in a minority Sam. But do not be troubled. I am not like Mr Boswell. Death holds no terrors for me.'

'Then I should wish you long life so you could teach the same serenity to me.'

'There's little of that in this house.' Her hand shook so that some of her tea spilled. 'Nor ever will be. Sluts and blackamoors.'

'Come, Anna let us not dwell on that. Frank, pour Mrs Williams some more tea.'

I moved towards her chair but she waved me away.

'Agnes has been reading to you from Zachariah's book again. I hope it has brought you comfort.'

I followed my master's gaze to a small leather bound book lying close to the hearth. It was a volume I knew well, as did Agnes. Her mistress had taken to demanding long sections of it being read to her on rising in the morning. Agnes complained about it regularly.

'I canna understand a word. 'Tis all degrees o' this an' degrees o' that. There's nae sense to it.'

I knew what she meant. I had peeped into it one day when the shrew was in the kitchen arguing with the cook about the evening meal. The hot sound of their anger rose up the stairs. Inside were pages of diagrams and calculations which I could have fancied as some devilish instruction had I not recognised the narrative to be my master's. The book bore the title 'An account of an Attempt to ascertain the Longitude at Sea'. It meant little to me beyond what I learnt from common gossip, but I knew it to be a book composed by my master for the shrew's father, Zachariah. I remember him as living near my master when I first entered his service in Gough square. He was exceedingly old and in poor health, though kindly towards me. In all the world he cared only for two things: his daughter, whose sight was failing, and a manuscript which he carried ever about him as some men do a keepsake. He had journeyed from Wales to London in hopes both to save his daughter's sight and make his fortune with his work. In neither was he successful. As he lay dying he fretted endlessly about the poverty inflicted on his daughter.

'The calculations must be worth something Sam. Perhaps the Admiralty could be persuaded to award me a trifle.' His eyes fastened on my master.

'I fear their Lordships are in no mind to part with their money. Even Harris may end up with nothing for his labours. Nevertheless we will see if Dodsley will publish. There are mariners enough who may value it.'

Zachariah's gaze slackened. 'Bless you Sam. For Anna, you know.'

'She shall not be forgotten. Whilst I live my home will be hers.'

And so it was. But the book, over which master laboured many long hours, was published to almost total indifference, save in the eyes of Zachariah's daughter.

'Comfort!' she said, almost choking. 'The lass is practically illiterate and has the pronunciation of a heathen.'

'I have said many times that Frank could read to you, or I, if you should wish.'

'Frank is too giddy. He cannot be relied on. And you are busy enough with Mrs Thrale.'

I was thankful on this occasion for her ill opinion. The thought of reading under her supervision excited nothing but dread. However, it was true enough that I was better able than Agnes, her education consisting simply of what her father had been able to accomplish, a man scarce literate himself. But I do not think the shrew attended to the words. She knew the text by heart and simply wished to keep her maid occupied. And in time Agnes learnt the text herself, though what it meant remained a mystery.

'Your father would have rejoiced to see the problem of the longitude finally settled ma'am. It was a great feat, and although his own endeavours did not succeed, his researches played a part in its solution.'

'He had the benefit of your own services Sam.'

My master shrugged his shoulders.

'My father was interested in curiosities and had amassed a horde of material on nautical matters,' she said. 'But he would never have accomplished its publication.'

'Curiosity is the thing itself ma'am. How many men devoted themselves to speculation about the orbit of the planets before Galileo? Would he have succeeded without their prodigal curiosity?'

'Even so Sam, I fancy there are some pursuits in which curiosity is to be guarded against.'

I heard the sharp sound of my master's chair on the floor.

'If you are alluding to my chemical experiments ' he began testily.

'I am alluding Sam, to Poll. You cannot be ignorant of the effect she is having within the house.'

'She is raw and untutored and not accustomed to the civilities of a Christian household. That is all. Give her time ma'am.'

'It is not all, Sam. Nothing can be done with a girl like that. Have you forgotten that madness with Levet? And there is Frank to consider besides.'

I felt her eyes on my back as I turned to pour more tea.

'Levet has learned his lesson, and as for Frank, I do not think his interests tend that way. No ma'am, I thank you for your concern, but my mind is made up on this matter. Poll will stay.'

The shrew made no reply. From experience she knew when it was well to remain silent. Nevertheless, from this time my master took pains to keep me under observation, frequently enquiring of me what my duties for the day might be. Indeed I owe my meeting with Betsy to his diligence. It happened after this fashion. One morning as I was tidying my master's bedchamber after the rigours of the night I heard his voice rumble from under the bedclothes.

'Leave the papers Frank. They must not be moved. They are my new penance.'

A sheaf of paper was strewn across the floor. On the topmost page in bold lettering I saw the title 'A Dictionary of the English Language in which the words are deduced from their originals'. The rumble increased in volume.

'I am to be shackled to them until Providence mercifully releases one of us.'

I was used to such moods which often presaged the beginning of any new work on which my master was engaged. Mr Boswell used to say it was the only instance of true vanity which he could discern in him. A feverish noise of linen being thrown back announced that he was attempting to sit up.

'I have been persuaded to a revision of those facts about our language which those who don't know them will scarcely be improved by acquiring. I doubt the world will be the better for knowing that 'antiferous' means 'producing ducks'.

'Mr Boswell admires the dictionary greatly master. I have heard him say it is a work of genius.'

He snorted. 'It is news to me that he has read it. Lend a hand here Frank.'

I went over to the bedside and gripped him round the waist catching as I did so the fetid smell of his bed. He could not be persuaded to let his sheets be washed above once in every month.

'Gently Frank. The ministrations of Levet are still fresh.'

I eased him into his chair where he sat looking about him with a distracted air like a large cherub.

'D'you fancy a jaunt Frank? Mrs Thrale, dear lady, has invited me to one of her gatherings this weekend.'

I nodded in silence. He was not accustomed to imparting superfluous information.

'It will please me to leave all this behind.'

He waved his hand dismissively over the scattered papers.

'And on this occasion, you may accompany me Frank, providing of course that Mrs Williams can spare you.' '

I have no objection,' said the shrew when the proposal was put to her. 'He may as well be idle at Streatham as here, I suppose. But I thought you had determined not to take him again.'

'I had ma'am but in the circumstances there may be less opportunity for mischief. And the household will be less of a burden to you in our absence.'

She gave him a glance which seemed to encompass the entire situation.

'Give my compliments to Mrs Thrale, Sam. Do not forget us entirely when you are shining in polite society.'

'I have only one home, ma'am. It is just a few days.'

So I accompanied him to Streatham, a feat which I am persuaded would not have been so simple but for the presence of Poll. Streatham Park was gravel walks, green meadows, and fine prospects. The house was as unlike our cramped accommodation as a palace to a garret. Being a servant there would have meant little to Soubise, or even Costano, accustomed as they were to fine living, but to me, I could not imagine an existence more conducive to happiness. Mr Thrale, the presiding deity of this paradise, emerged on our arrival and embraced my master warmly. A florid, jolly man, he ushered us indoors as though fearful we might change our minds and depart.

'You are most welcome, Sam. Hesther has been anticipating your arrival since before dawn. The house is in uproar sir. We have need of your good offices.'

'I had rather hoped to avoid uproar by coming here, Henry, but what little I can do I shall be glad to perform.'

'The matter is of some delicacy, Sam'.

My master frowned severely, 'Then we had better retreat to your study.'

Left to myself I ventured down to the servant's quarters. The cook was preparing dinner with three young girls who I took to be scullions. They looked up from their work and scanned me quickly, as I entered the kitchen

'There's some scraps left on the joint, if it's food your after, young man,' said the cook, a homely looking woman with red elbows, struggling with some pastry. 'Otherwise I'll thank you not to distract my girls. It's little enough they do God knows.'

Thank you ma'am. I've eaten already.'

She stopped what she was doing and observed me.

'It's ma'am is it? You'll be some fine gentleman's valet I suppose.'

One of the girls began to snigger.

'I'm Dr Samuel Johnson's manservant ma'am.'

'That's as maybe. No one calls me ma'am 'less I say so. I'm Mrs. Sharp to the likes of you.'

'It's Frank,' said one of the maids, a thin dark haired girl who could not have been above sixteen years old. From the look of recognition she gave me I saw that I had not been completely forgotten. The cook, however, continued to regard me blankly.

'It don't mean nothing to me my dear and shouldn't to you neither Lizzy. No good can come of such things.'

'Lizzy's in love with a blackamoor,' sang a girl of about the same age, her voice full of youthful spite.

Lizzy blushed angrily.

'I'm not, I'm not,' she protested, blushing more in the process.

'Leave her be, Nancy,' said the cook. 'If she starts hollering the missus'll hear and we've been told strictly by master to keep quiet.'

'Lizzy's right,' said the third, a girl with an oval face edged with auburn curls and a pretty lace cap, who I judged to be about eighteen. 'You used to come in the beginning with Mr. Johnson.'

I nodded, beginning to feel foolish. I could not recall one of them.

'You have the advantage of me, I'm afraid. I do not remember any of you. Though to be sure I would not have forgotten such handsome ladies.'

Lizzy and Nancy dissolved in a fit of giggles while the cook just glowered suspiciously.

'I'll thank you to keep such talk for upstairs. There's no airs or graces down here.'

'I meant no offence Mrs Sharp.'

I was beginning to see the significance of her name. But in truth my compliment had been aimed at only one person in the room. For the cook had long ago lost any of her female charms, and as for Lizzy and Nancy, they were scarce more than children, though I was to discover that in some things they were more than adult.

'Where I live,' I went on, 'there are no such women as you. My master surrounds himself with those who excel in piety not beauty.' An image of Poll's bare thigh flashed through my mind and I looked away in confusion.

This had the desired effect on the cook, however, who straightaway softened.

'I'll not say anything against piety but there's no getting of children from it, as my husband used to say. Men don't want preaching.'

'What do they want Mrs Sharp?' asked Nancy, sprinkling water over a new batch of pastry.

'You'll know soon enough my girl. There's many a one been in too much haste.'

'I know what Will Taylor wants,' said Lizzy. 'He told me.'

This time it was Nancy's turn to redden. Mr Taylor was head footman at Streatham, a good looking fellow, with a wife and child in a village ten miles away whom he visited every fortnight.

'Will Taylor's no business wanting anything,' said the cook. 'Nor telling anyone neither.'

'It was just a kiss.' Lizzy retorted. 'Everyone knows he's fond of Nancy.'

Nancy threw the bowl she had been holding on the table. 'Well, I'm not fond of him and you can tell him so. I'd as soon kiss a black.'

The cook took hold of Nancy by the hair and pulled hard until she squealed.

'You'll get my hand if I have any more of your nonsense. Be thankful that bowl didn't break.'

When she let go Nancy looked down silently, her face fixed in a sullen mask.

'Pay no attention to them, Frank. They're nothing but giddy girls. Betsy is the only one with sense.' She motioned towards the girl with auburn hair.

Betsy was at the sink where she had been cleaning dishes during the previous skirmish. On hearing her name she turned and glanced across at me. I was struck again by how pretty she was. The delicate curve of her chin and slope of her nose reminded me of portraits in books of famous beauties. Her skin was as smooth and white as parchment.

'Is your master well?' she asked. 'Last time he was taken poorly. But you weren't here then.'

'My master is never well. Though since he has been bled he has improved.'

The mention of blood dismayed the company. Lizzy and Nancy looked away whilst the cook began rolling the pastry with more energy.

'And is that why you are here again Frank?' asked Betsy.

The sound of my name on her lips was low and intimate. In spite of myself I felt a stirring in my loins.

'He is concerned at his condition and requires me to attend on him constantly.'

'And others too, so they say' said the cook. 'Mistress is worn out by waiting on him.'

The cook was right. I had heard of Mrs Thrale's attentions to my master. Sometimes extending far into the night, in his bedchamber.

'She is much abused by him,' she continued. 'If a man needs nursing he should keep at home.'

'My master is much sought after for his conversation. I have heard Lord Sandwich call him a man of rare information.'

'That's as maybe, and I'll say nothing against your master. He speaks kindly to me and he likes my food well enough. But I can't abide seeing mistress worn down by the likes of anybody. She's enough to put up with, poor thing.'

Her words reminded me of the greeting we had received from Mr Thrale.

'Is something amiss in the house?' I asked.

'Nothing for the likes of you to gossip about. I'm not speaking out of turn.'

Lizzy and Nancy exchanged glances with each other and I thought I saw a smirk on Nancy's face. After a few moment's silence Lizzy spoke, her eyes fixed on the table in front of her. Her voice had a softer, coyer manner.

'Have you a sweetheart Frank?'

The effect of her enquiry was surprising. Cook burst out laughing and Nancy soon followed suit. As for Betsy I saw her put a hand to her mouth and look to one side. Lizzy flushed angrily.

'It was Nancy as said I should ask,' she said her face welling up towards tears.

The cook, sensing danger, moved quickly to prevent the outbreak.

'Don't you start hollering Lizzy. I won't have it. You should know better than to listen to her. She likes nothing more'n mischief making. You know that.'

Nancy, of whom this was clearly true, decided to protest at cook's opinion of her.

'You always take her part. I didn't say nothing. She's just a stupid slut.'

This was too much for Lizzy who flew at Nancy tearing at her face. Nancy was pushed against the table by the force of the attack. But she was the sturdier of the two and despite being winded by her attacker she stood her ground and began to lash back.

The resulting mayhem bore out the cook's worst fears. There came from Lizzy a strange howling sound, not unlike a cat makes when its tail is trodden on, which grew in volume until it filled the entire kitchen. The effect was remarkable. All fighting ceased and it became the object of everyone to stop the hideous noise coming from her mouth. The cook put her burly form between the two girls and attempted to fasten her hand over Lizzy's mouth. But Lizzy, who now feared she was going to be murdered by cook redoubled her efforts until she was in a state bordering on hysteria. Suddenly I saw Betsy seize cook's hand and remove it from Lizzy's face, then, swinging her arm back, she slapped the girl smartly round the cheek. All at once the howling stopped. There were a few moments of ominous silence followed by the sound of quiet sobbing as Lizzy's head fell on cook's shoulder. Now seemed a good time for me to take my leave, before the outbreak of any further hostilities. But I had been anticipated in this by the cook who looked accusingly at me over Lizzy's shoulder.

'This is your doing. No good ever came of letting a man in the kitchen. I knew this would happen. Be off with you. See he goes Betsy.'

I made my apologies as best I could and went into the corridor, followed by Betsy. I turned to her not knowing what to say but she put a finger to her lips and whispered,

'What shall I tell Lizzy is the answer to her question?'

I hesitated for a moment and then replied,

'The answer to Lizzy's question is 'no'. But I care not that you should tell her. I care only that you should know.'

She continued to look at me for a while then smiled and disappeared back into the kitchen.

I went up the narrow staircase to the main reception hall anxious to distance myself from the commotion in the kitchen. I emerged at the top, near to the broad staircase which led up to the main bedrooms. Across from the hall I could see into the dining room and out the through the large French windows into the garden. It was a bright spring day and the breeze stirring the curtains was sufficient to carry the scents from the garden. I fancied I could hear the lines from Alexander Pope, one of my master's favourites, which he was wont on occasions to quote: 'Wher'er you walk, cool gales shall fan the glade.' Here, if anywhere, was perfection. In the dining room I could see the forms of several footmen, among then Will Taylor. They were laying out cutlery on a long table. Master had impressed on me the necessity to make myself useful, an instruction I had failed so far to fulfil. He was not above sending me back to Johnson's Court if cook chose to complain to Mrs Thrale.

Will Taylor was leaning against the mantlepiece as I crossed the hall into the dining room. I saw him straighten himself quickly and then relax again.

'Devil take you Frank. What d'you mean by creeping about like that?'

His face creased slightly with irritation. A slight, unassuming man, he knew all that went on in the house and didn't take kindly to fools. The other two servants who were with him and who appeared to be setting the table under his supervision turned round.

'Lord save us,' said the elder of the two, a tall Irishman with a pronounced stoop which gave him the appearance of permanently bowing. 'You're a terrible man for surprising a fellow. Sure I didn't hear you at all.'

'I came to see if I could be of service Mr Taylor,' I replied. 'I had no wish to alarm you.'

'Well that's good, Frank,' he said, recovering his humour. 'Another pair of hands John. What d'you say?'

The Irishman looked me over.

'I think he'll do Mr Taylor. Though I don't like the colour of him.'

'As to that,' I replied, 'I have heard it said the Irish are the blacks of Britannia. You and I should be brothers.'

John stared. 'There's some truth in that too, by God.'

'An educated savage,' sneered the third servant, a pale young man of about twenty, whose face already bore the signs of debauchery, 'What next?'

'If he knows enough to stay sober he knows more than you Bob,' returned Will. 'Frank could give us all the jump. He knows his letters.'

'That's not all he knows I warrant,' said Bob. 'I warrant he knows the taste of men's flesh and all. I've heard tell of such things.'

The Irishman looked mockingly towards him, rolling his eyes and waving a knife. 'You should have nothing to fear on that score,' he said. 'Even a savage would not make a meal on your poxed English carcase.'

Bob flushed and clenched his fists. The prospect of causing yet more disturbance alarmed me.

'Bob is right. It is not unknown for men to eat those caught in battle. But my taste is for beef.'

'I'm your man there Frank,' said Will. 'A side of beef any day for my liking.'

Bob unclenched his hands and the fire went from his eyes. He returned to his task.

'He'll not share my bed, even so.'

'That will not be a problem for you Bob should your temper get the better of you again' said Will. He turned to me. 'Now I think of it Frank I believe the mistress wished to speak to you about your master. She went outside for some air a short while ago. You'd best be off.'

I thanked him and made my way out through the French window. It was late afternoon and the spring sun was declining. The trees which bordered the lawn cast long shadows across the velvet plain. It would soon be evening. A narrow gravel walk extended from the front of the house down to a large lake. In the distance I could make out the figure of a woman whom I saw from her deportment to be Mrs Thrale. As I approached she looked up from a book she had been studying. She was diminutive in stature, not above five foot, her features fine and sharply drawn. Some considered her a beauty but her face was lively and expressive rather than handsome. On first appearance she seemed slight, almost fragile, but the firmness of her gaze betrayed a sensibility of great resource. From the look with which she greeted me I saw that she was deeply agitated.

'Frank, I am glad that Dr Johnson has brought you with him on this occasion.'

'Yes, ma'am.'

'You know better than most the condition of his health.'

'Yes ma'am.'

'I am concerned about him Frank. How has he been of late?

'In much pain, scarce sleeping, calling out and disturbing the household. Dr. Levet has bled him several times but with little effect. I believe he gains much comfort from coming here ma'am.'

She frowned and looked across the lake. On the far side some ducks were in hot pursuit of each other, squawking and thrashing round in the water.

'I sometimes wonder whether his ailments are altogether physical, Frank.'

'Ma'am?'

'Afflictions of the mind are often more severe than those of the body.'

'Master has often expressed a fear of madness but the doctors have always pronounced him sound of mind.'

'And I believe them Frank. Dr Johnson is one of the most rational men of my acquaintance. But he seems much burdened in spirit. I am persuaded that he is tormented by some private sorrow. I know he holds you closer to his heart than any other.'

'Master has always treated me with kindness.'

'Indeed, and I am glad of it. The doctor depends on your services more than you are aware.'

'And on yours too ma'am.'

'There is little I can do. I have a family to care for and a household to run. Mr Thrale is no less demanding than your master of my attention.'

'I would willingly help master if I could.'

'I was certain of it Frank.'

'Ma'am?'

'I would like you to sleep in the Doctor's room while you are here. I shall tell the maids to make up a bed there.'

'Master may not be happy at the exchange.'

'He will accept it in time Frank and it will be easier for us all. Anything you need for him will be provided.'

'But if his illness is of the spirit ma'am?'

'You can do as much as the rest of us and more than most. The Doctor has a special affection for you Frank. I believe he means to make a substantial provision for you.'

The suddenness of this announcement amazed me as much as its content. I wondered both at my master's generosity, which I had scarce merited, and Mrs Thrale's indiscretion. My master would be much criticised for it. If the shrew knew of this it could but make her hatred greater. I shook my head.

'I am at a loss to know why he should do such a thing ma'am. He has never mentioned it to me.'

'Nor will he at the present time. And you are to say nothing. But I consider it right that you should know.'

By the time I returned to the house the changes Mrs Thrale had spoken of had already been made. My master's bedroom was on the second storey of the house, a large room above the library overlooking the lawn and lake. He seemed ill-disposed to Mrs Thrale's intervention when he greeted me.

'So, Frank, I am not to escape you even here,' he said as I entered the room. 'Mrs Thrale has seen fit to join us like a pair of lovers.'

'She feels I can be of more service to you if I am by your side.'

'Fiddlesticks. I know she is tired of looking after me herself. I am become an embarrassment. What had she to say of me?'

'Only that she is concerned about your health master.'

'Well, there's precious new in that. I am an old man, and old men are an encumbrance. Does she wish me to be gone Frank?'

He was seated on the edge of his bed twisting in his fingers a piece of orange peel. Beside him lay the remains of several oranges.

'Mrs Thrale said she considered you one of the most rational men of her acquaintance.'

He laughed at this as at a witticism.

'Reason and love keep little company together nowadays. A fact which Henry Thrale's behaviour amply demonstrates.'

He got up from the bed scattering the peel and walked over to a side table where he picked up a wig. It was singed at the edges from where a candle had caught it one day as he strained to read.

'A humble thing but my own, Frank. Mrs Thrale wishes me to be fashionable. She would dress me in one of her husband's powdered periwigs. If I wished to be fashionable, ma'am, I said, I would go into the city and get drunk with the best of them. It will do for this evening.'

I took the wig and slipped it over master's head. Several of the curls were close to unravelling and what little powder remained gave the wig a mottled look. Despite his protestations I knew Mrs Thrale would not let him appear in company in such a comical manner. He must have caught my expression for he began again on the subject.

'The first wig I wore when I came to London Frank was from a dip in Holborn. It was thrown in by a young clerk. It cost me threepence and lasted six months.'

In all likelihood the same one I thought. The idea was not so fanciful. Master disliked getting rid of things. His attachment to things from the past was legendary, although it was not usual for him to be sentimental.

'Mr Boswell has told me master of your early life in London. He is collecting materials.'

'Bozzy knows little and nothing of any real consequence. But after my death he may make a stir in the world. I could wish he were here now. I fear the company will be in need of entertainment this evening.'

'Mrs Thrale said that Mr. Garrick and Sir Joshua Reynolds are expected master.'

'Did she? But I warrant she made no mention of Miss Sophy Gordon. A late addition Frank. We must hope there are no more. Miss Gordon is a beauty. Keep clear of beautiful women Frank.'

'They keep clear of me master.'

'You are better so. "Beauty charms the eye but merit wins the soul". When you marry remember that.'

'Yes master,' I replied, determining at the same time to follow my own inclination on that matter. Indeed, he was not immune himself to a handsome face and a roving eye. I have often seen him hover round a pretty woman like a moth around a flame. He toyed with them and they with him. Master's own wife had been many years older than him and exceedingly plain, and their life together, so I had been told, had not been happy. But she was never spoken of except with reverence and the anniversary of her death was observed as a solemn vigil. For all that, I did not care to mention Betsy to him.

'Mrs Thrale is considered a beauty by some', I said.

There was a pause before he answered. And when it came it bore signs of having been much pondered on.

'Mrs Thrale's beauty is unique. Her beauty is in her virtue. I scarce could think of her in the way of other women. We must remember that she is a mother.'

As if it were possible to forget. Mrs Thrale had been in a state of almost continuous pregnancy for above eight years and had given birth to as many children.

'She has a very high regard for you master.'

'And I for her Frank. But she is much younger than I and youth does not see with the same eyes as age. There are some things which have to be borne. Henry Thrale is a great fool.'

'He seemed distracted on our arrival master.'

He looked sternly at me.

'You have been gossiping with Mrs Thrale's servants Frank. I am not to be tempted into gratifying vulgar curiosity. It is almost time for dinner. You had best go and make yourself useful. If you wish to see what blockheads men become in the presence of a handsome woman observe tonight's company.'

I went down the back staircase from the bedroom. At the bottom the corridor led in one direction to more stairs which went down to the kitchen, and in the other to the dining room. As I hesitated, a figure came from the direction of the dining room. It slowed a little on seeing me and I saw with pleasure that it was Betsy.

'It's you Frank,' she said, stopping before me. 'I didn't expect to see you here.'

'I have just come down from my master's room. Mrs Thrale has instructed me to sleep there.'

She shifted a large basket she was carrying to her other arm. I reached out to take it from her but she drew back.

'Let me help you,' I said. 'The stairs are very narrow.'

'It's nothing I can't manage. Dirty linen that's all. I'd best be getting on.'

She made to move past me but the basket obstructed her passage. It would have been a simple matter to retreat back up the stairs and allow her to pass. But I remained there whilst we jostled each other pleasurably.

'You are not one to give way, Frank.'

'We are well matched Betsy, neither are you.'

'I mean never to give way to a man.'

'I wish you would give way to me.'

'You are very forward.'

'I would do anything for you.'

She laughed.

'And ruin me in the process too belike.'

'Not for the world.'

A noise from downstairs made her stiffen suddenly.

'You must let me pass Frank. Cook is coming.'

'Promise to see me again first.'

'In the kitchen, tomorrow morning, at first light.'

I stepped aside. Her arm brushed against mine as she eased past me, and she was gone, leaving me astonished and more than a little concerned at my boldness. In the dining room Mrs Thrale was giving orders for the disposition of her guests. She seemed distracted and changed her mind several times. I was sent away to the drawing room to supervise the punch.

'Make sure the cinnamon has not been forgot Frank. Mr. Thrale made mention of it last time.'

Punch had formerly been one of my master's pleasures before he resigned himself to water. Like Mr. Thrale he was firmly persuaded of the importance of its preparation. The punch bowl was a large silver salver placed on a low table next to the fireplace. I could see immediately from its colour that it lacked sufficient brandy. To make my diagnosis sure I ventured a finger into the mixture and was in the process of stealing it into my mouth when two men came through the open doorway leading from the hall.

'We are here not a moment too soon Joshua. The servants are like to have drunk our wine.'

A sprightly man dressed in a green frock coat from which a heavily embroidered silk waistcoat peeped out came towards me. I recognised him as Mr. Garrick. Without any warning he stretched his right arm out and dipped his finger into the bowl.

'Definitely more brandy, Frank,' he said, licking his finger.

'If that is the same finger with which you were attending to your crotch in the coach Davy, I think I may remain sober this evening,' said his companion.

Sir Joshua walked over to the fire, turned his back to it, and spread the tails of his coat wide. He was a man in build not unlike my master. He wore a dark brown coat and tight fitting neckerchief, which put me in mind of a country lawyer.

'A sure sign of Sam's occupancy,' said Mr. Garrick, moving away from the fire. 'The house is like an oven. It must make you homesick Frank.'

'England is my home sir.'

'Spoken like a patriot. You have your reply, Davy,' said Sir Joshua.

Mr. Garrick smiled expansively. 'Indeed I have.'

I bowed quickly to them and left the room in search of brandy. On my return a few minutes later the rest of the company had arrived and a spirited discussion was in process about giving to beggars.

'You may say what you like Sam,' said Mr. Thrale, 'but giving to the idle merely keeps them idle. The country is in danger of being overrun. There are paupers on every corner.'

Mrs Thrale was looking down at her feet whilst her husband delivered this opinion, affecting to study the carpet closely. My master, who was at the centre of the company, wagged his head. A gesture which I knew indicated trouble.

'Not everyone is as fortunate as you Henry,' he replied. 'To be poor is to be miserable. And I would remind you sir that the relief of misery is a duty enjoined on us by the gospels.'

'So are we to give to every beggar that importunes us?'

'To wipe all tears from off all faces is a task too hard for mortals, but to alleviate misfortunes is within the power of most us.'

'But what signifies giving halfpence to beggars Sam,' put in Sir Joshua. 'they will only spend it on tobacco or gin.'

'And why should they be denied such sweeteners of existence?' replied my master. 'Life is a pill which none of us can bear to swallow without gilding; yet for the poor we delight in stripping it still barer. No sir, a little compassion costs us nothing and gains them much.' '

Mr. Johnson, do you believe that compassion is natural to us? I have read that in a purely natural state we should be as the animals.'

My master turned towards the speaker, a slender dark-haired woman of about twenty, who had been observing him with a childlike seriousness. She had said little, but her pale, sensitive face had been keenly alert to the progress of the conversation. This was Miss Sophy Gordon, and she was not as I expected.

'Compassion cannot be natural to us ma'am. It is a divine virtue. We experience it by grace not nature.'

'Then sir, in aspiring to this virtue are we not aspiring to be like God.'

My master looked thoughtful for a moment. His face creased in preparation for a frown but issued in a smile instead.

'You are right madam. There is no sin so subtle as that of pride. Let us say merely that I feel sorry for the poor and make an end of it.'

But the company evidently did not wish to make an end of it. Mr. Garrick, sensing an equivocation in my master spoke out.

'Come Sam, you are simply exchanging one word for another. What is sorrow but a species of compassion?'

'Miss Sophy can answer that for you Davy?'

Miss Gordon reddened slightly. 'I believe you are playing with me sir,' She said.

'Not in the least. There are not many as young as you who have thought on these matters. Let us hear your opinion.'

She coughed nervously and then spoke as if reading from a book.

'Sorrow is uneasiness of the mind at the loss of some good. Compassion is a painful sympathy, a tender solicitude for the miseries of others.'

'Bravo,' said Mr Thrale delightedly. 'You must look to your laurels Sam. You have a contender for your crown.'

'I think not Henry,' replied his wife, 'Miss Gordon is quoting the good doctor himself.'

'Indeed,' said Miss Gordon. 'It is from the dictionary.'

'And very prettily recited too,' put in Sir Joshua. 'Have you ever had your likeness taken my dear? With your permission I should like to attempt it.'

'The female philosopher,' said Mr. Garrick. 'A damned good title Joshua?'

'I should be grateful, however, if you did not attempt it now Sir Joshua,' said Mrs Thrale, 'There are more pressing matters at hand. Dinner awaits us.'

The company filed into the dining room. Mr Thrale escorted Sophy Gordon and placed her by his side at the long table which filled the room. The dinner was a modest affair by the standards of the household. Mrs Thrale had been alarmed by her husband's doctors sufficiently to attempt some moderation of his excessive eating habits. Even so he complained to her of the meagreness of the table.

'Are we to send our guests away hungry tonight, my dear?' he said as the first course, a steaming pigeon broth with dumplings was brought in.

'No one has ever found my table wanting, Mr. Thrale, except yourself.'

'It is certainly wanting of pigeons my dear. We have broth a-plenty but where are the birds? Have they been spared out of compassion?'

'Your wife's affection for you is such that she would not hasten your death for a brace of pigeons. Be thankful Henry,' said my master.

'Well we shall have more wine then,' returned Mr. Thrale. 'We may die of starvation but not of thirst. Frank, see to our glasses.'

It was evident from Mr. Thrale's manner, if not his countenance, that he had already consumed a good measure of punch. I busied myself in pouring more wine and caught the eye of Will Taylor as he came in with the second course, a large goose glazed with honey and set with fruit. At the sight of this Mr. Thrale's spirits rallied.

'I see you were teasing us my dear. This is a splendid goose.

'It is the privilege of a wife sir to play with a man's appetite,' said Mr. Garrick.

My master glanced apprehensively at Mrs Thrale but her voice when she spoke was strong and high pitched.

'I fancy you take your standard of behaviour too much from the stage Mr. Garrick. It maybe the practice to play with such things there, but in real life it is wise to treat them with caution.'

'I would not dissent from you ma'am,' replied Mr. Garrick, piercing a slice of goose flesh with his fork, 'but you must remember that the theatre holds a mirror up to nature.'

'Ay, and a cracked one in your case Davy,' said my master, grunting gleefully.

His merriment was cut short by Miss Gordon who seemed anxious not to let slip the opportunity afforded by the turn in the conversation.

'But you would admit Mr. Johnson, that the stage has of late admitted some tender portraits of passion which even the nicest observer could not be offended by,' she said.

'The nicest observer might not ma'am, but I could. The stage is awash with sentimental nonsense. We are sorely in need of a decent comedy.'

'I fancy Kelly's *False Delicacy* has some merit in it,' put in Garrick.

'That's because you wrote half of it', replied my master.

Mr. Garrick put down his fork and looked round at the company, a gleam in his eye.

'I shall revive the play next season in Kelly's honour, and Miss Gordon shall play the part of Lady Lambton.'

'A capital idea,' said Mr. Thrale. Miss Gordon instantly demurred but the company would have none of her protestations.

'No, no. You would be perfect, my dear,' returned Mr. Thrale energetically. 'You have that combination of modesty, beauty and wit which the part demands. You must accept.'

'Perhaps Miss Gordon does not care for the profession of actress. It is scarcely a respectable one,' said Mrs Thrale.

'Oh, no ma'am,' replied Miss Gordon. 'I have no such prejudice I assure you. I believe the modern view is more enlightened.'

Mrs Thrale flushed suddenly and looked down at her plate.

'Go and see what has happened to the venison pie Frank. Why must we have to wait like this.' She waved her hand at me but there was no need for at that moment John appeared in the doorway, clutching a silver dish on which rested a pie, it's rich mahogany cut into thick slices. The juices were coursing out in a thin stream, forming a delta where the dish was inclined slightly.

'Be careful there John,' Mr. Thrale bellowed. 'Miss Gordon does not want to go home reeking of meat.'

'I'm sorry your honour. Cook's scalded her foot and I'm hurrying so I am.'

'Another triumph' said Mr. Garrick as John put the dish on the table. 'You have done us proud again ma'am.'

I served the slices out, reserving the thickest piece for Mr. Thrale who had been eyeing it keenly. His wife meanwhile determined to engage Miss Gordon in conversation.

'I believe you are new to the city Miss Gordon. I hope you will allow us to introduce you. We have many acquaintances whom it would amuse you to meet.'

'I do not go out much ma'am and I am but dull company I fear,' replied Miss Gordon.

'Then we must cure you of that,' said Mr. Garrick. 'To be in a city such as this and not taste its pleasures is a sin. One might as well be in the country.'

There was general laughter among the company punctuated by a loud snort from my master. Sir Joshua pushed his plate aside and contemplated his companion thoughtfully.

'You have an original view of sin Davy,' he said. 'What sin is committed in avoiding pleasure?'

'It is a breach of the first commandment,' replied Mr. Garrick wagging his head in the manner of my master. 'Go forth and multiply How can that be achieved by spurning the pleasures of society?'

'I think society requires warning Mr. Garrick, if your purpose in enjoying it is merely the propagation of the species,' put in Mrs Thrale.

'You are not in earnest Mr. Garrick,' said Miss Gordon. 'If you were you would consider that avoiding society is a virtue since it also allows us to avoid vice.'

My master, who had remained silent all this while, to all appearances preoccupied with mopping up the residue of gravy from his plate, unexpectedly raised his head and burst out.

'Nonsense ma'am. Sentimental twaddle. Solitude may prevent us from committing vicious acts but it cannot secure us from vicious thoughts. The chief benefit of society is that it keeps us from ourselves. What thinking being does not dread the hour when the last friend departs and he is left alone?'

'Well, Sam,' said Mr. Thrale his heavy lidded face creased in sudden delight. 'It appears you love our company because you hate your own. It is a good thing we do not share your opinion.'

'I am grateful that you and Hesther do not sir. I think you are well aware of it,' returned my master.'

'Indeed we are. And on the subject of Miss Gordon my dear,' he said, turning to his wife, 'you need not fear. If she will allow I shall take it upon myself to see she is not permitted to be dull. That will be my task and also pleasure.'

Mrs Thrale smiled across at her husband and folded her hands in her lap. By the time dessert appeared the company were exhibiting signs of repletion and seemed disinclined to do little more than peck at their food, all except my master and Mr. Thrale who made up for the reluctance of everyone else by sampling all three dishes: a hot buttered apple pie with pistacchio cream, a dish of candied fruits, and a tart filled with fresh raspberries. It has often been said that full stomachs and ready wits do not go together and I believe it to be true. With the ending of the meal the spirits of the company began to flag. Various topics of conversation were embarked on but no one seemed sufficiently animated to advance more than commonplace opinions. At last Mrs Thrale attempted to rally everyone with an amusement of her daughters in which every guest had to say what sort of animal the others resembled. To much laughter Mr. Garrick considered my master to be an elephant. A likeness he said he was not unhappy with as elephants were deemed to have prodigious memories and for his part he could remember when Davy was nothing but a street urchin with little more than two halfpennies to rub together. In return, my master said Mr. Garrick resembled a cat in that he had died so many times on stage but still managed to escape the hostility of the critics. Mrs Thrale he said was clearly a squirrel, and all agreed that with her small features and bushy hair it was indeed a good likeness. On being pressed to say what species of squirrel she was he replied 'Why the American of course. They are the fiercest and most protective of their territory.'

'And what of me Dr. Johnson,' said Miss Gordon. 'What animal do I put you in mind of?'

He peered closely at her pretending to examine her through a magnifying glass.

'As to that Miss Sophy,' he replied, 'no animal at all.'

'That is cheating,' she said.

'No animal, but a fish,' he continued. 'One of those bright, darting, creatures which dazzle the observer and slip through their fingers. What do you say Henry.'

He looked over the table to where the figure of Mr. Thrale sat slumped in his chair. From the way his head was sunk on his chest and the low noise coming out of his mouth it was clear to the company that he had succumbed to sleep.

'Henry is giving us an admirable imitation of a walrus, I think', said Mr. Garrick, observing the heaving chest and expanding cheeks of Mr. Thrale.

'Or a toad,' put in Mrs Thrale sourly.

It was midnight before Sir Joshua, Mr. Garrick and Miss Gordon departed from Streatham leaving my master and Mr. and Mrs. Thrale to bid good night to each other and make their several ways to bed. The evening had not passed without strain and I could see from my master's face he was glad proceedings had not been prolonged further.

'Well done Hesther,' I heard him say quietly to Mrs. Thrale, 'Everything was carried off to perfection.'

'I have behaved as Henry wished me to,' she replied.

'He knows his duty. Never fear it.' He said, 'All will appear brighter in the morning. Frank, I shall need some hot water tonight.'

Later, in his room, I helped him undress and prepare for bed. Despite the clemency of the weather there was a fire in the grate and a large pile of logs to one side. He was quieter than usual and I had hopes that he might choose to abate his habit of evening prayers and go straight to bed. But he was as regular in this as in all things and we knelt together while he importuned God to have mercy on our frailty and to preserve us from evil. Afterwards he experienced great difficulty in arising. I looped my arm around his waist and took his weight whilst he steadied himself for the effort of standing.

'I sometimes think our creator may have erred in making us go on two legs,' he said. 'The animal kingdom has adopted the greater wisdom of keeping to four.'

It was an old problem which afflicted him. Dr. Levet called it rheumaticks. It generally started in his loins and caused him much pain both in sitting and standing. I prayed God it would not pass to his stomach, a circumstance which would deprive us both of sleep. I gave him a little of the hot water to drink as a preventative and he sipped it like a cat lapping milk.

'I think I shall lie in flannel tonight Frank', he said.

'Mrs. Thrale has laid it out ready master,' I replied.

It was his custom at the onset of the cramps which afflicted him to wrap his body in flannel and sleep like one of the mummies of ancient times. I helped swathe him in a large flannel sheet rolled up at the foot of the bed and watched as he settled stiffly into his cocoon. Then, the ceremonies of the night over, I slipped into my own makeshift bed, a pair of sheets laid upon cushions, and attempted to sleep. But it was slow in coming. I lay in the darkness, listening to the fitful snoring of my master, and thinking how strange it was that the same house held the destinies of so many. I thought again of Betsy. The events of the evening had pushed her to one side, but I had not forgotten the sound of her voice and the touch of her arm on mine. I went over again every detail of our encounter. Despite her urgency to be gone, she had been reluctant to relinquish my company. The knowledge that she was sleeping close by stirred me until my flesh began to rise. I fancied her near me in the darkness, her breath on my skin, her promise to meet me echoing in my ears. At length, exhausted by such imaginings, I drifted into sleep.

I was woken abruptly by the sound of moaning. A low, pitiful sound, not unlike that of a wounded animal, was coming from the direction of my master's bed. I sat up and listened, wondering if he was hurt. The noise persisted in the monotonous, droning way, common to those disturbed in their slumbers. Now and again it would rise in volume and I feared lest he should waken others in the house. I got up and went over to his bed, drawing the curtain a little, so that I could see him more clearly. There was a full moon outside and the light fell over the upper part of his face. His eyes were staring straight at me as though he was dreaming, yet wide-awake. I called to him softly but he showed no recognition. After a few moments I approached and touched his shoulder. His nightshirt was soaking and yet he was trembling continuously as if in extreme cold. His head stirred as I touched him and I saw his lips begin to move.

'Is that you Hesther?' he whispered.

'It is Frank, master.'

'You have come. Under the bed. Be quick.'

'Master?'

His voice rose in sudden agitation.

'Hurry Hesther. They are coming.'

He began to move his arms feverishly as if warding off blows. I held him down hoping the fit would soon pass but he was stronger than I, and my restraint only served to redouble his wildness. His whisperings meanwhile grew louder, and he repeated continuously, 'under the bed' and 'hurry', his eyes fixed at something above my shoulder. I had been used, as had all of us at Johnson's Court, to his sudden shouting out in sleep, but there was something in this frenzy I had not observed before, some new terror which pursued him. He was evidently not to be calmed but by my obedience to his commands. I released his arms and he became a little quieter, his voice subsiding into incoherent mumbling. But as the terror receded from his voice it grew elsewhere. He had kicked off the flannel sheet and his legs and arms now began to wave in concert like some giant insect caught on its back. I knelt down quickly and reached under the bed as he bade me. At first all I could feel was the chamber pot. It had been my first thought that he was calling for this, but the sour smell from the bed signalled he no longer had need of that. Behind the pot was a wooden box, about the size of the one in which master kept his pens. I drew it out and opened it. In the light from the window I could make out a strong padlock like those used to secure prisoners and, attached to it, a length of chain. Immediately my master saw it his eyes sharpened, and his breathing became quicker. It was plainly the object of his urgent entreaties. He held out his arms to me, wrists together in a supplicating posture, and I saw that he intended I should bind him. I hesitated. The idea of padlocking my master like a common criminal filled me with abhorrence. But he persisted in his entreaty until I foresaw that it alone would quieten him. I wound the chain round his outstretched wrists as gently as I could and was about to fasten on the padlock when he moved his body against the metal railing of the bed-head. It was plainly his intention to be secured there. I did as I was bid and was rewarded by seeing the terror in his eyes begin to fade. He looked a pitiable creature more like a caged animal than my master. He must have seen the horror in my countenance for he said in a softened manner,

'We are safe now. Bless you Hesther.'

After a few minutes more he lapsed into a slumber and I soon heard the regular sound of his breathing.

I went back to my bed greatly perturbed in spirit. I could not settle. What demon was it that tormented my master? I remembered my black nurse in the slave compound warning me about wicked men who stole the spirits of others and inhabited their bodies. Once in the plantation I had seen a victim of their craft. A woman who men said was cursed with a demon. I remember her sitting stiffly on the ground her eyes fixed on the horizon, rocking herself gently. Her body bore the marks of many wounds where she had harmed herself. A priest from the village tried to cast out the spirit, but she attacked him with a strength equal to that of many men. The next day she was found lifeless at the bottom of a deep ravine. Was my master the victim of such a curse? If so, he would need more than human aid to preserve him. The last time I had seen a padlock of such size was on the shackles of new slaves brought to the plantation. To uncover the spirit's source and release him from its power would be a valuable service indeed.

By the time sleep beckoned, the first light of morning was edging through the window. It would soon be day, and I had been awake for what seemed like hours. Everything felt heavy as lead and my senses were dulled as though with sickness. Gratefully my body sank towards oblivion. But I could not afford to let my eyelids close, not if I was to keep my assignation with Betsy. Much as I wished for sleep, the urge to see her was stronger. I forced myself to get up. There was still a little of the water left which I had brought up for my master. I splashed what remained over my face and head and shook myself dry. My master still lay huddled in sleep, his body bound by his fetters to the bed. I ventured over and slackened the chain. He didn't stir but his face showed none of the anguish of the night.

Out in the corridor all was still, save for the faint sound of snoring from a distant part of the house, and, further off, a church bell tolling the hour. Five o'clock. Betsy would probably be in the kitchen kindling the fires which heated the large vats of water. I went silently along the corridor and down the stairs at the back of the house to the floor below. I was now in the narrow passage leading to the dining room in which I had encountered Betsy. I went quickly in the other direction. At the head of the kitchen stairs I stopped and listened. From below came the steady unhurried sound of someone working, a regular noise like the beating of a carpet. I continued down, treading carefully. My purpose, if possible was to surprise Betsy who had by now most likely given up all thought of my coming. I entered the kitchen and saw with surprise a man, his back towards me, bent over the kitchen table. From the manner of his dress and the outline of his form I recognised him as Will Taylor. The noise was coming from the table itself which Will appeared to be pushing against very hard. He turned round as I came in. Over his shoulder I saw another face, its head thrown back as if in pain. Will stopped his exertions and the head came upright. In the dim kitchen light I caught a glimpse of dishevelled hair and abandoned eyes. The silence was broken by the girl's hoarse whisper.

'Don't stop now Will. It's only the blackamoor.'

I stayed just long enough to assure myself of the speaker, and then rushed out of the kitchen, stumbling up the stairs in my hurry to be gone. At the top I paused briefly, breathing heavily. Where was Betsy? Why had she suggested the kitchen? I tried to focus on Betsy's face, but the girl's kept getting in the way. Her loose insolent look as she whispered her disdain set me trembling. I was roused and angry. I hated her and wanted her in the same moment. It was the second time she had mocked me. I thought where I had heard that taunting voice before, the same wantonness and casual indifference, and found myself thinking of Poll. I saw Poll's laughing face and lifted skirts and for a moment was back in Johnson's Court. To be black was to be worthy of nothing more. Such women knew me, knew the contamination of my skin. And Betsy. How could I have been so foolish? She must despise me like the others. How could it be otherwise?

A great weariness came over me and I realised how little sleep I had had. Perhaps if I went back now I could snatch a couple of hours before my master awoke. As I roused myself my attention was caught by a shape moving at the far end of the corridor by the entrance to the dining room. It had the form and movements of a woman. There was only one person I expected to meet here at such an hour, but now I feared such an encounter. I walked hesitantly towards the middle of the passage to where the stairs ascended to my master's floor and waited. The figure moved determinedly towards me. As it approached it spoke to me and I recognised the anxious tones of Mrs Thrale.

'Frank, I thought it was you. Are you on an errand for Dr. Johnson?'

'Yes, ma'am. He wished for more water.'

Fortunately, she seemed to take no notice of my reply, for a moment's survey would have revealed that my hands were empty.

'How has he passed the night?'

'Very ill, ma'am.'

'Yes, I thought as much. You have been forced to use the padlock?'

She must have seen my look of surprise, for she continued quickly.

'I have been into his room and released him. I have myself been unable to sleep and decided to rise early. Was he very agitated.'

'I have never seen him so afflicted ma'am. I was afraid for him. He seemed like a soul in torment.'

'Precisely so Frank. And you must help him. You may think this is the task of his friends. And so it is. We do what we can to comfort and assist him. But we are only his audience. He performs for us.'

'I cannot see why it should be different with me ma'am.'

'Perhaps not. But you have approached nearer tonight and may approach nearer yet.'

I bowed to her not fully understanding. In some strange fashion we had become accomplices. In reply she bade me good morning and urged me not to be long away from my master for he had shown signs of stirring. I turned and started up the stairs. At the top the corridor was even more still and vacant than before. The sound of distant snoring had ceased and the house seemed to have returned to its somnolent state. It would not be so for much longer. Soon doors would be banging and the endless round of household duties would begin. There were two other doors before my master's. Both had been firmly closed on my descent to the kitchen. But as I approached the first of them I could see it stood slightly open. My first thought was to close it, but upon grasping the handle I was surprised to feel some resistance on the other side. I pulled a little harder and there was a corresponding pull back. Alarmed I called out, 'who's there' in a voice intended to sound bold. This was greeted by a stifled laugh from behind the door.

'Cannot you guess Frank?'

I pushed open the door and saw the teasing face of Betsy.

'I went to the kitchen,' I said.

'I know. I saw you go down.' 'Why did you not stop me?'

Instead of answering she opened the door wider.

'You'd better come in,' she said. 'The house will be stirring soon.'

I stepped inside and she closed the door behind me. The curtains were still drawn and the room was cast in shadow. I looked around uncertainly.

'Don't be afraid,' she said. 'This room is not used.'

She looked up at me. The smile had gone and I felt her eyes searching my face in the half-light.

'Did you think it was me – with Will?

'I wasn't sure. Possibly. I don't know,' I said, feeling foolish.

'Is that what you think of me? Is that what you want Frank?'

'No. Of course not.'

'Liar,' she said, pulling me towards her. 'I've seen the way you look at me.'

'I like you Betsy. Where is the harm in that?'

'Plenty for Nancy. She'll be with child soon and Will won't want her anymore.'

She was close enough for me to feel her breath on my lips. What I said now must not be counterfeit.

'I cannot answer for Will,' I began. 'He possesses something I do not. He has both wife and children. And I pity him if he is discontented in them. For my part, I could wish for nothing more. Not if it was with you.'

'Where did you learn such pretty manners Frank? Not from your master I warrant.'

'My master has an eye the same as any man's. I have heard him say he misses the company of a wife, though I do not think he regrets being childless.'

'They say he is fond of my mistress, which is well for her, since Mr.Thrale no longer is. I could think of no worse fate than to be scorned where I had once been loved.'

'And no better one,' I returned, 'than to be loved in place of scorn.'

'Then we are of the same mind Frank and you had better kiss me.'

I folded my arms around her and drew her gently towards me. There was the slightest of pressures on my mouth and then, as her lips parted, I began falling, away from myself into her. After what seemed an age she pulled away from me, and without another word darted out of the room.

Back in my master's room I found him seated by the fire, clothed and in a peevish mood. He looked up as I came in. There were no signs of the padlock or chain and his bed had been freshly made. He threw me a quizzical glance.

'Off gallivanting Frank?'

'Master?'

'I have seen that look on only one man's face. Can you surmise it's owner Frank?'

I shook my head in bewilderment.

'Jamie Boswell.'

'What look is that Master?'

'Why, triumph, Frank. Triumph.'

3

London

1741

January 31. Dreamt again of Natty. Heaven preserve me and keep me from idle thoughts.

Slept but little. Stayed abed till twelve o'clock when noise from below roused us. Phillips making his usual racket. Breakfasted with Tetty on the remains of boiled tripe and a small portion of bread. Afterwards to work on my translation of *The Jests of Hierocles*. A singular work but quite without humour. Cave has commanded it for the end of the week. Tetty in low spirits again. The perpetual smoke troubles her. I shall ask the landlord for a room on the ground-floor though it is two-pence a week more. A garret may be nearer the heavens, but the accumulation of inconveniences renders them closer to hell. I ventured this witticism on Tetty to cheer her but we acknowledged it too feeble and too much a confirmation of our present woes. I should not have persuaded her to remove from Hampstead. She has since become delicate and full of complaint. Nothing pleases her. She has taken it of late that my interest in her is waning because I am no longer so attentive and concerned to please her. What must she expect? She is not a giddy girl nor I a moon-struck boy. But her reply is that I am cruel, that I regret marrying someone so much older than myself. There is no reasoning with her, though I am grateful she does not allege more. She does not assert what is evidently true: that I have married her and ruined her. She has abandoned the quiet satisfactions of a widowed life for poverty and distress.

About five o'clock ventured out carrying portions of my translation and the manuscript of Irene. Knocked on Phillips's door on my way down and requested him to consider his neighbours. Rewarded by him coming to the door flushed and possessed of a hammer. He said no man was more mindful of his neighbours, but cobbling was an honourable trade and a man had to earn a living. For his part he would be pleased if Mrs Johnson and I could consider that some human voices were equal to the sound of a hammer, particularly when those voices were raised in dispute, that he had no wish to be a party to our marital misfortunes, but if called upon to be a witness at any time he would have to assert that Mrs Johnson was in the right. He concluded by saying that if I had any further matter of complaint he would be pleased to step outside and knock me down. Such is the character of the fellow. I bade him good morning and passed on. At the ground floor was met by the lobster. Full of complaint about the stairs, her arthritis being bad again. I undertook to bring our linen to her in future. She said to make sure I brought enough soap; mistress had scarce sufficient last time. Without soap it was but rinsing dirt out and rinsing it back in again. I nodded at her but said nothing. It has lately been a matter of contention between Tetty and me. I upbraided her for squandering near sevenpence a week on soap, enough to maintain us in bread and butter. 'We are not gentry that we should concern ourselves with excessively clean linen Tetty,' I remarked. She, with equal spirit, replied, 'You need not remind me Sam of what every day brings abundant evidence, but there are standards to maintain. You may wear old stockings but you will not smell of them.' It pleased me on this occasion to remain silent.

Out into the Strand at last and across to Charing Cross. Magnificent sight. Truly the greatest series of shops in the world. Away to Tom King's coffee house in Covent Garden where I was accosted in the square by Dr. Rock. Asked him did I look as though I needed his vile potions. It was well to be prepared, he said, for even the wisest of men was subject to temptation. I replied that the wisest of men would hardly part with a month's rent for the privilege of being poisoned. Six shillings for mercury mixed with rhubarb and salt of vipers! This is the second time he has accosted me with his 'cathartic electuary'. I fear he has seen me and thinks I am venereal.

Met Guthrie in King's observing some gamesters at cards. I expressed myself much surprised to see him there knowing his aversion to games of chance. He said he 'wasna consarned aboot the game' but he had just come 'hither from the Hoose' and had been struck by the resemblance between parliament and a gaming den; both exhibited the passions in their worst light and were places where men sought the ruin of others. Guthrie is a good, decent Scot, ill-suited to the task Cave has given him. We sat down at a table to conduct our business.

'Cave wishes for something particular from Lilliput for the Gentleman's magazine next month,' I began.

'He doesna pay enough. Sixpence for my information. We could baith be pilloried Sam. The reports are nae legal.'

'Parliament is too occupied with the business of the war to worry about our reports Will. Besides, who can say with any certainty that the 'debates from the senate of Lilliput' are those conducted in the Commons. All the speakers are disguised.'

He looked at me scornfully.

'Aye, "Walepop", instead of "Walpole". Nae one would guess that!'

'If you are concerned about it I will speak to Cave. He has influence with the doorkeepers and has people in his employ ready enough to sleep away an afternoon in the gallery.'

'Mebbe', he grunted. 'But it's nae just that Sam. I dinna laik the deception. People dinna ken we make the speeches up.'

'You need have no trouble on that score Will. You do not invent them, I do. Your task is simply to relate what has been said. In that you are as truthful as your notes and memory will allow. If there is blame Cave and I must bear it.'

He nodded, but plainly I have not convinced him. The truth is Guthrie's reports, though faithful, are excessively dull. Cave, after his blunt fashion, says if he printed what Guthrie gave him, he might as well call in the bailiffs. I believe I have enlivened them sufficiently to render the magazine of more interest to the town. As for the prospect of prosecution, it is a whim of Guthrie's. He is jealous of my polishing. Guthrie is a reporter, but I am a writer. His speakers are hucksters, mine are statesmen. Cave is of the opinion he is treating with the government for a pension and fears the Debates may put this in jeopardy. It maybe so. Guthrie is not without principle, but he would keep to the trees rather than brave the wilderness. He is from a nation which knows the value of coin.

Away about seven to Moorfields to see poor Sam Boyse. Discovered him in the most wretched of conditions, almost naked and confined to his bed for warmth. Presented him with a meat pie from Porridge Island, at which tears started from his eyes. He is owed money by Cadell for a translation of La Fontaine's fables. Meantime he has been forced to put his clothes in pawn to purchase a few necessities. Such is his extremity that he has cut holes in his blanket to allow him to write. I confess that the sight of him sitting upright, with his naked arms thrust through the coarse cloth, endeavouring to work amidst the barren waste of his room, created such a comical effect that I could not refrain from laughter, which he poor fellow was good enough to indulge me in. He asked about *Irene*. I replied that I had retouched several parts and would be glad of his opinion.

'Willingly, Sam', he said, 'though the dramatic arts are not those in which I excel.'

'I intend it as a verse drama, for which action is not essential,' I replied. 'It will affect the mind read like a play acted.'

'Forgive me, Sam, but without action a play is not likely to succeed. Our modern audiences crave it more than words, which in many cases they are unable to hear.'

I now advanced my principal argument, the truth of which he could not but acknowledge.

'The stage,' I said, 'is sunk in superfluities and excesses. Pantomimes and farces are its common fare. But when we think of Shakespeare, in what does his greatness rest, if not language? I intend to revive the tragic muse, without the obscurities and barbarisms of Shakespeare's time.'

'And what did Fleetwood say? Would he consider it for Drury Lane?'

'He would not read it sir, such is the man's incorrigible dullness.'

Boyse shook his head, 'I fear the stage may not be ready for *Irene* Sam. I would advise a private printing, which when accomplished, and the play read by men of more shining parts than Fleetwood, may persuade the world to give it a fair trial. Apply to Tom Birch for assistance. He may be persuaded to use his influence with the Society.'

I thanked him for his advice but confessed my disappointment at the action he suggested. *Irene* is the fruit of much labour, as dear to me as any natural child. I cannot abandon it. My face must have betrayed my feelings for he apologised for any hurt his words had occasioned. He said I could take comfort in being a fine poet, that my poem *London* had been received with general acclaim and gave ample promise that the verse of *Irene* would not displease. He begged me to read some of the play to him, as I had first meant to do. I pulled the manuscript out of my pocket and read to him my revisions of the last scene in which Irene is put to death. He professed himself much moved by her death and by the tribute to the laws and freedoms of the British constitution which I have put into the mouth of Cali Bassa.

My reading used up the last piece of candle which Boyse possessed and I was much aggrieved that he must spend the remainder of the evening in complete darkness. He said it was no matter. He had trained himself to write in the absence of light, and that if ever he should have the misfortune to lose his sight he should still be able to maintain his trade, providing he could hire one to read to him. The demonstration of such fortitude determined me to help him. I undertook to raise the money needed to redeem his clothes, and as a pledge offered sixpence from my own pocket. He thanked me profusely, but said if I was in earnest I should keep the money till I had the entire sum, for such was his weakness he was liable to squander it. He had a liking for truffles which no amount of prudent advice could make him forego.

Away near ten to The White Hart near St Bride's. Streets less busy being cleared of hawkers and pedlars, though troubled by a drover with his sheep returning late to the country from Smithfield. Toiling up Ludgate Hill it began to rain. Almost knocked down by a sedan, the chairmen running; their charge, a corpulent periwigged Lord, leaning out of the window berating them for their tardiness. Reached the tavern just as the bell of St Paul's was tolling midnight. A great city is like a mistress; its pleasures are many, but they must be paid for. I had but one shilling in all the world. Sixpence was reserved for Sam Boyse, and the remainder, conscience told me, for Tetty. Decided I could spare one penny on bread.

The White Hart full of young bravos from the Middle Temple, lawyers with braying voices clutching briefs. Moses Browne in a corner, his head slumped over a table. I greeted him heartily and he lifted his head. Eyes heavy and empty, but still he recognised me, and raised his hand in greeting. Two women, who had been observing him, smiled to each other and returned to their tankards.

'Welcome Sam,' he began. 'I fear I am not at my best.'

'My arrival is propitious Moses,' I replied. 'A moment more and you were like to be dunned.'

He waved his hand dismissively, muttering loudly about 'thieves and whores'. Several of the young bucks heard him and turned round sniggering.

'Go home to your drab and brats fellow, and leave the drinking to men,' said one.

I saw a shadow cross Moses's brow. He does not suffer abuse lightly. The last man who attempted it lost several teeth. I laid my hand on his shoulder, but there was no need. The fire had plainly gone from his belly. Only one cause was sufficient to depress him so.

'Commonplace. He said my images are commonplace.'

'Who Moses?'

'Cave, of course. Who else? The ignoramus. What does he know about invention?'

I fear Moses' star is not in the ascendant. Cave's enthusiasm for his verses has waned. He now praises them as pleasant or pretty, where before they had been striking. This is not without warrant. If Moses has a fault it lies in writing too much. He can spin a verse extempore on any topic, but polishing brings no improvement. 'I make my verses as bees make honey,' he says. 'Just so', I tell him, 'but the making of honey costs the bee a deal of labour.' On this occasion it appears Cave has objected to Moses' seasonal verses on Winter.

'He says they are stuffed with sheep and shepherdesses. I attempted to explain that my intention was to revive the manner of Alexander Pope. But the fool would not listen.'

'Pope's pastorals are not the best of his productions,' I said. 'The world is tired of trees that tremble and zephyrs which blow. Every day brings us more immediate images which assault our senses. Winter in the Fleet prison – now there's a subject.'

This interested him, and the dullness which had overcast his eyes began to lift. A minute more and he would extemporise. I held up my hand in admonition.

'No, Moses. Wine is the better for fermenting.'

I caught his fancy sufficient to blunt his anger and disappointment and he accepted my advice better than I feared. I cannot but marvel at the change in our fortunes. A few years past I was the apprentice and he the master craftsman. Now he takes advice from me. 'There is a destiny which shapes our ends' as the bard has it. Though in my own case the end remains singularly blunt.

The effort of conversation was enough to dispel some of the worst effects of the wine and we began to converse more generally. Moses explained his ambition to write some longer work which would secure him from the perils of destitution. He is accustomed on several occasions to sleep in a glass factory in Southwark where the furnaces remained warm till morning. To this end he is embarking on an epic poem after the ancient fashion but is in want of a subject. Milton, he said, had stolen the only subjects worthy of epic treatment. I answered that no-one achieved greatness simply by imitation. The world was full of new subjects to exercise the vigorous fancy of a man such as he. He thanked me most gratefully but said he feared his genius for composition had gone. He could no longer do it in the old manner. 'Then find a new one Moses,' I said. 'Tear up everything and start again. Destroy even your nearest and dearest.'

He nodded slowly and then said,

'And what news of *Irene* Sam. Are we to see it performed?'

'I fear not,' I replied. 'Fleetwood is of the opinion it would depress the audience. I intend to dispose of it for publication.'

'Tragedy and epic. They are like maiden aunts Sam. No one wants them. The age craves amusement.'

I shook my head. 'The truth is Moses, the work is a failure. I cannot pretend otherwise. The audience would not be depressed, as Fleetwood fears, it would be indifferent.'

'Your genius is not for the dramatic as mine is not for epic, that is all.'

'Unfortunately Mrs Johnson is not persuaded that I possess a genius for anything. I sometimes think I did her a great wrong by marrying her.'

'Authors should never marry Sam. We're all whores and parasites. We should stick to our own kind.'

He looked at me pointedly for a few moments, belched and got to his feet unsteadily. Then tossing a few coins to the landlord he bade me farewell. I debated whether to task him with sixpence for poor Boyse but thought better of it. As he stumbled out the two women who had been watching us followed him.

Away about midnight towards home. The night exceedingly cold. I walked fast, stepping out of the way of a corpulent man with several children in tow, their faces blackened and red-eyed. Crossing Covent Garden, I turned down Hanging Mill Alley. Annie was waiting for me and greeted me after her usual fashion.

'You took your time,' she said. 'I thought you wasn't coming.'

She was wearing a thin muslin shawl over a faded cotton dress. Her face was chapped by the cold which the application of powder had failed to hide. Even in the dark of the alley I could see the signs of sickness in her features.

'I would have come to your room,' I said. 'You need not have waited here.'

'I've other gentleman to service. A girl's got to live.'

I followed her down the alley to a side door. Inside, a flight of steps went up to a small landing off which led several rooms. We entered the first one and she lit a candle. Her face mooned by the light looked feverish, her eyes sunken and unnaturally bright.

'Same price as usual,' she said. 'You can have half an hour, no more.'

I put a couple of coins on the table and sat down on the only chair in the small room. Annie lay on the bed. She coughed hoarsely for a few seconds then beckoned me to start. I got out a pen, some paper, and a little jar of ink. The thought occurred to me that she might die soon and I had only half her story.

'You came to London at thirteen?' I said, 'from the country.'

'There was too many of us at home. When mother died we was put in a workhouse. I wasn't having any of that, so I stowed away on a cart and came here. Best thing I ever did. The rest died within a few months.'

I wonder what Cave will think of her narrative. It is my idea to present in the Magazine a series of real life stories from the less fortunate in the capital, of whom Annie is most evidently one. She has lived by whoring since childhood.

'Ten years I stayed with my keeper. She was a good sort. Never let me go with no-one who wasn't a gentleman. Till I got smallpox and lost me looks. Then she couldn't keep me no more. I've been on the streets ever since. Me and Lucy share this room. She's in the same trade.'

'And children?' I queried. 'Have you never had to provide for them?'

She laughed. 'I know how to provide for them right enough. There's plenty of tricks gentlemen don't know about. I got caught once but it died soon after. Never again.'

She stirred herself from the bed, coughing loudly as she got up.

'You've had your time,' she said. 'Unless you want some business. No charge. Compliments of the house.' she laughed again.

I shook my head and thanked her. Sensing I might not see her again I had the desire to say something. Her eyes rested on me briefly.

'I wasn't always like this,' she said. 'The first gentleman I went with said I was the handsomest girl ever.' She blew out the candle and led the way to the door.

Arrived home just before dawn. Tetty snoring peacefully. Attempted to sleep but troubled again by thoughts of misery. Dozed fitfully and dreamt of the Fleet. Thought that if I died tonight society would not be the poorer. I had been in the city above four years and achieved nothing. 'Little Natty', the first words I can remember spelling. He lies dead now in Lichfield church. How I hate the darkness. Father stirring betimes to tidy the shop before opening, mother fretting at his noise and nuisance. The smell and sound of failure. Can it be pride to wish for something better? Father standing in the rain with his books. He would have smiled at me now. And Tetty? Must I admit I was deluded? 'An old dray horse' Nathaniel called her. But it was well for him, a lively, noisy fellow, always a favourite with women. She was the first who did

64

not look upon me with dislike, who listened to my fancies. Is it wrong to say she seems older to me now? Older and more foolish? If I should go tonight my epitaph will be 'He died a disappointed man.' Like my father, and brother too.

February 20: Annie died yesterday. I pray God she has found peace. Death is our final enemy. His terrors hang greatly upon me. Tetty much put out with me this morning 'for 'moping'. The truth is I have failed in my attempt to secure a room on the ground floor and know not how to break it to her. The landlord is an inveterate rogue. I am required to pay four-pence extra a week for the room. When I reminded him this was twice the sum mentioned he pretended it was already promised to a linen draper and that he would have to charge me for the injury to his conscience in breaking the agreement. The villain! I know the draper does not exist. I made my feelings plain and said besides that if he was content to injure his conscience for the sake of a few paltry coppers it was proof enough he had none. He proceeded to abuse me heartily, and not content with this, made lewd comments about Tetty. I replied by boxing him smartly about the ears and had the satisfaction of seeing him fall to the ground.

February 21: About noon, Tetty's sweeping interrupted by two men entering the room without ceremony and announcing that information had been laid against me on a charge of attempted murder. Tetty sank into a fit of hysterics and said she always suspected this would happen. What could be expected from staying out all hours and refusing to seek a respectable profession? I said there had clearly been a mistake which would take but a few minutes to clear up. The officers replied they feared the victim had narrowly escaped death and I should not presume to get off lightly from the charge. This set Tetty's fit into yet greater motion. She roared and said what should become of her without me, that she had been widowed once and was like to be again. I comforted her as well as I could and then accompanied the men to the court, where I was thrown into a cell and told I should face my accuser within the hour. About the middle of the afternoon I was carried before the magistrate and the charge read to me which I readily disputed, whereupon the magistrate instructed the landlord to stand forward. At that moment four men appeared in court carrying a bed on which lay the prostrate form of the landlord, his head heavily swathed in bandages. He commenced, in a feeble voice to tell how on being denied a room I had savagely set upon him, and that but for the assistance of those attending him he was convinced I would have done for him. He said I was known to keep low company and suspected I made my living from pimping.

I saw now the fellow had designs on my life and began to protest my innocence loudly. The judge said it was clear I knew little of the law else I would know that the weight of evidence was against me. My accuser's presence in court was testimony to the vicious attack upon his person, and moreover, he had witnesses who could testify to what had happened. I replied that I knew the witnesses to be members of his family and that as for the injuries he had sustained I did not believe them. How could I inflict them on him whilst his brothers were all standing by? The judge was not immune to the force of my reasoning and was for commanding a doctor to be present to inspect the wounds. At this the landlord began to protest loudly saying I was attempting his life a second time because he would surely bleed to death if the bandages were opened. The judge said the removal of all the bandaging was not required, just sufficient to indicate the extent of the injuries. Seeing how the land lay, my accuser said he was not willing to secure my conviction at the hazard of his life and would withdraw the charge against me. I know not how to account for the sequel to this farce, but I was so enraged by the coolness of the fellow in first being willing to see me hang and then denying me justice, that I determined to take my own revenge.

'You are a liar and a scoundrel,' I said, 'If the law cannot compel you to confess, I will.'

So saying I snatched up a sword from one of the officers and rushed towards him. At which, the injured man jumped up from his bed with amazing alacrity and ran out of the court.

February 24: forced to quit our lodgings. The landlord declared himself unwilling to harbour a man of such violent temper as me. Tetty begged me to apologise and seek an accommodation with the villain but I refused. We have not sunk so low as to parley with such men. The truth is my exploit caused him much loss of face and for two days he could not venture out for fear of exposing himself to laughter. The incident has reinforced my conviction that men immune to conscience are not immune to ridicule. For my part I was greatly admired for exposing such a trick. Phillips accosted me as I was going downstairs.

'Bravo Mr. Johnson. You are a man of spirit sir. You and I must be at odds no longer. I should be honoured if you and Mrs. Johnson would take tea with me.'

Amazing how such a simple circumstance can effect a change. This man has been a thorn in my side since we began lodging here, and now, he treats me as a hero. I could wish Tetty saw matters in such a light. The story of my intended assault shocked her exceedingly.

'What would have become of us if you had run him through Sam? Is your wife of so little importance that you could deprive her of your company forever and see her destitute and abandoned?'

I was stung by this accusation sufficiently to speak harshly to her, saying that it was for her sake I laboured night and day to keep us from the streets, that I married her because I loved and respected her, but that if she was no longer convinced of this we had better part and I would return her to Birmingham. She, poor thing, became wretched at my speech and immediately begged my forgiveness declaring she did not doubt the fervency of my regard for her but that the circumstances of our life caused her constant anxiety. I forgave her but felt a coldness at my heart. I fear her spirit is broken. Attempted to cheer her with a little ceruse purchased from the apothecary and was rewarded by seeing her pleasure. She immediately set to applying it, whitening her countenance until she seemed to my eyes almost ten years younger. It is unfortunate that the smell of this preparation is not equally rewarding, and indeed its taste, is truly nauseous. I complimented her nevertheless on her appearance.

'You remind me my dear of the morning of our marriage. What a pretty young miss you were when I came to fetch you.'

'A young miss of forty-six and past child bearing Sam. Hardly a good prospect.'

'No more was I. The importunate son of an impoverished bookseller.'

'You have never needed to fear my attachment Sam. It is the strongest bond.'

'I am grateful to God for your affection.'

I put my arms round her and drew her close.

'We are both blockheads and deserve whipping,' I said. 'It is plain as could be that we are an ideal match. Where could be found two such self-doubters as we?'

She smiled at me. The paint around her mouth creased slightly and dropped a few crumbs of powder.

'And it does not distress you too much that I am not clever and well read?'

'Nonsense, Tetty,' I replied. 'A man is in general better pleased when he has a good dinner upon the table than when his wife talks Greek.'

'There maybe some who can manage both.'

'And there are some who can manage neither. Come Tetty let us be easy with one another. We have taken each other for better or worse.'

She pulled away from me slightly.

'What is it now?' I said.

She shook her head as if waving away a bothersome fly.

'It is no matter. You have interrupted me. I have yet to complete my transformation.'

So saying she withdrew a small phial of lip salve from the top drawer of her dressing table and applied the contents sparingly to her lips. The effect was remarkable. Her mouth was suffused with a violent red as though a flower had opened in her face.

'It is a recipe from Miss Eliza Smith's book,' she said seeing my expression. 'A distillation from alkanet root. I have not been entirely idle during your absences. Pretty isn't it? There needs one touch to finish.'

She took a pouch from the dressing table top and slipped her hand inside. Then she pressed a finger against her right cheek and I saw a black patch appear just below her eye. She looked me in the eyes and giggled. For a moment the face looked familiar. I remembered Annie. She hesitated for a moment then beckoned to me. I took the outstretched hand and went with her to bed.

February 25: Have taken a room with Boyce in Moorfields. Tetty very disheartened at our change in fortune. Since finishing the Hierocles and polishing the Debates for Cave there has been little enough to do. I fear we may be pressed to pawn what little stock we have. *Irene* will not make my fortune and I must look to something else. Journey to Moorfields exceedingly mournful. Managed to hire a fishmonger's cart which required much scrubbing to rid it of the stench of offal. The owner attempted to dun me for sixpence, but I held out for fourpence. Even so I fancy we shall be accompanied by the smell of fish for several days. Phillips was sad at our departure and Tetty shed tears. There is something affecting in leaving even the most desperate of places which one has been accustomed to call home. I have heard it said that even criminals weep to leave Newgate, or the Fleet. Whether it be habit, or a fear of what lies before us, I know not, but life gives us abundant examples that man is an inconstant creature.

Our progress across the city delayed by a sharp fall of snow in the night which rendered the roads treacherous. Crossing Cornhill held up by several wagons pulled by as many as eight shire horses, the owners cursing as the wheels slipped on the rapidly forming ice. Bitterly cold and in continual fear of harming ourselves. Arrived about seven in the evening at Moorfields with the snow beginning again. Boyce's garret is three floors up but he has secured for us a large room on the second floor. The rent is sixpence less than the Strand but the area is sprawling and dirty. Began a fire as soon as we arrived and Tetty set to cleaning the room. The previous inhabitant, a printer's apprentice, stored ink, and there are few items which are not stained a deathly black. Much scrubbing by Tetty to lighten the colour, but to no avail. I fear we must spend our days entombed. Tetty is of the opinion that I like our new surroundings and have purposed to bring us here.

About ten visited poor Boyce and found him in surprising good spirits. Though still in bed he was clothed and busy writing in the dim light from a window set above the bed. He greeted me cheerily and thanked me for getting his clothes out of pawn for he knew what it must have cost me. I said it was little enough, but all his friends had willingly given sixpence and together it had been sufficient. He was moved at the thought of such generosity and vowed to be more prudent. He was spending his time in bed to avoid the necessity of lighting a fire. As for food, inactivity was the best saving yet invented, since there was but little opportunity to develop an appetite when the body was at rest. However, he had been assured by Cadell that he would soon be paid for his translation, and he would like nothing better than to entertain me and Mrs Johnson. If hope be considered one of the cardinal Christian virtues, Boyce is certainly in the way of being a better Christian than the Archbishop.

February 26: obliged to put my christening cup into pawn. The last of our plate and the only remaining memorial of my childhood. Obtained two shillings for it which was sufficient to purchase some pieces of mutton, a few loaves of bread and a quantity of candles. The remainder I set aside to pay our landlord who, God be praised, is a sober upright man not given to base trickery. Scolded by Tetty for wasting our substance on candles which we could ill afford in our present poverty. I reminded her that I was not like Boyse, who could compose by moonlight. This led to a spirited exchange about the lowness of my trade. She said we were surrounded with evidence on every side that writing was an ignoble profession which if I continued in would see us die in the Fleet. When she married me I had ambition but now I seemed content to emulate Boyse. I was angry at hearing poor Boyse treated in this fashion and reminded her that men of talent were often the sport of fortune but that Boyse would undoubtedly triumph in the end.

'If you believe that you are a bigger fool than I took you for,' she said.

'I am glad to be a fool in the company of such as Sam Boyse,' I replied.

Mercifully she did not mention *Irene*. All my hopes are lost in that direction. I fear Tetty knows it and wishes me to return to school mastering. That way madness lies. She cannot have forgotten the ignominy of Appleby. I have not an M.A. so there's an end of it. If I fail now at least my wounds shall be all before.

Away about 5 o'clock to the Potters Arms. The evening raw and the streets icy. Tetty peevish at my exit but the city called and there was business to attend to. Left her reading a romance and the fire roaring. Reached the tavern at Old Street about 6 o'clock, without mishap save for a few bricks loosened by the extreme weather hurtling onto the street near Mixen Lane. I was observing the constellation of Orion and was fortunate to see them coming: 'Our fortune is in our stars good Horatio'. A fellow leaned out of a top floor window, enlarged by the fall, and shook his fist, though at who or what I could not determine. Arrived to find Tom Birch ensconced. He greeted me handsomely and I saw from his countenance he was already well oiled, as the saying is. Considered raising the matter of *Irene* but my heart misgave me. In his present good humour Birch would promise anything but I doubt his influence with the Society is as great as Boyce thinks.

'You are surrounded by your trophies sir. Like the great panjandrum.' I pointed to the litter of empty tankards on the table.

'I am celebrating the downfall of vice and corruption Sam.'

'And in a fair way of encouraging it.'

'You have not heard the news. A general election is declared. Walpole is finished. He cannot survive.'

'Perhaps not, but he will be replaced by those warmongers, Newcastle and Hardwicke. There is little comfort in that.'

'Things improve by degrees. Except for the landlord's ale.' He pulled a face and belched heavily.

'I wish you could persuade Tetty of that. She is of the contrary opinion.'

'And is in the right of it,' said a solemn voice behind us. 'This world wears out to nought gentlemen.'

I looked round and saw Psalmanasar and Hoole bearing down on us. Psalmanasar leaning on Hoole as if for dear life, his white hair streaming down onto his shoulders like one of the patriarchs. The man is an incorrigible fraud but it is difficult not to admire the tenacity of his deception.

'You seem to be wearing out poor Hoole, George,' said Birch with amusement, watching the couple sit down.

'He's nothing but skin and bones,' said Hoole. 'He'll not eat more than a few mouthfuls a day.'

'If you had seen the world as I have you would know how little is necessary to sustain life. We consume too much,' replied Psalmanasar.

'But come George,' said Birch. 'We are not commanded to be miserable. A little ale, a good meal. These are the innocent delights of life.'

Psalmanasar looked pityingly at Birch.

'I do not deny these things to such as need them. But no great action has ever been performed in pursuit of appetite.'

'Then you should have been with me last evening George,' replied Birch laughing. 'There was more action than the sacking of Rome. My prowess in the art of love was amazing. Three women, and in the space of one hour.' '

71

You will not convince him,' said Hoole to Psalmanasar. 'Tom is not over fond of the virtuous life.'

'I am not over fond of long faces and hypocrisy,' said Birch edgily. 'George is only a late convert himself.'

Hoole protested at this allusion to Psalmanasar's youth which he considered ungentlemanly. But Psalmansar held up a hand in mild acknowledgement.

'Tom is in the right of it,' he said. 'My early life was wretched. I thank God I have lived long enough to repent of it. Virtue is the privilege of age.'

'Then you may safely leave off pursuing it Tom for another ten years,' I said, to general laughter.

'The pleasures of the city cannot be understood by those who have not experienced them,' replied Birch. 'Your own life Sam, as you have already told us, was not blameless on first arriving in this metropolis.'

'Sir, I was wild and with a wild companion. Richard Savage and I roamed the streets like devils seeking whom we might devour. My consolation is that Tetty remained at home and knew nothing.'

'Do not reproach yourself, Sam,' said Psalmanasar. 'You came to London as many before you, to seek your fortune, and found instead of a Paradise, a jungle.'

He spoke aright, but God knows I have repented my folly. Much affected by the turn in the conversation and remained silent for the remainder of the evening.

As we got up to leave the tavern Birch laid his hand on my shoulder.

'Devil take me Sam I had almost forgotten. I have information for you.' He snapped his fingers jubilantly. 'Guthrie is giving up the Debates.'

'This is good news?'

'The very best Sam. Cave wishes to see you. It can only mean one thing. You are to take charge of them.'

Parted from the company about midnight and hurried home. Streets chill and thronging with carriages and late night revellers. Making my way from St. Paul's the streets were emptier. Held my stick firm. The previous night a man was set upon and left for dead. Robbed of one shilling and his shoes. Arrived home after an hour, the fire out and Tetty snoring in bed. On the dressing table, an empty bottle on its side, the wood damp. Pray God it is not starting again.

March 6: Tetty scarce sensible since my excursion. I have endeavoured to discover her source without success. She has pawned some few bits of jewellery. A brooch I gave her on our wedding and some trinkets. Remonstrated with her severely but of what use is it? There are no women of her station in society here and she must spend her days with little occupation but sweeping. Moses is right - I should never have married. Tetty wishes for diversion and entertainment. She would visit and be visited. And I wish to make my way, to bend the city to my will. It is my adversary which I must wrestle with. I will not let go till, like Jacob's angel, it blesses me. Whether it is that being tied together, though in the holiest of bonds, is an enemy to that freedom on which the appetite depends, or whether the familiarity of repeated pleasures dulls the edge of bliss, I know not. But we have long since dwindled from lovers to friends. I pray daily for the renewal of those intimacies on which our attachment was first formed but I fear the accusation in her face. The city has been our nemesis. She resents the life of indigence and temporary expedients I have brought her to and has become sickly and nervous. She is shunned by polite society and drinks to amuse herself during my absences.

She affects to blame Savage for the decline in my affections. 'That man has debauched you,' she says, though that was not always her opinion. In the beginning she was charmed by his address and the pathetic nature of his condition. That a gentleman should be forced to live on the streets and take refuge with thieves and scoundrels because he was denied his rightful inheritance was like a story from one of the romances of which she had grown fond.

'The Countess of Macclesfield has much to answer for sir,' she said when first introduced. 'Her treatment of you has been barbarous.'

'You are very kind ma'am. I fear that to my mother I am become a reminder of her past misconduct. I am sent out like Cain with the stain of my dishonour.'

'The stain is not yours. Her liaison with the Earl was criminal indeed but the abandonment of her offspring is a worse crime. I know what it is to lose a son sir. My eldest child, Jervis, could never reconcile himself to my union with

Sam. I have not seen or heard from him these past five years. It is a bitter pill. That the Countess should choose to swallow it is unaccountable. It is against nature.'

Savage was gratified by such voluble evidence of Tetty's favour and I loved her the more for her partiality. To meet such a man on first coming to the city, the celebrated author of The Wanderer, and a nobleman in all but title, seemed an omen of good fortune. She bade me follow and learn from him. But then came tales of his profligacy and quarrelsomeness. If I returned home late she would question me repeatedly about the events of the night.

'Has he borrowed money of you again, Sam?'

'Only a trifle,' I would reply.

'A trifle. On whores and gambling. We shan't see it returned I'll warrant. He is treating you like a fool.'

'I cannot refuse him my dear. He would not refuse me were I in need.'

'A situation which grows hourly. That man will ruin you. I say nothing about his misfortunes. I pity him for those. But he will take us down with him.'

So it continued until I came home less and spent my days and nights with Savage, raging against the corruption of the times.

'If you continue as an author Sam,' he would say, 'you will either die miserably in a rat infested hole, or become a government hireling and expire in a palace. As for me, I choose exile. I shall become a hermit and live out my life in a welsh cave. But until then there are the pleasures of the brothel and if I am not mistaken, here is one hard by.'

Our sallies usually ended thus. He knew my scruples about the pleasures of the flesh and twitted me constantly. I would follow him anywhere, night cellars, shop doorways, taverns, the bulks, but not into a whore's bedchamber. Except, of course, for Hannah. She was called Hannah by the woman who kept the brothel, but her African name was Ehuoma, far more beautiful to my ears. Whether because she was not from these shores, or because she had not the practised eye and manner of the tavern whore, I had not the same fears of her. I was persuaded into her room to hear her story. She could not have been above twenty years of age, though her eyes looked far older. Ancient, sad eyes, they seemed, for which a man might commit any kind of folly. My fascination was not lost on her keeper, a wily old woman, hard as seasoned timber, though kindly enough in her way.

'Your friend has an eye for beauty after all, Mr. Savage sir', she said. '

I fancy he has, though it runs not after my taste,' replied Savage.

'We are all different sir. The appetite cannot be fixed. It takes gentlemen in strange ways.'

'Strange or not Mrs Holmes, I believe you are right. What d'you say Sam? Will the blackamoor serve your turn?'

'You forget I am a married man sir,' I replied.

'Indeed, and with very good reason. Marriage is a condition which is better forgotten. My mother managed it on numerous occasions.'

'And caused much heartache and confusion, as you yourself can bear witness.'

'True Sam, but you must acknowledge that if my mother had not so far forgotten her marriage vows as to take a lover I should not exist and, though I may regret her subsequent actions, I cannot wish that circumstance undone.'

'I tink de genel'mun don't like me.' The voice surprised us, coming, as it seemed, sideways into the room. She was standing loosely against the wall with a look almost of insolence on her face. Mrs. Holmes frowned.

'He will like you a lot better if you learn to hold your tongue girl.'

'On the contrary Mrs Holmes,' I said. 'I like her well enough as it is. Let her speak.'

'If that's your fancy sir. But I warn you she's a deal too much to say for herself.'

'Then she will please me excellently,' I replied.

'Capital,' said Savage. 'Whilst you are conversing with Hannah, I shall converse, if it please Mrs Holmes, with Lucy.'

'As you wish, sir. I shall send for her directly.'

I followed Hannah into a small room. She began undressing immediately, facing away from me towards a small window overlooking the street. Something in the mechanical way she did it unnerved me.

'Mrs Holmes said you were a talker,' I said.

'She tink me stupid. Like dem others.'

'What others?'

'Lucy, Chloe, Doris. Dey simper and purr like old she cats. Tink dats what men want. Dey not live long. None of us live long.'

She came towards me, her body moving lightly like a shadow through the room. She was unmarked and could not have been long in the trade.

'You be quick, or slow?' she asked.

'Slow', I replied Her teeth glinted in the darkened room.

'Your fren' not like dat. He pay for quick.'

'I will settle with Mrs Holmes.'

'She old she-devil. Tink I not earn enough.'

'Mrs Holmes knows her profession well enough. You may be sure she knows your worth.'

'She tink she own me cos she bought me from my massa. But no one own me. Not in dis countree.'

'If Mrs Holmes is treating you harshly I shall speak to her.'

She grunted contemptuously.

'But you fuck me first eh? Like genel'mun, like my massa do?

She stretched out her arm and touched my cheek, her fingers tracing gently round my mouth. I flinched slightly as if I had been struck. She laughed and dropped her arm.

'You don't like black flesh? You tink maybe I put curse on you, like I do on my massa?'

'No, of course not. I am not a believer in superstition and neither I think are you.'

'White man always tink he know best. But know nuthin'.'

'I know that Providence has given you youth and beauty.'

'You speak like priest. My massa rape me, then when he finis' sell me to dis woman. Always the same.'

'If you wish to leave this place I will help you. You can live with my wife until you secure a position in a respectable household.'

I cannot properly describe the look she gave me. It seemed to weigh and dismiss me in an instant.

'Dis wife know you are here?'

'Not exactly. She will understand.'

'She understan' one ting. You prefer fuck black woman dan her. You here cos you tire of her.'

I was about to protest when with a sudden motion she put her hand between my thighs. I drew my breath in sharply as my member began to harden.

'She don' touch you like dis,' she said.

Her words stirred me beyond anything I had known. Taunting and inviting at once. I have long sought to excuse the aftermath. My abstinence with Tetty, the girl's brazenness, the late hour and effects of ale. Whatever the case, I suppressed the secret whisperings of conscience more easily than I thought possible. I allowed myself to be taken to the narrow bed, where she did things previously unknown to me in the lexicon of love. Afterwards, as I lay in her arms, I learnt her real name.

'What does it mean?' I asked.

'Child of de sun.'

This was the first of many such visits. Men may speak of the addictive pleasures of the bottle or the gambling den but there is nothing so consuming or so devastating as the appetite of love.

March 7: We are saved! Cave has asked me to undertake sole authorship of the Debates. I am to receive £20 per month. Told Tetty, who has taken steps for our immediate removal to Cavendish Square. I am from today an author in regular employment. God grant me success.

4

Soubise stretched himself indolently along the mantlepiece in Johnson's Court.

'I am to be banished,' he announced tragically. 'I must prepare myself for oblivion.'

Obadiah observed him soberly. It was three months since the Christian Fraternity of Negroes had held its first and only public meeting at the Dog and Partridge, yet Soubise still continued his reckless career of pleasure. He had just regaled us with a story of his adventures with a Scottish lady disguised as a sultana whom he had met at a masquerade.

'It was the first time I did the deed with a woman blacker than myself,' he said laughing

'Do you wonder Soubise that you are being sent abroad?' said Obadiah, shaking his head. 'You bring disrepute and scandal on the Duke and Duchess of Queensberry. What else can they do?'

'You know nothing of fashionable society,' retorted Soubise, 'otherwise you would not say such stuff. Who do you think has been my chief mistress this past year? She has tired of me as I have of her.'

'She can afford to tire of you, but you cannot of her,' said Obadiah. 'You are fortunate in not being cut off completely.'

'Is not being sent to India being cut off?'

'India is a country of enterprise and commerce. A man may make his way there.'

'Obadiah is right,' put in Costano, who had remained silent for most of the evening. 'It could be worse. The Duchess will not send you empty–handed. You will have the means to establish yourself in a modest way. And besides did you not say that it is merely a threat at the moment?'

'But I believe she means to enforce it. I shall catch some terrible disease and die in agony,' said Soubise. 'My constitution is too delicate for the climate.'

Costano grunted, 'Your constitution must be stronger than that mantlepiece to withstand the repeated assaults made on it in the past five years. You will outlive us all.'

'Is it true Soubise that you have tried to lighten your complexion?' asked Famistan suddenly.

Soubise glanced at him and shrugged his shoulders. 'What of it?' he said.

'No matter. I was curious to know if the reports were true.'

'What reports?'

'It is said you were intent on marrying a woman of rank for whom the only obstacle was your colour.'

'A few washes and preparations, that's all. Women like their lovers black but prefer their husbands white,' said Soubise. 'Such is the hypocrisy of fashionable life. I tried and failed.'

'And always will,' said Obadiah. 'When will you learn to accept your condition?'

Soubise looked scornfully at him.

'My condition? What is my condition?'

'One of privilege,' replied Obadiah. 'If your master had not valued your quick tongue and ready wit you would still be in the plantation.'

'Lord Queensberry found me serviceable, that is all. He consults his own interests, as do all men. Why else were we slaves? He thinks, now he has done with me, to fling me back on the dung heap.'

'Hardly,' said Costano. 'Come Soubise, there is nothing to complain of. You have enjoyed your run of pleasure, but now it is over. Your mistake was to forget that we are here on sufferance.'

'My mistake,' replied Soubise bitterly, 'was to forget I am black.'

'Just so' said Costano.

I looked closely at him. Since the night at the Dog and Partridge a change had come over Costano. He appeared weary and resigned. His features still had their aristocratic fineness, but veiled now, like the haze which obscures the sun at evening. His first action after that night had been to write to the editor of *The Morning Post* protesting at the events which had occurred. The letter had been composed by us all, but his had been the guiding hand. Afterwards we all congratulated him on its tone of eloquent complaint. 'Sir,' it began,

> *Last night occurred an event which brings shame on those who perpetrated it. Some persons of a malicious disposition, taking advantage of a notice previously posted in this paper concerning a meeting of the fraternity of Christian negroes, caused the meeting to be broken up by a group of ruffians under the guise of a press gang. The participants were rudely treated and subjected to much abuse before being set at liberty. We are persuaded that readers of this paper will join the undersigned in condemning the outrage as unworthy that of a civilised nation.*

The letter appeared prominently in *The Post* and drew much notice. Even my master commented on it, in his dry fashion.

'You have turned correspondent, Frank. I wish you luck of it. There is little to be gained from advancing one's cause in the public press.'

I was a little nettled at this and spoke freely in reply.

'Must there be no hope then in changing the minds of the ignorant, master.'

'None whatsoever. If the ignorant could be persuaded by reason we had long ago achieved a utopia. There lies the necessity of law, to control by force where we cannot persuade by reason.'

'But what if the law itself is ignorant, master?'

'Then our hope is in the eye of heaven. There can be no perfect justice on earth Frank. To expect such is to live in a state of constant disappointment.'

I was discomforted by his complaisance and of a mind to say it was well for those who had not to endure the discomforts of slavery to say such. But I stayed silent. And in truth his judgements were always of a general than a personal nature. On the subject of newspaper correspondence, however, he was not mistaken. Costano's letter drew forth nothing but vitriol. In the week following its publication five letters appeared wondering at the insolence of negroes in pretending to ape their betters. The most mortifying of these was signed 'An English Christian':

Sir: when I behold a set of blackamoors who have so far forgotten their duty to their masters as to lecture us on the subject of civility, it vexes me beyond patience. Has this 'fraternity of Christian negroes' forgotten from what darkness and brutishness they were rescued, and what nation it was that accomplished this deed? Had they remained in their native wilderness what unnatural and bestial lives would have been theirs, far from the light of the gospel? Not only have their masters freed them from a life of endless misery and an expectation of eternal damnation, but they have elevated them to a condition where they may enjoy the comforts and blessings of a prosperous and enlightened nation. And what is their reward but to see their charges dressed in the borrowed robes of their betters parading their impudence in the public press? What are we to expect by way of dessert to this absurd display? A negro member of parliament? A blackamoor Archbishop? Let your correspondents reflect that their masters have a remedy for ingratitude and pride. The ship awaits in the harbour that can return them from whence they came. Let them think on that and be silent.

Costano first showed me this letter the morning it appeared and I could scarce read it through so unsteady was my hand. We were all accustomed to the casual abuse of the streets. It hung over us like a vulture over a carcase. But to be assaulted in public, before the world, and for that in which we most took pride. Worst of all, for our names to be known and indelibly associated with English Christian's scorn. Two days later appeared a second letter almost the equal of the first from someone signing himself 'a patriot':

Sir: Your correspondent 'An English Christian' in his letter on that absurdity calling itself 'The fraternity of Christian

Negroes' advanced a solution to such knavery which I would urge your readers to take seriously. There are at this present time upward of ten thousand negroes in this city, few of whom are in real employ. Many of these tawny sons and daughters of Afric's shores are runaways who, having cheated their masters of their lawful service now impose their unwanted advances on every innocent passer-by. I was, but yesterday, importuned in the street by a blackamoor beggar soliciting for money, who, when I refused him, abused me in the most vile manner. Have we not beggars enough of our own without importing the dregs of other nations? We hear everyday that our colonies are in desperate need of labour which the trade from Africa can scarce supply. By returning our negroes thence we could make them sound and useful members of the commonwealth and free ourselves from an unwholesome and unnecessary encumbrance.

It was but a short time afterwards that Soubise learned of his plight. Though not given to superstition he saw it as a judgement and blamed Costano as the author of his distress.

'I have become an embarrassment to Lady Qeensberry. I am teased mercilessly by her visitors asking when I expect to become Archbishop. It is too much. Though my Lady feigns amusement her annoyance is plain.'

'If the Duchess sent everyone away who displeased her there would scarce be anyone left in London,' said Costano. 'It would have come to this eventually Soubise. You have tried to live as a white man.'

'It is the only way to rise in society and gain respect,' said Famistan.

'Then it has failed,' returned Costano.

'What would you have us do?' asked Famistan. 'Talk in low English and behave like savages. That is what men expect of us.'

'What do we expect of ourselves?' asked Costano.

'I expect you to get off your black arses and leave the house immediately.'

The voice broke in upon us suddenly. I recognised its rasping shrewish tone.

'As for you Frank, Mr Johnson shall know of your riotous behaviour. Giving a bunch of good for nothing niggers the run of the house as though they owned it.'

She stood in the doorway, her face bloated with rage, so that I fancied she might any moment explode and cover us all with her bile. I winced instinctively at the thought but collected myself enough to say,

'You will find Mrs Williams, that Master gave me permission to entertain a few friends in his and your absence.'

'Did he indeed, well I am not absent now Frank. I am very much present, and either your companions leave peaceably or I shall call the watch and have them thrown into the gutter.'

She advanced into the room, her diminutive form bobbing like a cork around the occupants. Despite her virtual blindness she seemed to know exactly how many of us there were.

'Please sit down ma'am,' said Soubise with rather obvious courtesy. 'We had no wish to inconvenience you.'

She peered stiffly in his direction, but her tone when she replied was a trifle mollified.

'No thank you. I do not need to be invited to sit down in my own home. I daresay you all have masters to go to. I bid you return to them now.'

'Frank informed us ma'am that you were in the country, otherwise we should not have trespassed,' put in Famistan.

'I daresay he did. He's a talent for knowing things that don't concern him. But this is the private house of a gentleman, not a meeting place for the likes of you. You will oblige me by quitting it immediately.'

Later that evening when my master returned she began her wail again.

'Blackamoors Sam, as large as life, sprawling in our chairs, prancing about with their airs and graces like the gentry. It is insupportable Sam; it is monstrous.'

She paused, speechless with indignation, as if the sheer enormity exceeded all power of normal expression.

'I did give Frank my permission ma'am,' replied my master. 'It is surely not an unnatural desire for him to meet with his friends. I acknowledge it had not occurred to me you might return early from the country. But you must not allow yourself to be discomposed by this. Had you remained in the country you would have known nothing of it.'

'That much is evident Sam. I begin to think you wish me out of the way as much as Frank. I am sorry to disappoint you by coming back inconveniently. I have ever considered Johnson's Court my home. Perhaps I have been foolish to allow myself that indulgence.'

'Come now Anna, you and I do not need to stand upon ceremony in this fashion. You are closer than a sister, and my home is yours for as long as you choose. But I have a duty to Frank too. You must consider ma'am that he exists among us as an exile.'

'Stuff and nonsense Sam. You spoil the boy. He's as idle as the day is long. Since he accompanied you to Mrs Thrale's he moons about writing verses. I knew it was a mistake.'

This last barb was too much. I felt my blood rise.

'With respect Mrs Williams, I am not a boy,' I said.

She eyed me coolly. 'There is more to being a man than getting a wench with child,' she said.

A shadow crossed my master's face.

'What's this Frank?' he asked. 'What tomfoolery have you been up to?'

'The same as any man,' I was tempted to reply, 'The same as you would with Mrs Thrale'.

I surmised what the shrew was referring to, but the truth was I had been seeing Betsy for only a short while and our encounters had not progressed to the degree of intimacy of which she accused me. After our tryst at Mrs Thrale's I thought she would soon admit me again to her person, but I reckoned without the reticence of women and without the obstacles besetting us. As Costano observed to me, servants have little freedom and no privacy. Those brief moments in the bedroom had to serve as the only token of our connection for several weeks. I saw her constantly in the days afterwards, but she was always performing some errand, and gave me little sign of recognition let alone fondness. I saw her carrying dishes to the kitchen, or changing linen in the bedrooms, her gaze fixed in front of her, as though nothing else existed, and my heart burned. If I chanced to see the curve of her neck or the dark well of her underarm as she bent to her task, the day was richer yet more barren. I took to waiting in corridors and traversing stairways on spurious errands hoping to waylay her, but to no avail. She eluded the careful traps I laid for her and seemed to have foreknowledge of my whereabouts. In my desperation I suspected there were passageways around the house I knew nothing of and when I was sure no one was observing me I would tap and feel my way round the interiors of rooms. But my behaviour did not go altogether unnoticed.

'You have become a great walker Frank,' observed my master one day. 'Everywhere I look, there you are. I begin to think there is more than one of you.'

'You instructed me to make myself useful to the household, master. There are many duties I am sent on.'

He stopped peeling the orange he was holding and peered at me.

'You are not the only servant here Frank. How is it that you are so much occupied?'

'There is more for everybody to do since the departure of Will Taylor.'

He nodded and resumed peeling his orange.

'Of course, I had forgotten that unfortunate incident.'

As had I until that moment. Will had been obliged to leave the house shortly after the dinner at which Mr Garrick, Sir Joshua and Miss Sophy Gordon had been present. Unfortunately for him wind of his dalliance with Nancy had reached Will's wife who suddenly appeared at the house in a great rage and proceeded to box Nancy's ears so hard she howled like a scalded cat. The resulting commotion brought Mrs Thrale into the kitchen who ascertained the situation instantly and summarily dismissed Nancy. Will was sent for and confessed immediately throwing himself on the mercy of Mrs Thrale. He was a great favourite with her, but she held firm. He had been equally to blame as Nancy, she said, and must go. Will's wife began to plead with Mrs Thrale saying she had not meant to cause trouble, only to get rid of the slut who had seduced her husband. But Mrs Thrale was not in a mood to change her mind and the couple departed, with Will berating his wife for her foolishness in getting him turned off.

Will's departure cast a shadow over the house. At first I thought Betsy's avoidance of me was because she feared a similar fate. But as time went by and it became clear no-one knew our secret, I began to be plagued by darker thoughts. They kept me awake at night, so that between my master's tossing and my own, I got very little sleep at all. Perhaps Betsy had simply been amusing herself. I had seen enough to know she had an impish sense of humour. It was foolish to think she had no aversion to my colour. Perhaps Soubise was right about women. I would have no peace till I knew the truth, and I determined to confront her.

The servant's quarters lay at the top of the house, up a flight of narrow stairs leading from the second floor landing. There were several small rooms, one of which accommodated Betsy, Nancy and Lizzy. The idea of slipping in to see Betsy had occurred to me very early on but, whilst Nancy had been in residence, the thing was impossible. The pleasure of discovering us to the household would have been too great a temptation. But, with Nancy's departure, the idea regained its former hold. There was undoubtedly a risk, since it would mean ensuring the silence of Lizzy, by no means a straightforward matter. But I was convinced she was not without a sentimental side to her nature and capable of persuasion. Besides, I believed she had a fancy for me which, if managed aright, would assist my design. One evening I caught her as she was coming up from the kitchen bearing in her hands a soup tureen.

'A word with you Lizzy,' I said, detaining her with my hand.

She flushed slightly and dropped her eyes.

'What do you want? Missus has called for the soup.'

'I won't keep you long. I need your assistance.'

She looked surprised.

'What for? Ask one of the men. I've got me 'ands full.'

'It's something only you can do,' I said in a lowered voice.

I was rewarded by seeing a sly smile.

'You're a close one Frank Barber. You'll be getting me into trouble.'

'Not for the world Lizzy. Meet me in the kitchen garden after supper.'

'I'm not such a fool as Nancy. I know what you're after.'

'Trust me Lizzy please. You'll come to no harm. There is something I must ask you.'

She hesitated. At the far end of the passage a door began to open.

'Well, you may wait for me if you like. Whether I'll come or not I can't say. Now you'd best let me pass.'

Two hours later, as darkness was descending I made my way out to the small garden at the rear of the kitchen. It was an area used for growing herbs but there were some fruit trees and strawberry bushes at the far end. It was there I concealed myself. Shortly after dusk a figure emerged from the kitchen door. The light was too poor for me to see who it was and I was about to call out when I saw a taper glow followed by a plume of smoke. I moved further back into the bushes. After a few minutes there was a shout from the house and the figure threw something onto the ground and disappeared inside. By now the only light in the garden came from a weak and indistinct moon barely visible through the dark clouds. It was getting colder and the scent of rain was heavy in the air. I had almost decided to abandon my quest for the evening when I heard a noise behind.

'Frank,' a voice whispered urgently. 'Is that you?'

I turned and caught a glimpse of a pale face covered by a hood.

'Lizzy?'

'Stay there. I can't be long. Tell me what you want.'

'I need to speak to Betsy. It's important.'

There was a short pause.

'What's that to me?'

'My master is returning home soon and I may not come again.'

'Missus has forbid it. She says there's been too much goings on.'

'I only wish to talk to her. Nothing more.'

'I can't do nothing. You'll have to manage as you can.'

'I need to see her alone. I mean to come to her bedchamber tonight.'

She shook her head violently.

'I'll lose my place and Betsy as well.'

'Just five minutes, that is all. I beg of you. I have a guinea given to me by my master. You shall have it.'

'Save your money for your black whores.'

She moved further back into the bushes and I began to fear I had miscalculated.

'Wait, please,' I cried. 'I did not intend to insult you. I meant merely to show how much in earnest I am.'

When she spoke again her voice was lower and more deliberate.

'If I help you it's for Betsy's sake.'

'Of course.'

'You must stay for five minutes, no more.'

'I will do whatever you say.'

'Listen then. When the church clock strikes midnight I will leave the bedchamber. You must wait by the stairs till I come. I will keep watch while you go in. If anyone stirs I will deny all knowledge and declare I thought you had come to rob us.'

'Agreed.'

'Very well,' she replied. 'A guinea, you said.'

I passed the hours until midnight in a torment. I was not convinced Lizzy could be trusted. If Betsy should be turned off because of me I would lose her completely. Besides, I did not know how my intrusion would appear to her at such an hour. I fancied the house full of screaming women and myself carried before the judge on a charge of attempting a rape. Still, I was of a mind to hazard all. I could not remain in my present state of ignorance. It was not to be borne. My master meanwhile was thankfully too concerned about the well-being of his host to notice my agitated condition. He had been all day closeted with Mr Thrale in the library. From time to time I was sent for to fetch more wine for him and tea for my master. About ten in the evening I approached the library to see if they required more refreshment, when the door burst open and my master emerged in a high state of passion.

'Pack the bags Frank,' he said, his face twitching fiercely. 'We shall not be staying a moment longer in this bedlam.'

I looked stupidly at him. My mouth opened but all I could manage was a croak.

'What's the matter Frank? Have you become as witless as Thrale?'

'But master. It is almost midnight. There are no carriages.'

'Then we will walk. You have had practice enough of late. Or has profligacy and indulgence reduced you also to a sot.'

'Sam, Sam,' came a voice from inside. 'Let us not part like this. I am sorry for my foolishness.'

The unbuttoned figure of Mr Thrale appeared unsteadily in the doorway.

'Listen to Frank here. You cannot leave tonight.'

'You could not sir. But I can. There is no more that reason and common decency can do in this house. If you are determined to abandon those who are most dear to you then I have done with you.'

Mr Thrale looked miserably at my master.

'Tell me what to do Sam and I swear by God it shall be done.'

'You know what you must do. You must confess all to Hesther and beg her forgiveness.'

'Very well.'

'Then you must attend seriously to your business for unless you do you will end on the streets.'

Mr Thrale nodded grimly.

'I can always depend on you for the truth Sam.'

'I am no flatterer,' said my master. 'I leave that province to Miss Sophy Gordon.'

After a few minutes more they retired into the library again. I knew enough of my master's moods to know the immediate danger was past, but also that he was perfectly capable of attempting the walk back to London should Mr Thrale annoy him further. A circumstance which I am sure Mr Thrale well knew. Indeed I fancied his sudden contrition was due as much to his wish to prevent such an occurrence as any intention to reform his behaviour. My master was fond of narrating his prowess at walking, though in truth I always suspected his accounts were a little varnished. But for the moment I was safe. My master would not stir from the library now till after midnight. I returned along the corridor towards the back staircase. Much of the house was in darkness. Mrs Thrale had taken of late to ordering the wall candles to be extinguished early, one of several small economies which had recently rendered the house less comfortable. I went up the stairs to the middle landing and made my way to my master's bedchamber, thinking to spend the intervening time preparing the room for the night. He was given to complaining if the fire was not banked up enough even in summer. To my astonishment the door was already open and standing in front of the fire was Mrs Thrale.

'Frank,' she said. 'It is you. I thought perhaps it was Dr Johnson.'

'No ma'am. He is still with Mr Thrale in the library.'

'Yes,' she replied.

I looked at her hands. She was twisting a handkerchief as though tying a very difficult knot.

'Shall I tell him you are waiting for him ma'am?'

'No. Frank, there is no need.'

She paused a while and then said.

'Do you ever wonder who your parents were Frank?'

'No ma'am.'

'Not even your mother? Surely you must wonder about her?'

'When I was a boy I dreamt about her sometimes. But she died when I was very young. I don't remember her.'

'And your father. What about him?'

'Nothing ma'am.'

'Nothing at all?'

'The Colonel said my mother died on the boat from Africa to the plantation and nothing was known of my father.'

'How sad to have no one.'

'There are many like me ma'am.'

'I suppose so.'

'At least I am free.'

'Yes, the Colonel did that for you.'

'Master says there is always something to be thankful for if you look hard enough.'

She stopped twisting her handkerchief and looked thoughtful.

'You are a philosopher Frank.'

'No ma'am.'

'But you are right. Thank you. I will go now. You need not tell Dr. Johnson I was here.'

She went out softly, leaving behind her the faint scent of lavender. I busied myself about the room, laying out the flannel and raking the embers in the grate. On the stroke of midnight I left the room and went along the corridor to the landing by the foot of the stairs leading to the garret. After a few minutes I heard the sound of light footsteps descending the stairs and made out the ghostly shape of Lizzy enveloped in a large nightgown. I heard her curse quietly as she stubbed her toe in the dark.

'I must be bloody mad,' she said as she reached the landing. 'It's black as coal up them stairs.'

'Thank you Lizzy I said. I won't forget this.'

'No more will I,' she said. 'You better hurry up or I shall catch me death.'

I started up the stairs as quickly and silently as I could manage, my heart beating violently. Was this wise? I wondered. But I had gone too far to turn back now. At the top I soon found the door of Lizzy's room. It was standing open. Inside a faint light shone through the corner of a ragged curtain hanging at an angle against a small window. I could just make out two beds, one empty, the other with the shape of a sleeping body. I went cautiously over and bent down.

'Betsy,' I whispered shaking her gently. 'Betsy, wake up.'

One eye opened and then, as recognition slowly dawned, the other.

'Frank,' she said, sitting bolt upright. 'What in God's name are you doing? Go away, now.'

'Not until you listen to me.'

'You must go. Lizzy will be back soon. You'll have me turned off.'

'Don't worry about Lizzy. I have taken care of her.'

'What do you mean?'

'We have five minutes Betsy.'

'For what Frank? What are you here for?'

I took her question as a sign that she had accepted my presence, for the time at least. But now that I had gained my object I was at a loss how to begin. I had rehearsed this moment many times but suddenly the words escaped me. I was struck by the ridiculousness of my situation, crouched at the bedside of a woman I hardly knew in the middle of the night. She seemed to sense my dilemma and spoke first.

'I hope, Frank Barber, you have not disturbed my sleep for no reason.'

The old note of teasing in her voice served to embolden me.

'It is you who have been disturbing my sleep,' I began. 'I cannot rest for thinking of you.'

'Then you are not busy enough Frank. If you had to be up before dawn fetching and carrying all day you would not find sleep difficult.'

'You know my meaning well enough Betsy.'

'Perhaps I don't choose to know it. What is it to me if you can't sleep?'

She tossed her words in my direction in a hard, careless manner which was new to me.

'I don't understand,' I said. 'You were not like this the last time we met.'

'That was different.'

'Why?'

She shrugged her shoulders.

'Why?' I repeated.

'I allowed myself a little freedom. As did you. That is all. You make too much of it.'

I felt her eyes settle on mine in the darkness with a bold, almost defiant gaze.

'I do not believe you,' I said. 'There is something else. You have formed another connection.'

She laughed softly.

'You are a fool Frank.'

'Well then,' I blurted out. 'You are offended by my colour.'

Her body stiffened and she drew the sheet more tightly round her.

'If you wish to think that then very well. We have no more to say to each other. Go back to bed Frank.'

'What would you have me think? You cast me off like some nuisance in the street.'

I spoke more bitterly than I intended but it served to give me courage. Buoyed up by my sense of injustice, I whispered fiercely at her.

'I am possessed by you.'

There was a pause. I had announced clumsily what I had rehearsed in calmer moments as a considered statement. When she replied her manner was gentler without being more encouraging.

'What did you expect Frank? That I should become your mistress?'

'I thought I was not unpleasing to you.'

'I'm not so foolish as Nancy. I cannot afford to lose my place.'

'I would not put your place in peril for the world.'

'But you do Frank. Just by being here. Do you think I'm a serving maid by choice? I was meant to be a governess. I have an education, of sorts, Frank.'

I nodded. The difference between her and the other maids now became clear.

'My father had money until he drank it away, and with it my schooling. I was forced to leave and take up the situation I am now in. I was fortunate. Many employers would not take a girl who knew her letters. But Mr and Mrs Thrale were different. I cannot complain of my position.'

'I mean to improve your situation Betsy, if you will let me.'

I was rewarded by another laugh, not wholly scornful.

'How? Would you have me marry a poor black servant with a madman as his master?'

'He is not so mad nor I so poor,' I said. 'I am heir to his estate and shall one day have a modest fortune of my own.'

'You are a dreamer Frank. When I marry it must be for more than idle fancies.'

'Then I was mistaken,' I said stiffly. 'And I'm sorry I disturbed your sleep.'

I got up quietly and made to leave. But she interrupted my progress.

'You make a very poor lover, Frank. You are meant to implore my pity.'

Indignant as I was, I could not but notice the hint of teasing again.

'I know nothing of those games Betsy. I came hoping you were the same woman who professed love for me. I was wrong and shall not trouble you more.'

'If you abandon your cause so easily then perhaps you are not for me after all. Goodnight Frank.'

There was a rustle of sheets as she settled down into bed again. I turned towards her.

'For mercy's sake Betsy. Tell me what to do and I will do it.'

'Speak to your master. Tell him you want me.' She said in a muffled voice.

'What shall I say to him?'

'That you are a great booby Frank. If we are to see each other it has to be with his and my mistress's consent. Now go, and let me sleep.'

At that moment the figure of Lizzy appeared at the door.

'I can't be waiting anymore,' she said irritably. 'You've had fifteen minutes near enough.'

'Thank you Lizzy. I'm going now.'

I moved past her in the doorway. As I did so she put out her hand.

'Aren't you forgetting something?'

I reached into my pocket and drew out the guinea.

'I hope it was worth it,' she said, with a grin.

'Yes, most certainly. I would gladly have given as much again.'

'Oh,' she replied, crestfallen. 'I shall know not to cheapen myself next time.'

Speaking to my master was easier to contemplate than accomplish. Over the next week he was continually occupied.

'Not now, Frank,' he said to me as I accosted him one day in the garden. 'I cannot attend to domestic matters at present. Talk to Mrs Thrale if you must.'

'It is a personal matter master.'

'Well speak to me tomorrow. It can wait till then I hope?'

But it was the same story the next day, and the next. Indeed it was not till we were back at Johnson's Court that I had an opportunity to break my news to him. When I did his manner was less than encouraging.

'So, you have fallen for a pretty face, Frank. I cannot say I am surprised. And is the girl of a like mind?'

'Yes, master, I believe so.'

'Believe! This is not mere fancy Frank is it? Remember poor Levet. He believed his wench was enamoured of him, only to discover his money was a greater attraction. Though little he had of that.'

'And I even less, master.'

True,' he grunted.

'All the same, take your time Frank. Remember the proverb, "marry in haste, repent at leisure".'

At length it was agreed that he would speak to Mrs Thrale, and if there was no obstacle, that I should woo Betsy. After our next visit he spoke to me again.

'I have pleaded your cause to Mrs Thrale, Frank. She is not over fond of such arrangements and less than happy at the prospect of losing another servant. However, I prevailed at the last. You may court your paramour.'

So it was that Betsy and I were allowed to meet, though the opportunities we had were still infrequent and brief. Despite my master visiting Streatham regularly, Betsy had her liberty for just one hour after sunset. We would walk in the servants' garden away from prying eyes, and on occasions hold hands, and even kiss. More was scarcely possible without great subterfuge. Since Nancy's downfall the household was kept under strict watch. Besides, Betsy was reluctant to permit those favours until we should have the prospect of a closer bond. This became the daily subject of our talk until we could converse about little else. Whether it was my impatience or Betsy's common sense, one of us would be sure to stumble over it.

'We shall be very wise Betsy when at last we marry. That should be a comfort to us. Old people are supposed to be wise and we shall certainly be old.'

I had meant this to be humorous but the note of sourness was detectable even to my ears.

'Not so Frank, for I shall have lost my looks by then and you will have tired of wooing me and found out a fresher mate. But I shall always love you and die a maid.'

Our wooing continued for some time in this artful manner. We fancied ourselves lovers in Mr Cumberland's play *The Fashionable Lover*, an account of which had reached us from a servant who had been permitted to accompany Mrs Thrale to the theatre. I took to wearing black and writing impassioned notes to Betsy at whose insistence, I called 'Augusta'. I believe it was my master's impatience at this which persuaded him to hasten things. He spoke to me on the subject one day as I was changing the coals in his bedroom at Streatham Park.

'Frank, the business of attending to the fire does not require you to stare into it so interminably. It will not burn the brighter.'

I turned towards him and saw with surprise that he was watching me keenly from above the covers of a book.

'Yes master,' I said. 'I wished to make sure the fire was safe before leaving.'

'Since you have not yet lit it the question of its safety would not seem a fruitful object of thought.'

I was at a loss to reply to this and contented myself with mumbling, 'Yes,master' again.

'You have been caught out Frank. You stand convicted, in the common phrase, of 'daydreaming'. What have you to say for yourself?' He paused. 'Nothing, of course, because there is nothing to be said. Mrs Thrale is quite right; when servants fancy themselves in love they become entirely useless. I am beginning to be of the same mind as Mrs Williams in considering your education a waste of money. I did not pay £300 to Reverend Joseph Clapp's establishment merely for your mind to become infected by the idiocies of the modern stage. What is this mode of dress Frank? Why must you appear like an undertaker?'

I was stung by his rebuke and answered him warmly.

'If you complain of my work master, then I am sorry and beg your forgiveness. As for my dress, my passion for Betsy is of such a kind as I expect no one to understand who has not felt as I do.'

'You consider that I am too old and decayed in my faculties to know anything of the torments of love I fancy?'

He paused and blew out his cheeks. When he spoke again his voice was low and animated. 'Love is a thorn in the flesh Frank. It grows with age. It can never be removed. Take it from one who knows.'

'You do not approve of my love for Betsy master?'

'I do not approve of you mooning about all day like a calf deprived of its mother. If the only cure is your marriage we had better get on with it. Though where and how you are to live is a problem worthy of Socrates. Johnson's Court is already more akin to a rabbit warren than either comfort or convenience will allow.'

This was as much as I could hope for from my master by way of permission and I knew it must be seized on. He was as likely as not to have forgotten the incident entirely in a few days. His extraordinary feats of memory for which he was renowned did not extend to the domestic circumstances of his servants. Later that day when I met Betsy in the garden I told her what master had said, omitting some of his less flattering observations. To my surprise she was not so enamoured at the prospect of an early marriage as I had fancied. She seemed to be much of my master's opinion.

'And where shall we live Frank? Have you considered that? What did your master say?'

'Merely that room would be found. Johnson's Court is a large house and besides Poll will probably move out soon. As for the others, Mrs Williams cannot be long for this world, nor Mr Levet neither. We may be confined to begin with but not for long.'

Despite my air of confidence I fancy she saw through my deceptions. She returned again to the problem of accommodation.

'And what if we have children Frank? The occupants of Johnson's Court are elderly and not likely to welcome the sound of bawling infants.'

It was on the tip of my tongue to say that one set more of bawling inhabitants would not be noticed but I foresaw that such an observation would not increase the attractiveness of Johnson's Court in Betsy's eyes.

'Then I shall ask my master to find us lodgings until such time as we can conveniently move into Johnson's Court.'

'He will do this for us?'

'Yes, he has as good as said so. I know he means to make provision for me.'

After much persuasion Betsy agreed that I should approach her mistress with the proposition. I asked to speak to her the following day after Mr Thrale had left to attend a morning levee at Lady Southampton's. I found her sitting by a small table with a pack of cards in her hand, my master having not yet arisen.

'So, Frank,' she said when I had explained my errand. 'Like most men you have grown impatient. Well I hope you remain as eager for the company of your mistress once she has become your wife.'

'I cannot think of being parted from her ma'am.'

'No, Mr Thrale said something similar to me. But you should be warned Frank. Betsy is a girl of spirit.'

'I know ma'am and I honour her for it.'

'Good. I am glad to hear it. Spirit is something you will both need. The world is not as tolerant as your master. It would have been better had you kept to your own kind. People will point the finger at a blackamoor with a white girl, and your children also, should you be so fortunate.'

'We are ready for that ma'am. We shall outlast all scorn.'

'Very well. Let it be soon then. I shall speak to Dr. Johnson.

The news that Betsy and I were to be married was not entirely unexpected at Johnson's Court and neither was it entirely welcome. I heard Mrs Desmoulins, an old impoverished friend of master who lodged locally with her daughter bestowing her wisdom on the scullery maid. Master alleviated her poverty by giving her a weekly allowance and she repaid his generosity by interfering in the kitchen. She was informing her that in Eastern countries, where blackamoors were slaves, they had usually been rendered unserviceable for women first, and it was a custom she could wish had been adopted in England. The shrew, however, was the most vocal in her opposition. She berated my master mercilessly with the inconveniences which would be incurred.

'Picanninnies Sam. It does not bear thinking of. We shall be overrun. Stealing food, tormenting the cat, cheeking their betters. Is it your wish to turn this house into a colony. And have you considered the effect on the morals of the house of two people co-habiting?'

'Morals, ma'am? I fear your drift is not obvious. Marriage is an honourable condition I believe. What can you allege against it?'

'You know very well, Sam. This is not marriage. It is fornication. It is unnatural. We are made so that we keep to our own kind. The Bible is very clear on this.'

'If that is so ma'am then you and I read the Bible very differently for I can observe nothing in it which would forbid the union of Frank and Betsy. Have you forgot the first commandment ma'am "Go forth and multiply"?'

'But they are not going forth Sam. They are coming here.'

And so it continued. My marriage became like one of the labours of Hercules. I was at least fortunate in that Betsy heard nothing of the tumult, and I was careful in my meetings with her to say as little as possible. It was well that I did for there was yet another obstacle to our setting up house at Johnson's Court which I had not foreseen. Poll. Since the time on the landing I had kept my distance from her, a circumstance helped by my frequent visits to Streatham. But at home I was always aware of her eyes on me, mocking and playful, like a cat with its prey. I felt clumsy and awkward in her presence. If I spilt some milk or dropped a cup she was sure to be there. Master never noticed her except when she had one of her tyrannical rages against the shrew. On those occasions the house was full of her screaming till I fancied she would run mad and kill someone. Her life on the streets had been burned into her like a brand. But she had certainly changed in one respect since Master had dragged her home. She had looked then as if death could not be far off. Smallpox, starvation and the clap had taken their toll and left her a wretched thing. Within a few weeks, however, she had recovered her health, and, after a few months, her looks. Her face, though plain, was regular and well featured, and she had a habit when talking of puckering her cheeks in a most becoming manner. Her shape, which was thin and raw-boned when first she arrived, was, by the end of the year, round and firm once more. Even Dr. Levet, who had been disgusted by her appearance, could now be observed glancing secretly at her. But when the shrew accused her one day of attempting to seduce the doctor, she laughed and said she would gladly resign those pleasures to her, who might enjoy coupling with a death's head. As for herself, she preferred younger meat. The truth is that Poll had little enough to occupy her time. She was intended to help in the kitchen, but after several noisy encounters with Mrs Desmoulins it was agreed by all to let her be. Complaints to my master only drew from him the response, 'She will mend. Give her time. I cannot cast her out.' But she didn't.

Poll greeted the news about Betsy with great glee. All at once she had been given fresh material with which to plague me. She took to whispering to me as I passed her in the corridor or on the landing 'Have you dipped your nigger wick yet Frank?' She would look at me from a distance and insert a finger slowly into her mouth. Once when I was carrying a tray upstairs she blocked my path while she undid her bosom and displayed her breasts. I felt the tray tremble in my grasp and then a call from my master demanding to know what was delaying his tea freed me. But I reasoned that I had very little to fear from Poll. The house was generally too busy to allow her much scope for her tricks. Very rarely was anyone truly alone and little occurred which could be kept secret. However, I reckoned without her ingenuity. One morning, very early, I had occasion to go to the cellar to fetch coals for the fires upstairs. The cellar was a small enclosed space with barely room to stand up. I had just entered when I heard someone follow me in. I turned to look, but the door was quickly slammed shut. My first thought was that a thief had broken into the house and was seeking to hide there, but the rustle of skirts and my name called in a low intimate manner soon disabused me.

'Don't be frightened Frank. It's only me.'

'For God's sake Poll. This is not a joke.'

I took hold of her to push her aside and open the door.

'If you do that I'll scream rape. Then you'll never have your Betsy.'

'What do you want? We shall be discovered soon.'

She didn't answer but slipped her hand between my legs. I heard her laugh softly.

'You're harder than that block of coal.'

She pulled me towards her hoisting her skirts. The image of another encounter in a darkened room some months before flashed before me and my flesh began to stir. I tried to push her away, but she had hold of me now and my protests were too obviously feeble. With the instinct of her trade she knew what I desired and went about the task professionally. She quickly guided me towards her as if threading a needle and I felt with my tip the soft opening between her legs. I thought briefly of Betsy, but I knew it was too late. She arched backwards and lifted one leg, but, at that moment, the sound of the door handle turning made us both stop. We waited, expecting someone to appear at any second. The door opened a few inches and a small black object hurtled through.

'Stay in there where you belong, curse you,' said a voice in the raised tones of the shrew, her irritation a sign that Hodge must have performed one of his frequent feats of fouling again. Then the door slammed shut.

I let out a sigh and drew away from Poll. Her only reply was to take her hand from me and wipe it on my coat.

'You good for nothing nigger.'

'Come Frank,' my master said. 'I ask again, what tomfoolery have you been up to? When I gave you leave to marry Betsy I did not expect you had already ploughed the furrow.'

'Betsy is not with child master. Mrs Williams is, on this occasion, mistaken.'

'I am never mistaken,' she replied. 'I was talking of Poll.'

My master looked more sad than angry at this news.

'Poll? Are you certain Anna?'

'The girl is three months gone Sam. If you had not been so taken up with the Thrales you would have noticed.'

'Is this your work Frank?' He asked, turning to me.

I shook my head vigorously.

'No master. Poll is nothing to me. It is not mine.'

The shrew snorted scornfully.

'Of course it is his. He hangs around her like a dog after a bitch.'

'Don't believe her master. She has always hated me.' '

Ask the girl herself Sam. She says Frank forced her.'

'It's a lie,' I replied, my voice rising in volume. 'Poll is a damned liar.'

'I must confess Anna,' said my master, 'that the idea of anyone forcing Poll does not seem likely.'

'Maybe so,' she replied grudgingly. 'But it is his nevertheless. You can be sure of that.'

'Have the goodness to fetch Poll ma'am. We shall hear what she has to say.'

The shrew went outside onto the landing and after a round of screeching Poll appeared, her stomach unmistakably swollen. She entered the room, not looking at anyone, her eyes cast to the floor.

'How long have you been in this condition?' asked my master.

'Three months sir.'

'Tell Mr. Johnson whose the brat is.'

She nodded towards me.

'It's his,' she said. 'He's been at me ever since I came here.'

'You filthy whore. That's a lie,' I raged.

'If I'm a whore whose fault is that?' She said, lifting her head defiantly.

'Not mine. I never touched you.'

'Who's a liar now? You forced me – in the cellar. More'n once.'

'It could not be plainer Sam' said the shrew. 'Frank is not the innocent you take him for. He and the trollop are a good match.'

Poll was incensed at this. Forgetting me she turned on her old enemy.

'Trollop yourself,' she said. 'You'd give the master a jump any day if he didn't know better. Any man would sooner dangle his prick in a rotten piece of horseshit than fiddle with your cunny. At least I know what it's for.'

The shrew was momentarily taken aback by the force of this sudden assault, but she soon recovered herself.

'So does every man in London I dare say.' She turned to my master. 'You hear how she talks Sam. Of all the unfortunates who deserve your help, you chose to inflict on us the sweepings of the gutter. What possessed you?'

'In matters concerning my own house,' replied my master with some warmth, 'I am obliged to answer to my conscience and my God, but not to you. I will thank you to remember that.'

The shrew looked abashed. She could push my master so far before encountering a determination more resolute even than her own. Beyond all things, she cared for his good opinion. However, before she could retrieve the situation a new voice joined the fray. Dr. Levet, who had been on an errand to the far side of the city, and had just that moment entered the house, was alerted by the raised voices sufficiently to rouse his curiousity. His thin, bony head appeared suddenly in the doorway.

'In God's name Sam, what the devil is the cause of this racket?'

His intervention served to call us back to the matter in hand.

'You may well ask, Levet,' said my master. 'Poll here is with child and charges Frank with being the father.'

Levet made a noise as though clearing his throat, which I recognised as a laugh.

'Anyone but a blockhead would have known the wench was stuffed. As for the father it could be any of the bravos she's been with behind the Benbow every evening now for the past six months. She's back at her trade Sam.'

The consequence of this ado was ultimately to my advantage. My master agreed that Betsy and I could not, for the time being, live at Johnson's Court. To attempt such would be to make the contention in the house unbearable. As it was, the shrew was for turning Poll out onto the streets again, a turn which my master rejected, saying he had not taken her from a life of misery and poverty only to thrust her back again. As for the child she was carrying, the household and she were relieved of that burden by her miscarrying shortly afterwards, a consequence, so she said, of her tripping over Hodge and falling downstairs. As Dr Levet sarcastically remarked,

'There's most of us in this house either blind or decrepit, and it takes a young healthy wench to fall over what we have managed to avoid these ten years past.'

My master, meanwhile, determined that Betsy and I should occupy two small rooms further down the hill from Johnson's Court in a neat house close to St Paul's, owned by a milliner. The shrew exclaimed against my master's extravagance, saying I should get ideas above my rank, but seeing that his mind was made up, she took to reminding me of my need to be grateful.

'Dr Johnson has been very generous to you. Make sure you behave yourself Frank. I shall be watching you.'

The words 'with what?' sprang to my lips, but I held back and consoled myself with relishing the day when I could reply to her in kind.

So Betsy and I were married on a raw winter's day towards the end of January at St Dunstan's Church in Fleet Street at around four in the afternoon. Present at the ceremony were my master, Lizzy, Costano, Obadiah and Famistan. Afterwards, my master excused himself, and I took my bride to our new quarters where we entertained our friends with an early supper. When we had eaten our fill Costano said to me,

'We have a surprise for Betsy, Frank. Something to enliven the proceedings.'

So saying he went to the door and called to someone below. There was a quick answer followed by a sudden pounding on the stairs, and into the room hurtled a small hunchbacked man with black swarthy skin, carrying a fiddle. He bowed to us all and grinned, displaying a row of white, sharpened teeth. I saw Lizzy grimace and heard her whisper to Betsy.

'You are to be serenaded by a monkey Betsy dear.'

'This,' said Costano with a flourish, 'is the finest fiddle player in all England. He is called Sebastian, though no one knows his true name.'

'Well ask him. He's got a tongue in his head hasn't he?' said Lizzy.

'He did have,' said Costano. 'Until he lost it courtesy of the British navy.'

Lizzy went deathly pale, and as for the rest of us, we were sufficiently quietened to wonder what entertainment Costano had in store. Meanwhile, Sebastian was spinning round the room, his feet tapping out a delicate rhythm on the wooden floor. As he came round a second time to Betsy and me he struck up an accompanying tune on his fiddle. The music was fast and intricate, with an insistent repetitive tune, which would disappear and return and then vanish again, ducking and diving, as if fleeing for its life from a relentless pursuer. We were all of us caught up in it, clapping and hurrahing for dear life, until the hunchback motioned for us to join him in the dance. So, we followed in a chain, our feet skipping and twirling, as though possessed. Round and round we went, when, just as we could take no more, the music ended on a high flourish. I turned to Betsy and took her in my arms. Her face was glowing with delight.

'We have begun our marriage at a gallop, Mrs Barber,' I said, breathlessly.

'Pray we don't end it on a fall,' she replied.

'If it's as fast and furious as that she'll not complain I wager,' put in Famistan.

Betsy blushed slightly.

'I fancy she can stand the pace well enough,' said Lizzy, flashing a look at Famistan. 'Say what you like about us women we've more go in us than any man.'

Since first setting eyes on him at the church, Lizzy had been flirting steadily with Famistan. He was the handsomest of us all, and now that Soubise had gone he had taken on himself the role of a young blood. His master, the Earl of Dornwood, also a young man, had allowed Famistan to attire himself as a gentleman rather than a servant. For his part, Famistan had taken to letting it be known that in his own country, before enslavement, he had been the son of a prince, a circumstance which Costano treated with scorn.

'His father was a basket weaver, depend upon it,' he said. 'These airs and graces are sheer fantasy.'

But there was no denying Famistan's youthful good looks and boyish charm, the last of which had survived his initiation by Soubise into even the lowest of brothels. He was now, at the age of twenty, a black Adonis, and fully aware of Lizzy's fascination for him.

'You speak the truth Lizzy,' he said. 'I daresay you have more than enough go in you to satisfy any man. I am sure you could satisfy me.'

'That's as maybe, but you'll never find out. I shall be like Betsy and save myself for a husband.'

'Very sensible, my dear,' said Obadiah, who had said little throughout the day. 'These things are not to be taken lightly. You young people think only of the present. When you are my age you value constancy and companionship.'

'Constancy and companionship are to be had from a dog. I have heard the Earl say as much myself,' said Famistan.

'He is a very loose fellow I hear,' replied Obadiah.

'He is a man of the times Obadiah and I value his favour.'

'You deceive yourself Famistan,' said Costano. 'Have you forgotten Soubise?'

At that moment, our attention was caught by a shuffling noise from the side of the room. Sebastian was busy arranging the chairs so that a space was cleared in the middle.

'We are not to be allowed to rest,' I said. 'But something slower this time Sebastian, if you please.'

He bowed to me and began a mournful air on his violin which set us all looking exceedingly gloomy. Then with a laugh he launched into an Irish reel, almost as fast as before. Over by the door I spied the milliner and his wife who had heard the music and come to watch the festivities. I motioned to them to join us and we were soon handing each other around the room in high spirits. Towards evening we began to tire, when a fresh influx of people, attracted by the sound of the hunchback's fiddle, invaded the room.

'He has bewitched us all,' said Betsy laughing. 'Look out of the window.'

Outside, people were dancing gaily in twos and threes, holding up carriages and carts, impatient to get by.

'What did I tell you?' Costano said, when we had all danced our fill. 'Is he not the finest fiddler you have heard?'

'He has certainly worn us to the socket,' said Famistan. 'Poor Frank will be good for nothing. You will have Betsy at your heels if he does not stop.'

'At least she may get a good night's sleep,' said Lizzy archly.

By now Sebastian had ceased the jigs and reels of his earlier display and was playing a gentle melody which I knew as 'Lover's tryst', a popular ballad in the taverns of London. It had a wistful, haunting refrain, very sweet. I studied him more closely as he played, and noticed with surprise that he had the same markings on his face as Costano, but etched more coarsely, as though the skin had been gouged rather than carved. I felt a hand on my shoulder.

'Who would think something so ugly could create such beauty?'

I turned to face Costano. He had read my thoughts exactly.

'He is from your tribe, is he not?' I asked.

He nodded. 'I knew him in the old country. He was an outcast because of his deformity. My father took him into our household so we could laugh at him while we eat. After a time he became very skilled at performing tricks. He can play any instrument you care to mention, providing he can dance while he plays. If you removed his legs he would be as you or me. He used to sing too, once.'

'So you must know his real name?'

'He is called Adebayo. The sailors nicknamed him Sebastian after a monkey one of them had, which could climb the ropes and catch peanuts.'

'He is not a likely shape to be sold into slavery'.

'Adebayo was captured with me and when I was sold he was given to the captain of the ship as a present. One day he displeased the captain with one of his tricks and his tongue was cut out as a punishment. When the ship came to England the captain tried to sell him, but eventually threw him out to starve. But, as you see, he reckoned without Adebayo's ingenuity. He is much sought after for his playing.'

'I can well believe it. Betsy is much pleased with her present.'

'I am glad of that. But I did not bring him here simply for Betsy's pleasure, or yours.'

Costano paused. I waited for him to continue, but he seemed to find it difficult.

'What I am about to tell you is not meant to alarm you,' he went on.

'You have alarmed me already,' I said.

'Tell me what you mean.'

'I brought Adebayo here to meet you.'

'Why me?'

'Because he knew your mother.'

I did not at first take in what Costano was saying. It seemed almost as if he was talking of someone else. Someone who had a mother once, as I had not.

'Are you listening to me Frank? Did you hear what I said?'

I nodded but every instinct in me rejected what I had heard. My mother was a silver chain in my keeping, that was all. I had no memory of her and wanted none.

'It cannot be true,' I said. 'My mother died on the voyage to the plantations. Adebayo was brought to England. The thing is impossible.'

'England is where he met her. Believe me. This is true.'

I shook my head vigorously.

'She was taken from Africa. My first master, Colonel Bathurst told me. How could she have come here? It is someone else.'

'Listen to me Frank. Your mother did indeed die going to the plantations. That is true. But the ship was sailing from England, not Africa.'

'But why should the Colonel lie to me? What reason could he have?'

'Think Frank. Did he ever say exactly where the ship came from?'

I paused. In the stillness, I could hear my own breathing, faster than normal, as though I had been running. Adebayo was playing, but softly, as if at a great distance. The guests were moving like ghosts around the room, some slumped in chairs or on the floor. From the next room I could see Betsy looking across at me her face creased with anxiety.

'Frank', she called out, coming across, 'Are you alright?'

'Yes Betsy. I am just a bit faint after our exertions.'

I saw Lizzy smile knowingly at Famistan, and he smirked back at her. Obadiah, for his part shook his head.

'In my young days I could dance for hours. But my old bones won't let me now. Take things steadily, and make the most of life while you can Frank. That is my advice.'

'And very dreary advice it is too,' said Famistan.

'I must agree with Famistan,' said Costano. 'You are hardly an old man, and have danced this evening like a young buck. It is my fault Frank is tired. I have been wearying him with a tale about my boyhood.'

I was grateful for the interruption which seemed to serve as notice to everyone that the evening's entertainment was over. One by one our guests, whose number had swelled considerably during the evening, took their leave. Costano whispered to me as he withdrew to think about what he had said. A quite unnecessary admonition, since my mind was full of little else. Adebayo was one of the last to leave, giving Betsy a low bow, before vanishing through the door as spiritedly as he had come. I attempted to see from his manner whether he knew what Costano had told me, but his face remained the same grinning mask it had been all night. Afterwards, I sat on the bed while Betsy readied herself for the night. Costano's question ran riot in my mind like a mad dog. I feared to approach it lest it should injure me. I thought back to a time long distant. A memory stirred as though I had turned the yellowing pages of a book. I was in a large room, the curtains billowing slightly in the breeze, blowing from the garden. An elderly man was sitting at a desk to one side of the window. In front of him a small boy was listening as he spoke.

'Come closer Frank where I can see you properly.'

I moved round the desk and stood, obediently, at his side.

'I have been observing you Frank. You have been diligent and helpful around the house. I like that. Mama Du speaks well of your conduct. You are a good obedient child.'

He coughed, bringing his hand stiffly up to his mouth and wiping it with a silk kerchief. After a few moments he continued.

'You must know that I have decided to remove to England. I do not intend to return. I am telling you this because you will be accompanying me.'

He must have noticed the look of apprehension on my face because his manner unbent slightly, and he looked more kindly at me.

'There is nothing for you to fear. You will like your new home. The climate is more temperate, and the sun does not shine so incessantly. There are many good things to enjoy.'

'Yes master,' I ventured at last, at a loss to know what good there could be in such a place.

'Is England far away master?

'It is several days journey by ship Frank. We shall see what kind of sailor you are,' he smiled.

'Will I really like it master?' 'Yes Frank, for there you will no longer be a slave. Do you know what that means?'

I shook my head.

'Shall I become white like you master?'

'No, that can never happen. You will always be as you are. But it means you will be free. Freedom is something men prize above all else.'

He stopped, seeing me puzzled.

'Well, never mind. You will understand in time.'

'Were my mother and father free, master?

He coughed again, and wiped his mouth slowly with his kerchief.

'Your father I know nothing of Frank, but yes, he must have been free. Your mother, as I told you before, perished on the boat which was transporting her here.'

He opened a drawer in the desk and brought out a small packet which he turned upside down. Out of it fell a long silver chain made of delicate ringlets.

'This is yours,' he said pushing it towards me.

I stared at it. I knew that such a rare object could not be mine.

'Take it. It was your mother's. When she died the captain stole it from her. I recovered it and kept it for you.'

'What was Costano saying to you so earnestly, Frank,' said Betsy suddenly emerging from the other room towards me.

'Nothing of any consequence,' I lied, fingering the chain around my neck.

'He was telling me about Soubise. He has the pox and been sent away into the country to recover.'

'That is better than India, at least.' She replied.

'Yes.'

I got into bed beside her at a loss as to why I had not told her the truth. Some instinct in me whispered that things were best left alone. The past was dead, let it remain so. After all, my mother had meant nothing to me, and it was impossible to add to the joy I now felt. Any discovery I made could be of no significance. With the aid of such reflections, and the influence of my wife's caresses, I soon found the events of the evening receding.

The next few days and weeks passed in a trance. For much of the time, I seemed to be living another existence. Becoming a married man had, unknowingly, raised me in everyone's esteem. Even my master took notice of my new situation, choosing on occasions to call me Mr Barber. One day, as I was reading to him, a service I had increasingly been called upon to supply since the deterioration of his sight, he said,

'You will no longer be able to accompany me so freely to the Thrales now you have acquired the dignity of a husband.' He squinted at me. 'Betsy will not like you enjoying the company of Mrs Thrale's maids, and the lady herself will not be pleased should you carry off more of them.'

'My conquests have ceased with Betsy, master.'

'Good. Society will be a safer place now you are settled.' He emitted his usual grunt. 'And Mrs Barber? Is she happy with the bargain she has struck?'

'She says so master.'

'Keep it that way Frank. Women are heretics in their desires. They have a genius for mischief, and for knowing us better than we do ourselves.'

The eccentric mixture of censure and compliment in his reflection left me for a moment, unable to reply.

'Mr Boswell believes they are the better sex, master,' I said eventually.

He let out a roar at this.

'Does he? It is news to me that Jamie Boswell has any beliefs to speak of, though he carries off the pretence of them very well. Do not go to Bozzy for an opinion. He acquires them as children do baubles.'

He paused before continuing in more sombre mood.

'The lot of a woman is scarcely a happy one. She must live her life in subordination to others. If she is fortunate she will find a man who will not oppress her. Mrs Johnson and I rubbed along pretty well, but I fancy I did not bring her much happiness. Betsy seems a good girl. Stick to her Frank.'

This was the closest I got to receiving his approval of my marriage. As for Betsy, she continued to grow in favour. She was taken on very early to help in the kitchen, Poll having proved entirely useless. Mrs Desmoulins was at first not happy with the arrangement and complained to my master that instead of one idle girl to hinder her, she would now have two. But she soon learnt the value of her new kitchen maid, as did the rest of the house. Mrs Desmoulins' food was never wholesome at the best of times. Even the cat could be observed turning away from it in disgust. This mattered little to the shrew, who scarce ate above a mouthful of anything, but for the rest of us who had to endure her regime, the constant state of famine was insupportable. No cook lasted more than a few days under Mrs Desmoulins' watchful eye. She was always certain the food could be prepared more cheaply, and made to last longer. But within a few weeks she was content to leave the running of the kitchen to Betsy. The secret, I soon learned, of this revolution lay in Betsy's cunning. She let it be known to Mrs Desmoulins, that at Streatham Place, a lady of any rank would not stoop to working in a kitchen. The effect on Mrs Desmoulins was dramatic. Gradually she withdrew from the kitchen, keeping herself to the morning room where she busied herself in sewing.

'After all,' I heard her say, 'I may be in reduced circumstances, but I am still a lady.'

To Betsy, however, she said merely that she had been waiting for someone suitable to assume her responsibilities, and was happy to relinquish duties she had always found irksome. The rest of the house rejoiced in the change.

'Thank God the woman has seen sense at last,' said Dr.Levet. 'She is fortunate not to have been taken up on a charge of manslaughter.'

'Then she may join you Levet. Your concoctions are hardly less foul. I shall recommend her to set up as an apothecary,' said my master.

Dr. Levet looked stung at this.

'My preparations preserve life Sam, which can hardly be said for her poisonous brew.'

My master snapped his fingers.

'A pistol may preserve life but the world is not the better for its invention.'

'It is very well for you Sam. You have the privilege of escaping when you wish to the Thrales. Consider the lot of those who remain. Consider our stomachs sir.'

The shrew was the only one of our number unhappy with the new order. She assailed my master one day as he was taking tea with her in her room.

'So Mrs Desmoulins has decided that the kitchen is not suited to her station in life,' she began. 'Are we now to stand on ceremony with her? Will she expect to be curtsied to?'

'No Anna. There will be no change in the household arrangements except that Betsy will be asuming Elizabeth's duties for the time being. That is all. Her health has not been good of late, and this will allow her some respite.'

'You did not see fit to seek my opinion Sam, though I have been the one entrusted with household matters since your absences at the Thrales?'

'You have been not been well yourself ma'am. I thought to avoid inflicting further distress.'

She peered sharply at him over the rim of her cup and poked a bony finger in his direction.

'You have become a politician Sam. It does not suit you.'

'Then it is living here that has done it, ma'am. I fancy there are more factions in this house than in parliament itself.'

'You have only yourself to blame for that,' she replied. 'But I shall soon relieve you of your anxiety. I shall not be an encumbrance to you much longer.'

'Nay ma'am do not talk so. You will outlast us all.'

She shook her head, spilling some of her tea.

'I hope God is more merciful. I pray to him daily to end my days.'

'That would deprive me of my oldest friend.'

'It pleases you to say so, but I am not so foolish as to think I should be long mourned.'

'This is a morbid state of mind Anna.'

'There was a time Sam, after Tetty died.'

A look of alarm crossed my master's face and he twitched visibly in his chair.

'Have a care Anna. There are things better not remembered.'

She nodded and then looked over to me, busy clearing away the tea things.

'Meanwhile,' she said. 'We must all dance to Betsy's tune. I fancy she will soon be supplanting me.'

'Let us have no talk of 'supplanting' ma'am. Betsy will be a useful member of the household.'

'And another mouth to feed,' she replied scornfully.

But even the shrew found it impossible to maintain her dislike of Betsy for long. For her part, Betsy was careful to acknowledge her authority, deferring to her over any decisions to be made, and not answering back when she was in one of her black moods. One morning, as I was opening the shutters in the dining room, she said to me,

'Heaven alone knows how you managed it Frank, but you have married a clever woman. You are no better than a dolt if you do not acknowledge it.'

I told Betsy this and she laughed.

'See,' she said. 'Everyone can be managed. You just have to know how.'

Time slipped by and I began to forget about Adebayo until one evening as I was returning home from Johnson's Court to St Paul's. I was passing the Benbow, when I heard from inside the strains of a fiddle being played with great gusto. I stopped to listen for a while, and debated with myself whether to venture in. The playing brought back fond memories of my wedding day, and I half fancied that if I put my head round the open door I should see another couple dancing as Betsy and I had, so many weeks before. Eventually, curiosity got the better of me, and I went in.

The sight that met my eyes surprised me. Adebayo was there as I expected, playing and cavorting round the room to the furious clapping of the onlookers. But he was not alone. With him were at least ten more black people, mostly men, but a few women too. Some of them had instruments, which from the look of it they had been playing. Two of them were the strangest in appearance I had ever seen. The first, a small man, with an excessively large face and bloated cheeks, which made him look, for all the world like a roasted turnip, was lolling against a table with a scarf around his neck. As I watched, he mounted the table, and to a frenzied flourish from

Adebayo, quickly withdrew his scarf. There was a sudden gasp from the crowd. Across his neck was a deep wound, scarlet at the edges and purple, almost black, in the centre. While we stared, he opened his coat and plainly visible across his chest in bold lettering was the inscription:

Joseph Olugunde

Born: West Africa -1730

Hanged by the neck: Jamaica - 1770

When we had looked our fill at the gruesome wound, he bent down and beckoned to some of the women in the crowd to come and touch it. But none were so bold. The wound had the peculiar appearance of looking fresh, almost as though it might start bleeding again at any moment, even though it was several years old. After a few minutes, one of the men in the crowd pushed forward and throwing a coin into a cap on the table, reached out and ran two of his fingers gently round the rim of the wound.

'Go on Will. Stick em in. It's not real,' called out someone.

The man looked round grinning. Suddenly, Olugunde took hold of the man's hand and plunged it roughly against his flesh as though trying to insert it into his neck. Immediately, he pulled away in disgust. This set the crowd roaring.

'What's the matter Will? Scared of a nigger?' called out someone else.

'I ain't scared of nuthin,' replied Will. 'But it's real I tell you. Anyone who says it isn't is a bloody liar.'

He looked round angrily, defying anyone to contradict him. I looked again at the scar where it ran brutally round his throat. The edges, though fresh and vivid in hue, were thick and rubbery. The rope must have cut very deeply, almost to the bone. After displaying himself for a few minutes more, the man jumped down from the table. He was immediately replaced by his companion, a tall willowy woman, with an imposing, stately, figure. She would have been a most handsome woman, except for her colour. For although her features proclaimed her black, like her fellows, she was perfectly white, even to the hair. As we looked, she revealed parts of her body to us. All appeared bloodless, as though bleached. She seemed like someone from the grave. The only sign of life lay in her eyes which were pink and almost bloodshot. The murmuring from the onlookers indicated that this monstrosity was worse than the last. The women thought she must be a witch, while some of the men considered her to be the victim of some experiment.

'What did I say?' said a fierce, argumentative man, in the middle of the throng. 'They're all white underneath. I said so.'

There was general laughter at this which made the man even more pugnacious. He turned round as if squaring up for a fight.

'It's a fact. It's the sun turns 'em black.'

'It's paint,' said someone next to him. 'Any fool can see she's painted herself.'

The first man made his objections at being thought a fool very clear and matters might have become violent, when a suggestion that the skin be inspected calmed things down. Two of the women reached up and felt the woman's arms and legs.

'Look at her fanny. I bet it ain't white,' a voice called out.

There was a general chorus for the woman to be undressed, but the landlord appeared at that moment and said he was not going to have his inn turned into a brothel. Eventually, it was agreed that the women should take her to one side and privately inspect her. It took but a few moments to accomplish this and to announce the verdict, which confirmed that she was indeed white all over, and that it wasn't paint. The fierce man was triumphant.

'See,' he said. 'She's been peeled. I've seen it done before, with boiling sugar. The black just peels off.'

Most of the crowd remained unconvinced by this explanation, but some were for trying the experiment on one or more of those present, and had the landlord not stepped in to stop the display, they might very well have proceeded to some enormity. He bundled the troupe unceremoniously into the street, myself along with them, and I found myself at the centre of a very disgruntled group of blacks. I looked from one to the other.

'Dey rob us,' said Joseph Olugunde.

'Dey stole our money. Dey nuthin' but teeves.'

He wiped his throat with a cloth and I saw the freshness disappear from his wound. It looked now like a very old injury. He turned to me and ran his eyes briefly up and down. I could see contempt in his gaze.

'You got no place here nigger,' he said. 'You ain't one of us.'

Just as he said that, Adebayo came over to him and signed quickly. Joseph observed him closely, then grunted and turned away.

'What did Adebayo say?' I asked. 'Tell me what he said.'

The sound of Adebayo's name on my lips drew all their attention. When Joseph spoke again to me his tone was different.

'He say you look like a turd, you dress like a turd, but you ain't a turd.'

Adebayo stood by, grinning at me, as he said this. I nodded at him.

'I am grateful for your good opinion,' I said.

Adebayo signed again to Joseph. But this time it was the albino woman who translated for me.

'He say you talk like a turd too.'

I smiled at him and bowed, while he just grinned back. Then, without warning, he put two fingers in his mouth and whistled to the rest of the group, of which he seemed to be the leader, and they set off at a run up Fleet street. When I looked again they had disappeared down one of the numerous alleys, leaving me to make my way home and ponder on the strange encounter. That blacks like Adebayo and his companions existed I knew well enough. The city contained many such. Some were runaway slaves seeking to hide from their masters, trying to earn a living from any who would employ them. They would work almost for nothing, a circumstance which did not endear them to their white competitors. Others were cast off by their masters for some injury or deformity they had sustained, and left to fend for themselves. I would see them on the streets begging, or crouched in shop doorways seeking shelter. Soubise and Famistan always affected to despise them and would cross the street. As for me, I averted my gaze and quickened my pace. From time to time the shrew would delight in reminding me how slender was the thread dividing my fate from theirs.

'Have a care Frank,' she would say. 'If you are discontented with your service here there is always the street.'

Of troupes such as Adebayo's, though, I knew little. I had heard of them but this was the first I had witnessed. How did they live I wondered? I fancied them relying on their wits, travelling wherever profit was to be had from entertainment. A shiftless, uncertain life. With thoughts like these I arrived home to find Betsy waiting for me in a state of high anxiety.

'Wherever have you been Frank? I have been expecting you this past hour.'

I started on an explanation but soon found it was not needed. Betsy's anxiety was not caused by my delay, but by some information she had received from Streatham Place.

'Frank, you will not believe what I am about to tell you. There has been such goings on at Streatham. Mistress is beside herself. She says if it weren't for the children she could wish herself dead. And Lizzy too.'

'Calm yourself Betsy and tell me what has happened.'

'Miss Sophy Gordon is with child. And all the world knows it is Mr Thrale's.'

'Has he said so?' She looked scornfully at me.

'I should think he has not the effrontery to deny it.'

'All the world may be wrong, my dear. Miss Gordon may have other lovers.'

'I might expect you to take his part. My poor mistress. It is too shocking for her. And that is not all. There's Lizzy too.'

'Lizzy is with child as well.'

'Yes.'

'And by Mr Thrale?'

'No, you booby. By Famistan.'

5

'It is too much Sam,' said Mrs Thrale. 'Henry has made me a laughing stock. God knows I have been generous about his past infidelities. But this...' Her voice tailed off and she gestured despairingly.

'You know that he denies paternity ma'am'?' replied my master.

She looked scornfully at him.

'He has set her up in an establishment of her own. I do not imagine this arrangement was an act of charity.'

Master had gone to Streatham as soon as news broke of the turmoil at the Thrale's, stopping only to give instructions for certain papers and books, on which he was working, to be despatched after him. On this occasion he instructed also that I should accompany him. He said to Betsy that I would be useful to him as an amanuensis, assisting with the drafting of letters and other documents. But in truth there were other services I performed of which he was more commonly in need. He would of late lean more heavily and more often on me, so that had I not been present he must have called for assistance.

'You are become his walking stick,' Betsy joked. 'He will soon use you to beat tradesmen with.'

When we arrived at Streatham Mrs Thrale was in a distracted condition. My master was for sending me to the servants' quarters, but she waved her hand dismissively declaring that it was too late for discretion, Henry had seen to that.

'It will be my misfortune for the slut to give birth to a boy,' Mrs Thrale continued. 'Will Henry disown it then?'

She sat down wearily on a chair which my master placed for her and began dabbing at her eyes. Since the death of her son she had frequently been given to sudden uncontrollable bursts of weeping. Mr Thrale had been almost broken by the loss.

'What am I to do Sam? He has treated me with contempt. And my daughters too.'

'Henry has many faults Hesther but he will never desert his family. You must think that he has merely strayed and will return. He is weak, as men generally are, but he is not given to vice. If you forgive him you will show the rarer virtue.'

'I believe he loves her. I see it in his face.'

'Fiddlesticks. Henry is a middle aged man who finds his vanity soothed by a woman thirty years younger than himself. It is an occurrence the world knows well.'

'He has squandered money on her. Heaven knows how much. Perkins came to see me yesterday. He says Henry has been speculating in the funds and has lost heavily. We are ruined Sam, I know it.'

'If that is the case ma'am he will be of little further use to Sophy Gordon.'

'And of little use to my children either. They will be reduced to poverty. They have done nothing to deserve this.'

She picked up a glass from the table and drank the remaining few drops. When she spoke again her voice seemed old and beaten.

'I was a great fool to marry him.'

Later, as I helped my master attire himself for bed I saw him rub his loins and stomach in a manner which filled me with foreboding. He had been free from the rheumaticks for some weeks past, but I feared its onset daily. The suddenness with which we had left Johnson's Court, and the anxiety of his interview with Mrs Thrale had not been advantageous to him.

'I think I shall need the flannel tonight Frank,' he said as I helped him rise after saying prayers.

'I shall get them ready master,' I said.

'Yes, Frank.'

I hurried downstairs and begged some flannel from one of the scullery maids, reflecting as I did, how unusual it was for Mrs Thrale to overlook such a detail. As I came back into the room, my master was reading a passage from the Bible, his head bent so low to the page that the candle threatened to singe his wig. He looked up as I came in.

'What has occurred in this house should be a great lesson to you Frank,' he said.

'Yes, master,' I replied grimly, knowing he would not be content to leave the matter there.

'Mr and Mrs Thrale are blessed with all the advantages which living in a polite and prosperous nation can bring. They have wealth, a fine house, and are beloved by their friends and family. Yet they are not happy. In my youth my days were often filled with envying the great and fancying to myself a future condition of consummate happiness. What folly Frank. What folly.'

I laid out the flannel on the bed, and thought briefly as I did of Adebayo and his friends.

'But some conditions are happier than others master,' I protested. 'The life of a free man must be better than that of a slave.'

'Freedom is certainly better than slavery, yet a free man is not certainly happier than a slave.'

'What is happiness then master?'

'At the moment Frank it is to be rid of these troublesome rheumaticks,' he said rubbing himself ferociously. 'But if I were to answer in general I should say with Jonathan Swift that it is "the perpetual possession of being well deceived".'

I helped him into the flannel sheets, winding them round him as though tying a bandage. He was in a despondent mood, peevish and fretful. I attempted to cheer him with talk of Mr Boswell's visit last spring but he would not be drawn.

'Nay Frank, do not remind me of that which I cannot have. I would give half my pension for Jamie's company now.'

As I expected, he did not sleep well. He began with a fitful doze but around two in the morning his restlessness became almost feverish. I got up and went over to him. He was lying on his back with his hands and feet in perpetual motion. His eyes were open and he was staring upwards as though struggling to see something. He looked at me as I approached, the corners of his mouth twitching in the manner common to him when agitated.

'It seems I am not to be allowed any sleep. I have murdered it, as Shakespeare says. Get me up Frank, and I shall sit by the fire.'

I helped him rise and steered him gently to a large armchair in front of the fire. I knew by habit what his next command would be.

'Step down to the kitchen Frank and prepare me a dish of tea. And for yourself too.'

I made my way down to the kitchen which at this hour of the morning was deserted. The fire which burnt continually underneath the great chimney had sunk down, its embers flickering dully in the darkness. I quickly raked it through and put a large pan of water on the iron grill, thinking as I did so of Nancy, Lizzy and Betsy, all of whom, in a few short months, had departed from Streatham Place. Nancy had simply vanished. There were reports that she had gone north to one of the new cities and was working as a maid to a sea captain, but no one knew for certain. As for Lizzy, she had eloped to be with her lover. At least that is what the note she left for Mrs Thrale said. It was left with a small packet containing some trinkets given to her by Mrs Thrale. She would not have it said she had taken anything which did not belong to her. 'Foolish girl,' said Mrs Thrale when news of Lizzy's sudden departure was brought to her, 'she has exceeded even Nancy's stupidity. She has ruined herself.'

When I took the tea up to my master I found him attempting to read by the light of the fire.

'Ah Frank,' he said pettishly. 'You were gone so long I thought you had taken up residence in the kitchen.'

'The fire was low master. It needed stoking.'

'Well, now you are here you can read to me if you please. I fear my eyes have become strained and sore.'

I made the tea and began reading to him, thinking as I did so, what the world would make of such a scene. The great lexicographer, and editor of Shakespeare sitting helpless, his body continuously contorted like some deranged puppet, being read to as though a small child. What a subject it would have made for one of his *Rambler* essays. A similar thought must have crossed his mind, for after a short while, he glanced across at me with a smile playing round his lips.

'I fancy your friends, Soubise and Famistan, would find your present situation entertaining.'

'Master?'

121

'They are both fine bucks are they not? They frequent theatres and brothels with the regularity of lords so Boswell tells me.'

'Soubise has been sent abroad by his mistress. Of Famistan's habits I know little,' I replied stiffly.

'I am pleased to hear it Frank. Famistan should have a care. The Earl of Dornwood's tastes are of uncertain continuance. I knew his father, the late Earl - a man of vicious and libertine desires. He killed his groom for muddying his boots. There is no greater insolence than the insolence of power.'

'Is there not the protection of the law master?'

'The law is a blunt instrument Frank. Many a thing which is not right is tolerated. We need only consider the situation of your fellow countrymen.'

He shook his head gravely from side to side and his limbs ceased their twitching. When he spoke again it was in the solemn tones of a magistrate.

'No man is by nature the property of another. We suffer slavery to our shame in the West Indies, and it is certain that no English or Scottish law permits the institution here. But men and women are still traded as cattle. I cannot have many more years left to me Frank, but when I die you and your family will live independently. I will see to that.'

His words struck me forcibly. I looked up from the book I was holding and tears sprang to my eyes. I tried to speak but my tongue had become thick and heavy. He saw my distress and waved his hand airily.

'Nay Frank. Do not take on so. You must think that I have no son, no heir, to carry my name forward. The name of Johnson will die with me. If I had married again perhaps, but then my life would have followed a very different fortune.'

I tried again to express my gratitude, and this time managed a few halting words, but he would hear no more on the subject, and dismissed it by requesting me to carry on reading to him. This was ever his way. I knew by experience of his dislike for 'feelers'. So I picked up the book which I had let fall to the ground and attempted to continue. Fortunately, I had not to do so for very long. After a few minutes the low rumble of snoring interrupted my endeavours and I looked up to see his head slumped forward. I contemplated going back to my bed but the idea of movement left me unaccountably fatigued, and in thinking about getting up I fell into a deep slumber.

Morning found us both ensconced in our chairs, the rays of the mid-morning sun filtering through the curtains. The fire had burnt out in the night and I shivered with cold. When my master awoke, his slow and heavy movements showed that sleep had refreshed him little. He looked wearily round and addressed himself mournfully to me.

'We have survived another night Frank. Let us be thankful.'

The instant he said this his lethargy disappeared. He got up from his chair as though galvanised by one of Mr Priestley's electrical experiments, and announced himself ravenous. Such unaccountable bursts had become more frequent of late. Mr Boswell said he was one of those for whom rapid and sudden motion alleviated afflictions of the mind. I arose too and prepared to help him wash and dress, but he was too impatient, and hastily attiring himself, he went out of the room, muttering as he did so that he hoped breakfast had not fallen victim to Thrale's doltishness, otherwise he was like to turn cannibal.

Around mid-afternoon the household was disturbed by the arrival of Mr Thrale on horseback from the city. He arrived looking hot and flustered. I was the first to see him as he came into the entrance hall. He stopped and waved his finger at me, which I noticed bore signs of chewing.

'Ah Mr Barber,' he said, 'I see my wife has sent for her big gun. Well I am ready for him. I am not to be trifled with. Have the goodness to tell Mrs Thrale I am here, and tell Will to bring me a bottle of port in the library.'

'Will is no longer in service here sir,' I reminded him.

'Then bring it yourself. Must I do everything?'

I made towards the drawing room where I knew Mrs Thrale was, but she intercepted me at the doorway as her husband disappeared into the library.

'I am not at home to Mr Thrale Frank,' she said. 'Ask Dr Johnson to attend him in the library.'

'Mr Thrale wishes for a bottle of port ma'am.'

'It is his house. If he wishes to drink himself further into oblivion let him do so.'

I went out into the garden where I knew my master had gone after breakfast. It was one of those tranquil summer days when thoughts of disharmony seem to belong to another existence. I found him sitting under a willow tree down by the lake reading.

'I see from your countenance Frank that the miscreant has returned,' he said, looking up as I arrived.

'He is in the library master.' '

And in what temper?'

'Mr Thrale is out of temper.'

'Is he? Well, let us beard the villain in his den.'

He motioned me towards him and I held out my arm. He got up, wheezing slightly, and walked slowly along the gravel path towards the house. Inside, he waved me away, and went into the library, shutting the door behind him. After a decent interval had elapsed I knocked on the door and entered carrying a bottle of port which I had fetched from the cellar. My master was standing by the fireplace looking down on Mr Thrale who sat sprawling in an armchair, red-faced and decidedly ill at ease. They both turned in my direction as I came in.

'What the devil are you doing Frank?' said my master. 'Take that away. Mr Thrale will drink water or tea. Nothing else.'

'Stay there,' said Mr Thrale, pointing at me. 'I fancy I am still master here Sam and can command a bottle of port if I wish.'

'Then you must do so from one of your own servants sir. Mine will not assist you in sinking into insensibility.'

'But I have been mightily abused Sam. I have not fathered Sophy Gordon's child. It is a monstrous libel.'

'Maybe so, but the whole world believes it and with good reason. You have become her benefactor. A man does not buy a pretty woman clothes and jewels for nothing.'

'The whore deceived me. She simpered and purred with the best of them. But all the time she had her nose in another trough. I got nothing by her for my pains.'

'Nothing?'

Mr Thrale shrugged his shoulders.

'No. Except the clap.'

'In God's name Henry!'

'Not by her,' Mr Thrale said bitterly. 'I found consolation some nights ago in a bagnio.'

This last announcement stunned my master who looked up to see me still standing there, the port in my hand. But before he could order me away, we were interrupted by another voice coming from the open doorway.

'So sir, not content with dragging your family's name in the mire you would give me a dose of the clap as well.' It was Mrs Thrale white and trembling.

Mr Thrale got up to go to his wife but she held out her hand.

'No Henry, don't. I would not have believed it even of you.'

'I meant you no harm,' said Mr Thrale. 'I was drunk and miserable. I have confessed it now.' He opened his arms to her in an attitude of despair.

Mrs Thrale looked contemptuously at him 'I have borne you eight children sir. Four of them are dead. And I could wish that I were dead with them.'

'Don't say so Hesther. I have behaved badly. I acknowledge it. But it is over now.'

'Only because Miss Gordon has found another fool. Where is your constancy Henry? Where is your loyalty, if not to me then to your children?'

'I would never forsake my children Hesther. You cannot charge me with that.'

'You have already forsaken them. You would bring ruin and shame on their heads.'

My master, who had been standing silent during this exchange, now approached Hesther and took hold of one of her hands.

'Ma'am you and your children are too much loved by your friends, of whom I count myself the principal, for that to happen. The gossip of the town is mere flotsam on the surface of society. It will have its day and then pass. But your virtues, and those of your children are real and known and must triumph.'

Mrs Thrale looked at him in silence. But when she next spoke her voice was like steel.

'If it were simply a matter of fashionable opinion I could weather it. Henry's tastes are not new to me, nor, I fancy, to the town. But he has brought us to bankruptcy by his folly. God knows if even Streatham Place is safe. Where shall we go if we are forced to leave?'

Mr Thrale seemed to take heart from the turn in the conversation, and following my master's example, he came over to his wife and took her other hand, which she suffered to be held.

'Matters are not so bad my dear, whatever you have heard,' he said. 'We are in no danger of losing our house.'

'But according to Perkins,' she began.

'Perkins does not know everything,' interrupted Mr Thrale. 'He manages the business and knows what is good for him to know.'

Mrs Thrale shook her head.

'You keep me in the dark Henry. What am I supposed to think?'

'Hesther is in the right of it Henry,' said my master releasing Mrs Thrale's hand. 'Send for Perkins immediately and let us have a complete account of how things stand. Henry you must reveal all to us.'

'As you will,' replied Mr Thrale.

'And Frank will oblige us by bringing us tea in the drawing room,' said my master.

I withdrew quietly and returned the port to the cellar, thinking as I did what a sorry pass things had come to at Streatham. My sympathies were chiefly for Mrs Thrale, who had been grievously wronged. Betsy told me she had borne much in her marriage. Mr Thrale was often excessive in his appetites, and had grown tired of his wife's continual child bearing, although in truth he was a fond and doting parent. In her turn, Mrs Thrale had sought relief from the burden of maternity in making Streatham Place a centre for the London literati, an ambition considered presumptuous for the wife of a merchant. But her wit and talent for hospitality had silenced all opposition. For his part, Mr Thrale relished his wife's success, though latterly, as his business fortunes declined, he had come to resent it.

Mr and Mrs Thrale remained closeted with my master for the rest of the day, leaving me to spend the time as I wished. I wandered around the house and gardens gossiping to the servants I knew and trying to get some news of Lizzy. A change had come over Streatham Place since I had last been there. It had always been full of bustle. There was scarcely a day when guests were not expected for one of Mr Thrale's gargantuan dinners. And he was continually spending lavishly on new furnishings and costly ornaments. But there was now a pinched and parsimonious air about the house. The servants conducted themselves in a subdued and chastened manner as if sharing in the burdens of the owners. Entertaining still went on - the social round could not be interrupted merely for domestic inconvenience – but it was a dull and joyless affair, as the cook informed me when I visited her in the kitchen.

'We've had a deal of trouble since you were here Frank,' she said, her hand deep inside a goose she was dressing. 'Mistress has been at her wits end - keeping to her room and carrying on something pitiful. I'm sure I don't know what's got into Mr Thrale.'

'I think matters may be on the mend,' I replied. 'It seems he and Miss Gordon have fallen out.'

'Well, I'm glad of that. She's no better than she should be. Coming here as though butter wouldn't melt in her mouth. I don't know what the world's coming to. In my day she'd have been thrown into the Bridewell.'

She drew her hand out of the goose, disposing of a mass of bloody entrails in a bucket under the sink.

'Have you heard anything of Lizzy?' I enquired, eager to change the subject.

She spread her hands in a gesture of hopelessness.

'Another little madam,' she replied. 'Always after the men, as you well know. She's done for herself good and proper now. And with one of your lot too.'

'I hope Famistan won't abandon her.'

'From what I hear he's not likely to wed her. Not like you and Betsy. But then Betsy always did have her head screwed on. And your not a bad sort Frank.'

I thanked her for what seemed like a compliment and returned again to the subject of Lizzy.

'Do you know where she is living now?' I asked.

'No. She just upped and left. Told John, the footman, she'd got a cousin in Moorgate, but she never has. Silly little fool. Mistress wouldn't have turned her off. She's too soft-hearted.'

I was disappointed that she knew no more. Betsy had particularly asked me to discover her whereabouts. Lizzy was a headstrong girl who might throw away any chance of recovery for want of good advice. Despite her strident manner she looked up to Betsy and might listen to her. For my part, I feared, that if her hopes lay with Famistan, she reckoned without his ambitious nature. There seemed little I could do except speak to Mrs Thrale on her behalf. But there would be scant opportunity for that with the current crisis in the house. As fortune would have it, however, it was Mrs Thrale herself who raised the subject of Lizzy with me. It occurred towards evening. I was assisting John, who had taken over the duties of head footman since Will's departure, in preparing the table for dinner, when Mrs Thrale appeared in the doorway. She looked pale and drawn, and her manner, which was normally so spirited, was dull and lifeless. She motioned to me with her hand.

'A word with you Frank, if you please,' she said.

I went over to her and she drew me outside into the hallway.

'Dr. Johnson will be staying a few days to assist Mr Thrale and me.'

'Yes ma'am. I thought that would be so.'

'Quite. However, I have requested your master to release you for the time in order to perform a special service for me.'

'Ma'am?'

'You are aware of what has occurred with Lizzy, my scullery maid?'

I nodded.

'Yes ma'am. Betsy knew her well.'

'Of course. She has behaved like a hussy, and I have been minded to abandon her. But I cannot in conscience let her ruin herself without attempting one last effort to save her. I wish you to find her Frank, and let her know that she may return here to Streatham Place.'

'I will do what I can ma'am.'

'Good. You can leave first thing in the morning. If you find her let her know that she may keep the child.'

She glanced fleetingly at me and I caught in that moment a sense of the effort it cost her to make this concession. Lizzy had behaved no differently from Sophy Gordon, a coincidence which could not have been lost on her. Lizzy's child would be a perpetual reminder to Mrs Thrale of that other infant, over whose paternity there still hung, despite the vigorous denials of her husband, the scent of scandal. My master was keenly conscious of this as I helped him prepare for bed that night.

'Mrs Thrale is an example to us all of Christian charity Frank. There are not many employers in her situation who would concern themselves about a scullery maid.'

I was tempted to remind him of Poll, but held my tongue, uncertain where such an observation might lead.

'I cannot be certain of finding her master,' I said. 'There is little information of her whereabouts.'

'If the fox has gone to ground it will not be your fault. It is enough that you make the attempt. Mrs Thrale expects no more.'

'But who will attend you while I perform this errand master?'

'Pooh,' he replied dismissively.

'I can shift for myself. As for anything I might need, Mrs Thrale will supply it.'

He threw off this last announcement carelessly, but the reason for his ready acceptance of the proposal was now plainly revealed. My absence would increase his dependence on Mrs Thrale, a consequence which I knew would not be unwelcome to him, and to which I suspected Mrs Thrale herself had given only cursory consideration. I smiled inwardly at the transparency of his strategem and saw there was little to be gained in protesting further.

So it was, that very early next morning, I found myself on a cart being driven by Mrs Thrale's stableboy to the Horse and Hounds Inn at Streatham where I was to catch the London stage. All round me the fields were busy with the bending shapes of labourers, and heavy with the scent of ripening wheat. Along the lane into the village, cottagers were beginning the first of the day's many tasks. Life was stirring, and despite the nature of the task before me, my spirits stirred in answer. At the very least I would see Betsy again, and sooner than I had fancied. The inn was full of bustle with men, women and animals in a state of either arrival or departure, their voices vying with each other for attention. The scene resembled nothing so much as an auditorium before the commencement of a play. I was set down in the big courtyard and was instantly submerged by the dense undercurrent of its life. The stage arrived within half an hour and stayed just long enough for the horses to be changed and the coachman to sink a pint of ale before starting on the last leg of its journey to London. On board with me were two squires, a footman in livery, and a man and his wife in the sober costumes of quakers. They had all evidently travelled a considerable distance further than me and gave me only the briefest of glances as I mounted on the outside of the coach.

With fresh horses we covered the 8 miles to London in an hour and I was at home with Betsy in time to breakfast with her. She was in some consternation at seeing me so soon and thought some accident had occasioned my return. But I quickly set her mind at ease. After I had explained my errand she told me she had some news which might assist me. Lizzy had visited her two days ago and begged her for money. She was poorly attired and looked ill. Betsy had made her sit down and rest awhile but she would not stay long. Before she left she gave her address as Marsh Lane, Westminster.

'She has a bed in a lodging house there. She is in a very poor way Frank. Famistan has cast her off entirely and will have nothing more to do with her. She is close to despair and I fear may do something desperate.'

'Could you not persuade her to stay Betsy?'

She shook her head.

'It took all her courage to come at all. She is full of shame and eaten up with bitterness at Famistan's treachery. I gave her a guinea, which was all I had, and a few clothes and she left.'

Betsy's news dismayed me. I knew Marsh Lane as one of the poorest areas of the city. No one ventured there after dark alone. If Lizzy had become one of its denizens she would be very low indeed. I stayed with Betsy long enough to renew those tokens of affection between us and then hurried out into the street. The city was at the full tide of its busy life as I made my way up Fleet street towards Westminster. I crossed over the Strand and struck off through Charing Cross In the square I was held up by some cows blocking the road, much to the annoyance of two sedan chair carriers eager to get by. After much waving and shouting the carriers attempted to gain possession of the square and force their way through. This only served to startle the cows, which proceeded to push against the chairs, and tumble their occupants, gesticulating wildly, into the thoroughfare. I picked my way cautiously through the sprawling mass and was roundly abused by all parties, as though I had been the author of their misfortune.

It was about mid-day by the time I reached the maze of streets around Westminster and saw the Abbey rising above them, like a parent amid its offspring. Marsh Lane was a small turning about 50 yards from the Abbey. Its tall overhanging buildings shut out most of the sky and seemed to be debating which would topple over first. Down the middle of the lane ran an open ditch, just narrow enough for me to step over. As I did so I caught the stench of night soil and saw the rotting carcase of a dog, its single remaining eye turned towards me as if asking what my business was. A strange guardian so it seemed to me of this underworld. I asked the first inhabitant I met, a solitary man sitting in a doorway smoking a pipe, where the lodging house was, and he waved his arm carelessly in the air.

'Tek yer pick,' he said, looking me up and down. 'They'm all the same. But there ain't none of your sort 'ere, if that's what yer after.'

I shook my head.

'I'm looking for a young girl, small, dark-haired, called Lizzy.'

He pointed to the far end of the lane.

'Try there. They've allus got new uns,' he said.

I thanked him and made my way down to the end of the lane. The house was a narrow building, four storeys high, which wound upwards like a crooked plant. I went inside past a clutter of furniture and cases. Several doors led off into a number of rooms each with a row of beds, placed like dominoes with a few inches between them. Some had silent shapes on them in the attitude of sleep. Others were busy with children playing games. Round two beds clustered a family, the parents and two children, one an infant at the breast. I gazed in bewilderment at this scene of misery. Lizzy could be anywhere. As I stood there a woman approached. She had a thin frail figure and I thought at first she was a young girl, until she pulled back a shawl from her face and revealed a haggard, sharp-featured countenance. She fixed her eyes on me with an air of professional curiosity.

'Shilling a night for a bed,' she said. 'Room's two and sixpence. You pay now.'

'I'm not looking for accommodation,' I replied. 'I'm in search of someone. A girl.'

She sniffed loudly.

'This is a respectable house. If that's what you're after you won't find it here.'

'You misunderstand me. I'm looking for one of your residents. A young woman named Lizzy.'

The woman cleared her throat noisily and spat on the ground.

'That little slut. She went this morning and good riddance to her.'

This was very disappointing news. If only I had been earlier. But I reasoned that she could not have gone far. I must soon find her.

'Do you know where she has gone to?' I asked.

'That I do,' she replied vigorously. 'She's in the Fleet prison. And she'll rot there until she pays me what she owes.'

I stared in amazement at her, brimming as she was with virtuous indignation.

'You had her taken up for debt?' I asked.

'The slut tried to sneak out while my back was turned. But I'm too old to be fooled by the likes of her.'

'But in Christian charity ma'am,' I protested. 'She was with child.'

She spat on the floor again in disgust.

'That's little you know,' she said. 'She's a liar that one. Thought she could cheat me out of ten nights rent.'

Little of this made sense to me. Betsy had given Lizzy more than enough to have paid the hag with ease. I wondered whether Lizzy had been robbed, perhaps by her, and then thrown into prison as a ruse to avoid detection. But what could she mean by doubting her condition? Why should Lizzy lie about that?

Any further enquiry I might wish to make, however, was cut short by the woman, whose attention shifted from me to a shape stirring on a bed in the corner of the room. As I watched, she went over and pulled back a blanket gently from the sleeping head. I caught a glimpse of a tousled head, and heard the unmistakable sound of a consumptive cough, low and heavy. She replaced the blanket and bending down whispered soothingly to the figure, 'Go back to sleep Tom. Don't fret.' Then she turned and looked accusingly at me, as the one who had disturbed the boy's slumbers.

Outside, I debated with myself what to do. The Fleet was not far from my present lodgings and it struck me as a strange irony that Lizzy should be living nearby after all. The simplest expedient would be to go to there and discharge the debt myself. However, I had not the necessary sum about me. I would have to step to Johnson's Court and borrow the money from Dr. Levet. At the same time, I was not entirely convinced of the truth of what I had been told. I could not believe that Lizzy had already disposed of the money Betsy had given her, and half suspected the hag had mistaken her for another girl. I decided to seek out Lizzy in the prison and ascertain the facts for myself.

It had begun to rain as I set off for the Fleet. A steady drizzle which threatened to soak through my outer garments. Turning out of the lane I looked back and saw the ditch already filling with water, dispensing its contents over the narrow path. The carcase of the dog was submerged, it's one eye hidden beneath the mud and filth. It took me an hour of walking to reach the Liberties of the Fleet prison, where those who could afford to live outside, resided. The prison itself, with its thick walls and gloomy precincts, was reserved for the most impoverished debtors, among whom would most certainly be Lizzy. I could not help but think of the time, many years ago, when my master had been imprisoned in the Marshalsea. He spoke rarely of that period in his life, but the misfortune and shame of debt were subjects which could still bring tears to his eyes.

I knocked at a thick wooden door set into the wall of the prison and after a few minutes I heard the sound of a metal grille being opened and saw the grizzled face of the turnkey observing me.

'What's yer business?' said the face.

'I wish to see one of the inmates,' I replied.

'What for?'

'I have important information.'

'Name?'

'Francis Barber.'

'There ain't no one 'ere of that description.'

'No, the person I wish to visit is Miss Elizabeth Jones. She calls herself 'Lizzy'.

The door swung open and a heavily tattooed arm beckoned me to enter. I surmised that the turnkey had at one time been a sailor. A deduction confirmed by his invitation to me to 'come aboard'.

'No bottles, knives, cutlasses, allowed. Any suchlike must be stowed wi' me.'

He looked suspiciously at me as though I had been concealing an armoury.

'I have nothing of that nature I assure you.'

'Very well,' he said grudgingly. 'Follow me.'

He led me through a courtyard crowded with prisoners and their families, and past some children playing hopscotch with stones and a small piece of crayon. Over to one side there were several tradesmen trying, without much success, to sell their wares. But I was chiefly surprised by the number of clergymen in the courtyard, walking a little apart from the others as if to signal that they were not to be numbered as ordinary debtors. I asked my guide what reason there was for this abundance of parsons. He laughed hoarsely.

'There's more of 'em in 'ere than outside,' he said. 'They're devils for running up debt. Not that they don't do well in 'ere neither.'

'How can anyone do well in such a place?' I asked.

'There's money to be made the world over if you've an eye fer it.'

He pointed in the direction of a low, squat, wooden shed in the corner of the courtyard. Over the doorway hung a sign showing a male and female hand joined with the words 'marriages performed within' written beneath. Sitting outside was a parson in a tattered nightgown, his bloated countenance bearing the hallmarks of drink. He was clutching what looked like a prayer book and every now and then he would start up from his chair and accost any who approached him with ' Sir, will you be pleased to walk in and be married?'

'Cheapest place to get hitched if you've a mind to it. No church fees to pay in 'ere,' said the turnkey.

Facing onto the courtyard, behind the shed, was a large building several storeys high, dotted with small windows, which seemed like so many eyes gazing mournfully out. The turnkey gestured towards it.

'Bottom floor, on the right as you go in. If you stay beyond six o' clock you'll be locked in fer the night.'

I thanked him and carried on to the building. Inside, was exceedingly dark. The only light filtered through from the doorway and four small windows set high in the wall. Despite these apertures the air was stagnant and foul smelling, so that I was obliged to hold my hand to my mouth to prevent myself from choking.

The cell on the right was a large open area with a stone floor, and no furniture of any kind. On the floor and propped against the wall were several figures, some covered with thin blankets. I called out Lizzy's name, hoping that the turnkey had been mistaken and that none of these wretches could be her. At first, there was no reply and I was about to call again, when I heard a low murmur and a figure in one of the corners feebly raised a hand. I went over and bent down and saw the unmistakable features of Lizzy. She was thin and pale and looked infinitely weary, but it was undoubtedly her. She could barely talk, and her lips were parched and black, but her eyes as she looked at me showed signs of recognition. I reached out and smoothed away the hair from her face and noticed there were sores around her mouth. I wondered at the humanity which could cast such as her in a place like this. I put my finger gently on her lips and spoke quietly to her.

'Don't speak Lizzy. I shall get food and drink, and when you have eaten we shall talk. I will return in a few minutes.'

She nodded her head. I picked my way carefully round the sprawling bodies and went outside. To the right of the courtyard was a stall selling a few basic necessities from which I purchased some bread, cheese, and ale. When I returned with them to Lizzy I saw she had moved slightly and was now sitting more upright. Her face as I approached showed renewed signs of life. She held out her hands eagerly for the ale and it was all I could do to prevent her from draining the bottle at one go. When she had taken a good draught she ran her tongue over her lips and I saw the colour begin to return.

'Thank you Frank,' she whispered hoarsely.

She was about to speak more but I stopped her and made her eat some food. She eat slowly at first, swallowing with great effort, but then more easily. After a while, she sat back against the wall and rested her eyes on me.

'Why're you 'ere?' she asked.

'To take you back to Streatham,' I replied

She shook her head.

'No.'

'You must go back Lizzy. Mrs Thrale has sent me.'

'No,' she said, more forcibly. 'I can't never go back.'

'But you cannot remain here. Think of your condition.'

She smiled at me.

'My condition? What's that Frank?'

'Your child Lizzy. Consider your child if not yourself.'

My words affected her powerfully. Her eyes filled and I thought at first she would weep, but when she next spoke her manner was calm and indifferent.

'There ain't no child,' she said.

'No child?' I repeated. 'Betsy said you were with child.'

'You're such an innocent Frank.'

'Is it not true? And Famistan?'

Her face changed at the mention of his name.

'I've lost it.'

I stared at her uncomprehendingly.

'The child's dead Frank. Now do you understand?' she said angrily.

'I'm sorry Lizzy. I didn't know. But that is all the more reason for you to return to Streatham.'

She fell silent, and seemed to be giving fresh consideration to my proposal. But her reply, when it came, was not encouraging.

'If you want to help me Frank just get me out of this place, and then let me be.'

'Willingly Lizzy, but if you will not return to Streatham you must stay with Betsy and me. Why were you thrown in here? Betsy said she gave you enough money to pay for your lodgings, and more besides.'

'The old cow wanted more.'

'More? For renting a bed?'

'No. Not for that.'

She paused and shifted her weight slightly.

'She said she'd help me get rid of the kid if I paid her. Only when she'd done it she said I still owed her. Greedy bitch.'

'You got rid of it?'

'What d'you expect? I went to see Famistan. He couldn't give a cuss. Just laughed. I couldn't have a kid. It would have died anyway.'

'So might you. The old hag wouldn't have cared.'

'She knew enough to do it. It weren't her first time. Said she needed the money to buy a potion from the 'pothecary for her son.'

'Yes, I saw him. But such wickedness. To have you taken up for debt.'

'She got scared. Thought someone would find out. I don't owe her nuthin.'

The whole thing stood clear to me now. I tried to imagine the fear, the pain, the sheer misery of it all, but my mind misgave me. I looked at her, wretched and defiant, her face still bearing the marks of youth, and I could no longer see the sixteen year old girl I had met at Mrs Thrale's. For her part, Lizzy sank back, exhausted by her narrative, her eyes staring distractedly over my shoulder. I judged it time to leave. So, promising her I would come back the next day with money to secure her release, I got up and made my way into the courtyard. Looking back I saw that she had drifted off into sleep.

Outside, there was a steady stream of people making their way to the gate. The stall holders had packed away their goods and were getting ready to leave. Only the parson was still plying his trade. As I passed by he scrutinised me quickly and then looked away. By the time I reached the gate the warning bell had sounded and I thought of the horror of being incarcerated there even for one night. How precious a thing freedom was and how easily it could be forfeited The rain had eased off now and after the crowded prison the streets seemed empty. Walking at a steady pace I reached home in a little under the half hour and was soon relating to Betsy the events of the day.

My purpose was to return very early the following morning, but as fortune would have it, this proved to be impossible. I arose about six intending to go straight to Johnson's Court to borrow the sum necessary for Lizzy's release, when I felt suddenly dizzy. I tried to dress myself, but as I bent down a burning sensation in my chest and head left me gasping for breath. I sat down heavily on the bed, shaking all over, my body seemingly not my own. Betsy was roused by my discomfort and put her hand to my brow.

'You are on fire my dear. You must return to bed and I will send for Dr. Levet.'

I protested as well as I could and tried once again to rise, but she would not hear of my going out and commanded me back to bed. It was near mid-day when the doctor arrived and informed me that I had a fever.

'If you will go trudging round the most infested parts of the city, getting soaked into the bargain, you must expect nothing else Frank. You are fortunate it is no worse.'

As he was leaving I heard him whisper to Betsy. 'You must nurse him carefully Betsy. He will need constant attention. His condition is not dangerous, but fevers are fickle creatures.'

Betsy nodded and when Dr Levet had gone, came over to me. I took hold of her arm and attempted to speak but my voice when it came was a mere croak.

'I know Frank,' she said. 'Don't vex yourself about Lizzy. Dr Levet has left money to discharge the debt. I will see that she is set free.'

I thanked her as well as I could, and a short while after sank into a deep slumber. I have little recollection of the next few days. I burned and shivered through them as the fever ran its course, playing with me like a child with a toy, by turns shaking me to pieces and casting me aside. It was not until the fifth day that I returned to myself. It was a still, summer's morning. From outside, I could hear the sounds of the street, low and indistinct, like the murmur of distant water. For a moment I fancied myself a young boy again back on the plantation, waiting for Mama Du to dress me for the colonel. I called her mama, but I knew of course that my real mother was dead. I tried to remember the first time I had known it, but it was too difficult. Mama Du called me an 'orphan'. The word sounded strange to my ears. For a time I had imagined it to be my true name, not 'Frank', as the colonel called me, but 'orphan'. It was a secret which belonged only to me. I whispered it to myself, letting my tongue linger on its soft syllables. It was gentle, like a warm breeze, not harsh like 'bastard', which the overseer had called me once.

'You are awake, Frank,' said Betsy, placing a hand on my forehead. 'And much cooler, praise God.'

I looked up at her and the thought crossed my mind that I had been very ill.

'You have frightened us all my dear,' she continued. 'Even Dr Johnson has been to see you. But you are better now.'

'My master came? Why was I not woken?'

She smiled.

'You were scarce in a condition for company Frank. Dr. Levet told him of your illness and he came immediately.'

She helped me sit up and gave me some broth to eat. It was the first food I had tasted in days and my hand shook as I brought the spoon to my mouth. I took a sip of the warm soup and instantly remembered Lizzy.

'Has Lizzy been released?'

'Yes. The milliner's son took the money the same day.'

'Is she here? What has happened to her?'

Betsy shook her head.

'She could not be persuaded. She sent a message saying she was provided for.'

'Provided for? What does that mean?'

'I don't know. But we have done all we could. Lizzy is proud. It does not surprise me.'

Betsy was right. Yet I feared for her situation. Lizzy had been in a poor way when I saw her, and the only protector I could imagine for her was the street. I could see from Betsy's manner that I was not alone in my fears.

'I must find her,' I said. 'She has suffered enough.'

'When you are well Frank. And not before.'

It took a further three days before I was sufficiently well to return to the Fleet. It was not a prospect I relished. The memory of my previous visit was still fresh upon me. But, as soon as I was up and about, I purposed to return there. This did not meet with the approval of the shrew, however, who was already discomposed enough by my illness to consider I was taking advantage of my master's absence.

'Dr. Johnson did not intend you to spend your time running after good for nothing hussies', she said to me on my returning to Johnson's Court. 'He has been inconvenienced enough already by your sickness, as has poor Dr Levet.'

I had never before heard her describe Dr Levet in such fashion. Their mutual dislike was usually sufficient to inspire only the barest of acknowledgements. It was clear to me that the inconvenience she complained of was all her own. It was jealousy, and of the most blatant kind. Armed with such knowledge I determined to answer her in kind.

'I am carrying out my master's orders. He would not be pleased with me, nor with you ma'am, should they be set aside to satisfy the whims of others.'

She looked at me, her face suffused with anger.

'Whims!' Her sightless eyes almost danced in their sockets.

'You deserve whipping. Dr Johnson shall hear of your insolence. Get out.'

I gave her the briefest of bows and left. Despite her threat I knew, as did she, there would be little advantage in reporting the exchange to my master. The shrew's temper had become increasingly vexatious as her health declined, and my master had taken to ignoring the almost daily torrent of complaint which poured from her lips. She scolded Agnes terribly, who was scarce persuaded to remain with the shrew by my master's generosity.

Once away from Johnson's Court I could afford to smile at the encounter. The shrew's influence in the house was waning. This was something of which even she was aware. But like a shooting star she seemed to glow more fiercely at the end. She would not be mastered but by death. This thought put me in mind of Lizzy. I knew full well why I was reluctant to return to the Fleet. I feared to hear that she was dead.

It was about mid-day by the time I arrived at the prison. The turnkey looked at me wearily through the grille.

'Well,' he said irritably

'I came last week. To see Elizabeth Jones.'

'She's gone. Went out Friday.'

'Do you know where she is? It's important.'

He shook his head and was about to close the grille when I held out my hand. He looked quickly at the coins I was holding and after a few moments I heard the sound of the door being opened.

'Try the parson,' he said taking the money and inspecting it closely.

'The parson?'

He gave me a wink.

'She got wed afore she went,' he said.

I looked at him in astonishment. The thought of the poor wretch I had seen being able to walk let alone marry was scarcely believable. The turnkey seemed to know what was in my mind.

'Sailor's ain't choosy. Party of jolly lads came over Friday and one of 'em carried 'er off.'

'But she was ill,' I protested.

He smirked at me as if this was of no account.

'She scrubbed up well with the money you sent. She'll serve 'is turn alright.'

I made my way across the courtyard to the wooden shed still not believing what I had heard. The parson was sitting outside smoking a pipe as I approached. He was reluctant at first to assist me, muttering something about respecting the privacy of his customers, but his manner changed when I produced some money. He showed me inside to a small wooden table which I surmised served him as an altar, on which lay a large book. He turned over a few pages for me and indicated an entry made just a few days ago. There before me in a very uncertain hand I saw Lizzy's signature. At the side, in another hand was her occupation 'housemaid'. Her husband, so it appeared was a sailor named James Walsh who had signed himself by a cross.

'You didn't enquire of Miss Jones why she was getting married?' I asked.

'That would have been an impertinence sir. The lady was willing enough.'

'And where did he take her?'

'To Portsmouth I believe. His ship is in berth there.'

He closed the book and took me by the arm as an indication that the interview was at an end.

'Do you know the name of the ship?' I asked.

A puzzled look came over his face and he affected to scratch his head. I slipped another coin into his pocket.

'His Majesty's ship 'The Osprey'.' He replied, quickly enough.

I had gleaned as much as I could of Lizzy's fate. It seemed she had seized the first opportunity to escape her confinement in the Fleet and shake off the dust of London. But I feared the bargain she had struck with the sailor would only lead to fresh misery. I made my way home in a dismal mood. I had failed in the task Mrs Thrale had given me and I was angry with Famistan for abandoning Lizzy. All I could do now, I reasoned, was to write to her, reminding her that she had friends, if she needed them. Betsy helped me compose something suitable and we addressed it to Lizzy care of 'The Osprey'. Later that evening I caught the coach to Streatham and was soon relaying the news to my master and Mrs Thrale.

'Not content with one fever you must hazard your life a second time by visiting that infernal place,' said my master irritably. 'What the devil d'you mean by it Frank?'

'Dr Johnson was concerned by news of your illness Frank. He has berated me daily for sending you on such an errand,' interposed Mrs Thrale.

'Nonsense ma'am. He is not a boy to be mollycoddled. But the errand was foolish. I said so from the outset.'

After my master had retired I learnt from Mrs Thrale the true cause of his vexation. As I had expected, he had been hopeful she would reward his sacrifice of my services by attending on him herself. But in this he was disappointed. She had been circumspect enough to instruct her servants in his needs.

'He has been impossible Frank,' she said. 'The new maid has been at his beck and call night and day. The quantity of tea that has been consumed would drown a normal man.'

'And his nightmares ma'am? Has he been visited by them?'

The look she gave me was enough to confirm my fears.

'I sat up with him for two nights. He would have called on me more but I was too exhausted. He returns home tomorrow, and I shall not be sorry on this occasion.'

I gathered from this, that the immediate cause of my master's presence in the house had been sufficiently resolved to allow his departure. He confirmed this as I prepared his flannel.

'We return to Johnson's Court tomorrow Frank. Henry Thrale has recovered sufficient of his senses to put his affairs in order.'

'Mrs Thrale must be relieved master.'

He grunted. 'I fancy so. But her gratitude has not been greatly in evidence.'

I looked innocently at him.

'I have become a burden to the household,' he went on. 'The servants avoid me. They walk in the other direction if I approach. Mrs Thrale, if you please, considers it my fancy.'

'They have not been unaffected by events in the house master.'

'It is neglect. I cannot be deceived. But no matter. Old men can be tiresome. I must not become like Mrs Williams. I am pleased you have returned Frank.'

The next morning we set off very late. It was almost noon by the time we were seated in Mr Thrale's carriage. Before we left my master took an affecting farewell of his hosts. Mr Thrale embraced him warmly and shook him by the hand.

'Thank you Sam. I do not deserve such friendship.'

'Mere cant Henry,' replied my master, waving him away. 'Which of us deserves anything? It has pleased me to be here and to be of assistance to you.'

He turned to Mrs Thrale.

'And you ma'am are forbearance itself,' he said, raising her hand to his lips. 'You tower above us.'

Mrs Thrale whose slight figure, beside that of my master's, resembled nothing so much as a flower beneath an overgrown bush, smiled.

'If I did not know better Sam I should believe you were teasing me.'

'I am in earnest Hesther. You have stood firm amidst our folly.'

She bowed her head briefly, and a look of mutual understanding passed between them. A few minutes later we were bowling through the countryside both of us wrapt in silence. My master had about him an air of solemnity which usually betokened the onset of one of his many afflictions. I recognised this one as a bout of 'the black dog'.

'Marriage has many pains, but celibacy has few pleasures,' he said eventually. 'Do you know who wrote that Frank?'

'No master.'

'Me. Twenty years hence. Every day since then has confirmed the truth of it to me.'

Emboldened by his confidence I said.

'But did you never think to marry again master?'

'The loss of a wife is the greatest affliction to which a man is liable. I cannot look upon it with equanimity.'

'But a man does not marry a woman thinking she will die master,' I protested.

'Then he should,' he replied. 'Of two mortal beings one must lose the other. It is an object of contemplation more dreadful even than one's own dissolution. The continuity of being is lacerated. The day Mrs Johnson died my life stood suspended and motionless. It has been driven since by external causes into new channels. But when the current slackens the memory of that dreadful event returns like the Dutchman's ship.'

He continued in a similar vein for several minutes more before tailing off into silence and then sinking into a fitful slumber. I thought of his night-time terrors and wondered whether here, in the circumstances of Mrs Johnson's death, lay the source of my master's demons. It was shortly after this event that I had entered his household, and I could not but think, that in some way I had not yet divined, my life was entwined with that most solemn occasion. I could remember little of my early life in England. Soon after returning from the slave plantations the colonel had died and I passed into the service of my master. At whose prompting, or why, I had no knowledge. I thought of my mother. From the small silver chain which was my only possession I had formed an idea of her as small and delicate, too fine and good for this life. I had always assumed her story to be just another of those sad narratives familiar to slaves. She had been taken from her village in Africa and sold into slavery but had not been strong enough to survive the voyage and me. But now another story beckoned. If it were true, my mother had been living in England, and my own voyage into existence had begun, not in Africa, but here. Perhaps she had been white. In my childish fancy I had always thought of her as white. When I told this to Soubise one day he simply laughed.

'This is the advantage of being an orphan, Frank,' he said. 'You can invent your own parents. I wish mine had been considerate enough to die too.'

But, of course, I dismissed this as idle fancy. It was not unknown for white women to have black lovers, as Soubise and I could both bear witness, but my mother had been sent out on a slave ship to the plantations, a fate inflicted on no white woman. Besides, Costano had said she came originally from Africa. I was indulging a common enough fantasy, that my black skin was only temporary. When I grew up it would change to white. Its failure to do so made me, at first, sad, then resigned, unlike Soubise who always remained angry at his colour. I thought of what it had cost my mother to give birth to me. Had she lived long enough to give me a name? If so, why was I called 'Frank', why Barber? The colonel, who I had thought so kindly, now seemed to have denied me everything. Why had my mother been transported from England when she was heavy with child? Had some wrong been done her? I had always considered my true parentage unimportant, but perhaps it was intended I should think that. By the time we reached London my mind had woven a dozen different stories around the meagre facts of my birth, each more elaborate and preposterous than the last. But that short journey had accomplished a subtle alteration. By the time it was completed a mild curiosity about my history had become a determination to find out who and what I was. I cannot explain it other than the disclosure of something previously hidden, as though a shoot should break the surface in a seed bed. Whether the sad fate of Lizzy and her child had made me consider the circumstances of my own abandonment, or whether the conspicuous secrecy of Costano had excited me with fantasies about my origins, or whether I sensed that, as the heir of my master, I should know who I was, I cannot say. Whatever the explanation, I became possessed by a conviction that only by discovering my true history could I release my master from his own demons. My first decision was to open my mind to Betsy on the subject. The small deception of which I had been guilty on my wedding night had caused me some uneasiness. Now was an opportunity to make amends.

Her reaction was not unexpected. She urged caution. I should not entertain excessive hopes of discovery. It had been a long time and besides it was sometimes better not to know the truth. I knew this last to be the real reason for her lack of encouragement. It had occurred to me too. There could be no guarantee that unlocking the past would not disturb my present happiness. But I was not to be dissuaded. I remembered my master observing to Mr.Boswell that once a falsehood had been detected a man could not be content till it had been corrected.

'But a man might be better not correcting it,' objected Mr. Boswell. 'It might not contribute to his happiness.'

'Indeed sir, but you should consider that a man will sooner risk his life for the truth than he will for his own happiness. Consider Gallileo,' replied my master.

Once I had taken the decision I began by reviewing what I knew already and was immediately overcome with despair. The small threads of knowledge which I held hardly amounted to very much. Indeed I could not be sure of their veracity. All I had was Costano's narrative to rely on, and whilst I had no reason to doubt his honesty, his eagerness to disabuse me about my past concerned me. Whether it was simply the pleasure which superior knowledge bestows on the teller, or something less disinterested, I could not know. My master was fond of quoting a maxim of Rochefoucauld's 'There is something in the misfortunes of others which does not displease us'. Costano had always been envious of me. Although his master was richer than mine he treated Costano with a condescension which he found irksome. He knew of Costano's origin as a prince in his own country and delighted in displaying his black servant as a trophy.

'My master was a kitchen boy in his youth,' Costano said to me one day. 'He owes his elevation to a rich relation who died with no heir. He is as stupid as Balaam's ass and thinks to shine in the eyes of his fellows by treating me with contempt.' Costano's face glowed with a dull anger whenever he spoke of his master and I feared that one day it would get the better of him. But I could not believe that he intended me any ill. Besides his words to me on that fateful night at the Dog and Partridge had spoken of some good fortune that awaited me. Plainly I should start my search by talking to him. Accordingly, the morning following my return from Streatham I sent Costano a note asking him to meet me that evening at a tavern in the Strand.

I arrived at the tavern a little beforehand and chose a table towards the back of the tap room. The hour was too early for custom to be heavy, and the few who were there had the sunken look of all day drinkers. I received barely a glance as I approached the bar and bought two tankards of ale. Costano arrived after about fifteen minutes. Despite the gloomy interior he saw me almost immediately and came over. I thought from his countenance that he didn't look well. He had a strained and tired air, and his manner, which was normally brisk, appeared slow and careful. He saw my enquiring gaze and said,

'I am perfectly well Frank. There is no need to concern yourself. I have had a disagreement with my master, that is all.'

I pressed him to tell me what had occurred but he would not be drawn.

'Let us say that I am determined to leave his service as soon as I can,' he said.

'But what will you do?' I asked.

'Will he release you?'

He gave me a look which forbade further discussion of the subject and I knew better than to pursue it. Then he leaned back in his chair and took a long draught of ale, swallowing noisily.

'I wondered how long it would be before you came to see me,' he said, putting the tankard down.

'I almost didn't,' I replied.

He grunted disbelievingly.

'You have always preferred burying your head in the sand, Frank.'

I felt my irritation rise. He was evidently not in the best of moods.

'If you mean I have never been given to complaint then I don't mind confessing to that,' I replied.

'There are too many things you don't mind Frank.'

I looked at him, puzzled. There was a dangerous edge to his voice which I knew of old.

'What do you mean?' I asked.

He took another long pull at his ale, wiped his mouth, and seemed on the point of saying something but then changed his mind.

'It's of no consequence,' he said. 'You are here to ask me about Adebayo are you not?'

'Yes. Those things you told me at my wedding...'

'Are all true,' put in Costano. 'Your mother was transported to the plantations from England.'

'But who was she? Why was she sent there?'

He shrugged his shoulders.

'You will have to ask Adebayo that. But he may not have all the answers to your questions'

'Do you remember what you said to me outside the Dog and Partridge that evening?'

'Of course. I assumed you ignored it.'

'I didn't take it seriously then. We were none of us sober or in our right minds that evening.'

'Nevertheless, it was seriously meant.'

'You said I should ask my master about the colonel.'

He nodded.

'I didn't expect you would, or that anything would come of it if you did.'

'But ask him about what? The colonel took me in and gave me my freedom at his death. What more is there to know?'

'Perhaps that he was your father.'

He fingered his empty tankard calmly whilst delivering this blow, and the muscles around his mouth twitched with barely concealed pleasure. As for me, I stared stupidly at him.

'It's not possible,' I said at last.

'I don't believe it.'

'Very well,' he replied.

'Keep your head in the sand if that's what you prefer.'

He smiled, mockingly. I steadied myself and tried to think clearly as my master would do, but all my instincts were to hurl myself at him. What right had he to torment me? What harm had I ever done him?

'You are trying to make a fool of me,' I said.

He leant towards me until his face was just a few inches from mine. His eyes were cold and sharp like needle points.

'I was never more in earnest Frank. Think what you will of me, I have said nothing but the truth.'

There was something about his manner which carried conviction. I knew at least that he believed it to be true, whether or not it was so.

'How did you come by this?' I asked.

He leant back again and resumed his smiling composure.

'Another round first,' he said, pushing his tankard towards me.

I got up and made my way to the bar. The landlord, who had been observing us from a distance, gave me a knowing look as he served me. I fancied he thought us conspirators of some kind and was preparing in his mind information to lay against us should the occasion arise. I took the ale from him and returned to the table. To my consternation it was empty. Costano had taken advantage of my errand to make his exit, leaving me foolishly clutching two brimming tankards. I put them down carefully, and, as I did so, noticed a crumpled note lying near a puddle of ale. I smoothed it out and read its brief message. It said simply, 'Be careful Frank'.

6

The meeting with Costano, and its untimely end, left me confused and unnerved. What, or who, I should be careful of escaped me. I was inclined to think the warning a consequence of Costano's fevered state of mind. He was plainly alarmed, and I was not deceived by his assumed calmness to think him any other than a deeply worried man. As for his information I could scarcely credit it. The circumstances under which the colonel could have fathered me remained obscure and doubtful. I knew that many plantation owners fathered children by slave women. Such children were often scorned and abused by other slaves for their mixed parentage. Occasionally a child would be born completely of one colour. If white, they lived a strange half-life. Their sad pale faces a curse. If black, they shrunk away, as best they could, from discovery. But such was not my case. The colonel had taken possession of me after my mother's death. She had not set foot in Jamaica. How could he be my father? Costano had to be mistaken.

As for talking with my master, I could see nothing to be gained from it. I could not voice my doubts openly without seeming to accuse him of deception, the mere thought of which was sufficient to astonish me. When I tried to put them into words they seemed foolish. I could hear my master angrily dismissing Costano as a blockhead and me as a ninny. So I kept my peace for the time being. But the ideas which Costano had planted continued to nag at me like a sore tooth. What if the colonel had visited England before his final return? He had, after all, a son, named Richard, studying medicine at Cambridge, in the years before my birth. I had often heard my master speak of him as one of his dearest friends. After his death of a fever at the siege of Havana my master was for a long time in a black despair. Nothing could be more natural than that the colonel should wish to visit his son. I decided when the opportunity arose to make an innocent enquiry of my master.

It was a few days before I could attempt it, however, during which time I spent many hours considering how I might disguise the reason for my curiosity. But in the event, it was my master himself who provided the cover I needed. One afternoon I came upon him in his room at Johnson's Court working on the manuscript of his *Journey to the Western Isles of Scotland*. He was in good spirits, having just completed a section on his visit to the hut of a poor highland woman, and he called out to me as I carried a tray of refreshments into him.

'Frank, you are more welcome than the Good Samaritan to the man fallen among thieves.'

I handed him a dish of tea and some bread rolls which he took eagerly and began eating noisily.

'How many times I could have wished for tea and warm bread in the Highlands. Much is made of Scottish hospitality but it is nothing without the means.'

'You informed me yesterday that you lived well in Scotland' I said.

'Just so' he replied, removing a roll from his mouth. 'But you must remember that yesterday I was not hungry, today I am.'

'Can a man's opinion be altered by such trivial circumstances, master?'

'Every day brings evidence of it. The truth of oral accounts is seldom perfect. Even the narrative of a man's own life is not constant. It is subject to continual alteration and amendment. The only secure record Frank of what you and I thought and did yesterday is a diary. Every man should keep one if only to remind him of the frailty of recollection.'

'But may not a man still deceive himself in a diary?' I asked, pouring more tea.

'He is to imagine it is read by his maker alone. Any man who thinks he can deceive God is a fool. Then it should perish with him. That will be your task after I am gone.'

He drank his tea calmly, and I thought how frequently his conversation was drawn towards mortality, like a compass point seeking north. It was the first time he had referred openly to his own diary, although I had often seen him writing late at night in a book which he kept hidden. Once, Mr Boswell had come across it and read a few pages. My master was much discomposed by this and remonstrated with him severely. If only fate would cast such a document in my way. Here, if anywhere, might be the evidence I was looking for. But no sooner had I admitted the thought than I banished it. Such an event was unlikely to occur. Even could I obtain possession of it, the possibility of an uninterrupted viewing was very slight. Ours was a house with many eyes. Someone would be sure to inform on me and I shuddered at the thought of his wrath. There was no alternative but to try what intelligence I could gain by open enquiry.

'Did my first master keep a diary?' I asked.

He looked up from the second roll which he was just finishing. I fancied he hesitated before replying.

'The colonel?'

'Yes, master.'

'Bathurst was the least likely of all men to keep anything. He was most unmethodical and ruined his estates in Jamaica by poor management.'

'Is that why he returned home, master.'

'That, and failing health.'

He paused as if needing to say more.

'Bathurst was a good man Frank. Failure in him was more honourable than success. His opposition to the trade was inveterate. You owe his kindness to that.'

He said this with a finality which seemed to announce an end to further discussion of the topic. But I was determined not to let the matter rest.

'I have been thinking master, if Betsy and I should have children, what I could tell them when they ask about my early life. There is so little that I know.'

He grunted in a manner which did not suggest he shared my concern.

'Pray they are docile. An inquisitive child is a torment to its parents. I was a great trouble to mine.'

'But I should like to know more master,' I persisted.

'I can be of no assistance to you there Frank. I know little more of your history than I do of the solitary Highland lady who entertained us, to the tedium of which I am recalled by duty.'

With that he handed me back his tea, which he had let go cold, and shooed me out of the room. I had, after all, gained little for my pains. If my master had intelligence about my past he was not about to disclose it. But something in the manner with which he spoke exercised me. He seemed anxious to maintain my good opinion of the colonel. Could it be my fancy, or had there been a note of apology in his voice? I reflected again on the conversation, forcing the words into different shapes until I declared myself defeated. I was no further forward. I knew no more than before. Except that I had now announced openly, for the first time, my dissatisfaction at things as they stood. I had no name except that given me by my owners, and no conception of where I came from, or to whom I really belonged. My parents had been erased, and me with them as though my very existence was a mistake. This is what being an orphan meant. The word suddenly disclosed itself to me. It was, in the end, my true name.

I spent the next few days in a torment of uncertainty. A short while ago my parentage had been of small account to me. Now it was everything. To Betsy, who had watched me keenly over the past few days it was a sign that my fever had not entirely departed. She was in perpetual apprehension of its return. When I announced to her that I intended to seek out Adebayo, she protested.

'It is madness Frank. You are not yet returned to complete health. Dr. Levet has ordered that you take more rest.'

I smiled at her, knowing this to be a fiction of her own invention.

'Dr. Levet has been drunk this past week and incapable of anything sensible,' I replied.

I knew this to be true because the shrew had mounted a campaign of complaint against the condition of his room, which had suffered dreadfully from the effects of his recent debauch.

'Then you have a companion Frank,' she replied. 'For you are scarcely sensible yourself. You have fastened on this story of Costano's like a bird on a worm. Even if it is true who would believe it? And of what consequence can it be? It will make no difference to you or me. Let the past alone. We have enough with the present.'

As she said this she took me in her arms. I knew what she meant. What I had said to my master about children was not altogether a stratagem. Betsy and I had strong hopes of a family, and there were few days not occupied in some measure by preparations for such an event. They filled our waking hours and supplied much of our conversation. But how could I explain to Betsy that the more I thought about the future, the more I was drawn to the past? I too was someone's child. Someone had anticipated my coming into the world. There were threads linking lives together. For most people they were on the surface, like the pattern in a carpet. For me they were hidden, perhaps never to be found. I kissed Betsy tenderly on the mouth and felt the answering warmth of her lips.

'You are everything I could need of the present and the future,' I said. 'And perhaps it is a fruitless undertaking. But I cannot ignore what I have been told. I believe there is a purpose in it somewhere.'

She shook her head.

'You were always a dreamer, Frank. But you must do as you will. Just don't hope for too much,' she said, pulling away.

I considered this as much of a blessing as I could hope for from Betsy. And when all was said and done she was probably right. I could not satisfactorily explain to myself, let alone her, the compulsion I was under. But, having decided on my course of action, I was determined to pursue it. It was here that I encountered my first problem. I had innocently assumed that finding Adebayo would be a simple matter of asking Costano. It was not so. Costano, whom I fancied knew everything, on this occasion seemed to know nothing.

'I have no idea where he is,' he said in answer to my enquiry. 'Adebayo has no home. He and his company go wherever they can find employment.'

'But there must be places where he is regularly to be found. You discovered him easily enough for my wedding.'

'Sheer good fortune, Frank. I had not seen him for years before that.'

I groaned audibly. I could not believe Costano had excited my interest only to frustrate me. As if he could read my mind, he continued in a more hopeful vein.

'He usually performs in taverns and inns. Try the landlord of the Benbow, where you saw him last.'

I thanked him coolly, and at the earliest opportunity, sought out the landlord. Like most of his kind he was not the most communicative of people. His main concern being to part customers from their money, he was, from long practice, avaricious and suspicious. I took care, therefore, to provide myself with a few shillings before calling on him. In the event, they proved to be unnecessary, for I quickly discovered that he was sufficiently interested in questioning me about Poll, who had, until recently, been a frequenter of the inn, to make my enquiries about Adebayo perfectly acceptable to him.

'She was a game un,' he said, winking. 'Good for custom. But she don't come here no more.'

'My master has forbidden her,' I replied.

'Wants 'er for himself I dare say. Poll won't stand fer that. She's a game un', he repeated.

I decided it was politic not to correct him about my master and simply agreed about Poll. It soon became clear, however, that his interest in her was not limited to reminiscence. He wished to renew his acquaintance. To accomplish which he was eager to enlist my support.

'I allus liked 'er,' he said. 'She ain't fussy like some.'

I looked at his heavy face, jowelled like a bloodhound, and wondered how fussy Poll would have to be to refuse him.

'If you could tell 'er Tom's waiting.'

I nodded and said I would let her know. He appeared content with this, and mumbled something about 'a favour fer a favour'. As things turned out, however, there was little he could tell me about Adebayo. It seems he was in the habit of arriving unexpectedly and offering to entertain his customers. But after the last performance, which had threatened to become violent, the landlord said he would think twice about agreeing.

'I can't afford it,' he explained. 'Not on account of some niggers.'

I surmised that this was a frequent hazard and wondered whether Adebayo had been forced to venture further afield as a consequence. I gathered from the landlord that this was indeed the case. The last he had heard of Adebayo he was performing in the Midlands. My heart sank at this. I began to think I should never find him. The best the landlord could do was to give me a list of the principal inns in London where Adebayo had been known to perform. I looked forlornly at them. Some I knew, others were just names, but I guessed they were all low taverns like the Benbow. I saw myself wasting much time and effort in fruitless searching, trudging around the capital.

I continued in this anxious state for some weeks. Occasionally, I would venture out to one of the inns and make enquiries, only to be met with the same mixture of ignorance and indifference. I was on the verge of abandoning my quest as hopeless when, during the last of my visits, I came across a handbill advertising a fair to be held at Blackheath. There, amongst the fire-eaters and conjurers were notices of the 'white negress', and the 'hanged negro'. My pulse quickened and I looked further down the flyer. In bold lettering, at the bottom, was written, 'musical entertainment from Sebastian, the famous negro minstrel'. The date was Saturday August 12, a week hence. Little enough time to organise a visit. But there was no question that I should not go, manage it as I would. I knew, of course, how my master would respond. To him, such an entertainment was little more than a display of grossness.

'Jugglers and freaks Frank,' he said when I sought his permission. 'I am amazed you propose wasting your time on such absurdities. If you really are intent on it, Bedlam is a lot nearer, or the House of Commons. There is enough absurdity on view there to satisfy the lowest appetite.'

I summoned as much earnestness into my face as I could manage. I had been prepared for such an outburst. He would bluster and mock, but he was not always averse to such diversions and would listen keenly to Mr Boswell's account of cock fights.

'I thought to treat Betsy to an outing Master. The country air will do her good. And the entertainments are innocent.'

He gave his usual grunt.

'I credited Mrs Barber with more sense than to go chasing after trifles.' He said.

'I fancy you have not acquainted Mrs Williams with your design.'

'No master.'

'You thought to chance the lion's roar rather than the tiger's bite?'

'Yes master.'

'It may be she cannot spare you both on Saturday.'

'There is nothing which cannot be prepared on Friday, and you will be at Mrs Thrale's.'

'Very well, Frank. I shall undertake for you. But have a care of your person, and Betsy's. Such places are the haunt of thieves and vagabonds.'

Betsy was well pleased with my plan when I announced it to her. I said nothing of my real purpose in wishing to go but presented it in the same manner as I had to my master.

'An outing,' she said, clapping her hands. 'It is just what we need Frank. How clever of you. We can take some food and stay all day.'

When our landlords, the milliner and his wife, heard of it they declared their intention of going too, and we immediately determined to join forces. They were an amiable couple whose company would make the trip more sociable and agreeable, as well as allowing us to share the expense of a cart, a consideration not lost on both Betsy and me. I also reasoned that I could safely leave Betsy with them whilst I sought out Adebayo.

The day of our expedition was warm and humid. I sensed rain later, but not just yet. We made our way over to Smithfield market where we hired the services of a cart, returning into the country after an early morning delivery. Betsy held her nose as she climbed in, but by the time we reached the outskirts of the city, the odour of meat had sufficiently lessened to be only a mild annoyance. The ladies had bought thin muslin scarves for their faces, and it was well they did, for the dust from the high road caused us all to cough incessantly. The journey of ten miles took above two hours. Our horse was in no mood to hurry, having already covered the same distance hours before. Indeed, his stumbling was at times so acute as to put us in grave concern of ever reaching our destination safely, and what with the swearing of the driver and the jolting of the cart, we were so shaken on our arrival that we staggered at first like inebriates. But the inconveniences of the journey were exceedingly well rewarded by the sight of the fair itself. Even before we were set down we marvelled at its extent. It covered the common where it was situated, like a vast army encamped before a city. Tents of every size and colour sprawled like a rainbow across the plain. The field was awash with people. We stood and stared, awed, and if truth be told, a little disconcerted at what we saw. It was forcibly brought home to me how difficult my task would be. I might never find Adebayo in such a throng.

It was the milliner and his wife who first took the plunge. Without them Betsy and I might have remained transfixed all day. Clutching us by the hand they threaded their way through the stalls and tents at the edge of the fair towards the large open space at its centre. We passed a conjurer with a flock of doves and an oriental gentleman making paper dragons surrounded by eager children. Sandwiched between them was a raised platform on which stood a man haranguing a small group. As I looked he beckoned to me, and I recognised with horror the swollen countenance of the parson from the Fleet. I put my head down and forced my way on. Once in the centre of the fair, the crowd thinned and we were able to take our bearings. It was laid out like a clock face. In the middle lay the chief attraction, a square of turf marked out with ropes from which hung signs inviting passers-by to try their luck. Striding round this makeshift arena was a giant of a man, naked to the waist, who was taunting the crowd, which was returning his taunts with interest. Now and again a contender would come forward, urged on by his fellows, only to be helped out, limping and bloody after a few rounds. Straight up from the ring were the hucksters selling potions, washes, and nostrums To the left, from which we had entered, were conjurers, jugglers and tumblers, whilst to the right, were stalls selling food and ale. The freak shows with their rarities and monster exhibits, in which my interest lay, were situated at the bottom. Plainly I would need a stratagem if I was to accomplish my design of visiting them.

The milliner wished to visit the peddlers of 'cordial drops' and 'restorative pills' first. He had long been a sufferer from the gout, for which he and his wife were constantly seeking a remedy. Betsy whispered to me that it would be a kindness to them if we paid our respects in that quarter first. I readily concurred, but ventured to suggest that after two hours of travelling we were all in need of refreshment. This was patently true. However, one glance at the ale tent was sufficient to show we would not be accommodated speedily. I offered to make the purchase and join them as soon as I could. To my great satisfaction, this was taken up by all, and I parted from them, promising to be speedy.

Once out of view I hurried towards the bottom end of the common. I felt a twinge of conscience at my deception, but I reasoned that it was harmless enough. Betsy would not wish to accompany me, and besides I would not be gone long. As I drew near the tents I reviewed my plan. I had no wish to disrupt a performance or become a spectacle myself. I knew how volatile and unpredictable the crowd could be. I would seek out Adebayo, let him know my business, and ask where I might find him in future. Then I could rejoin Betsy by way of the ale tent. It was simplicity itself. I was just complimenting myself on this when I saw a crowd gathered outside the largest of five tents. In front of it was a large board fixed by a pole into the ground displaying a list of items, like a bill of fare in an eating house. At the top was 'The Human Porcupine'. A man 'covered', so the advertisement said 'from head to toe in solid quills'. Below him was 'The surprising wonderful Elephantiasis Woman'. A creature 'part woman and part fish'. And further down, past the man with arms four inches long, and the child with two heads were the exhibits I was looking for.

I cast about for a way of entering the tent which did not entail joining the general crush. At first glance it seemed impossible. The tent was solidly constructed all round, and at various points were stationed men whose bull-dog appearance was clearly meant to deter anyone with ideas similar to mine. I began to think there was no other way but to wait my turn. But then I noticed, to one side of the tent, a smaller one, which I guessed served as an attiring room for the performers. In the wall of it, nearest me, was a flap, tethered at the bottom by a peg. As I watched I saw the peg pulled up from inside and the flap moved back. The attention of the crowd was immediately drawn to this in hopes of securing a quicker entrance. But it soon appeared the movement was simply to allow those closeted inside a little air. From the gap emerged a figure, a pipe clenched firmly between his teeth. He looked around and surveyed the throng with obvious satisfaction, then removed his pipe and blew a generous coil of smoke into the air. After a few moments he turned to re-enter the tent, revealing as he did so a long scar running the length of his neck. I waved my arm energetically in his direction.

'Joseph,' I called out.

He stopped and looked back but seemed not to see me.

'Joseph,' I called again. Louder this time.

His eyes rested on me briefly and I saw he recognised me. For a moment I thought he was going to ignore me but then he raised his hand and beckoned. Some in the crowd murmured as I left their number and made my way over, but I strutted confidently towards him as though I were one of the performers. He pulled me quickly inside and replaced the flap firmly with the peg.

'Yo lucky dey don't lynch yo,' he said. 'Dey bin waiting lon' time.'

'I must speak with Adebayo. Is he here?'

'Yeah. He say yo come again.'

'Where is he?'

Joseph pointed towards the large tent. In my hurry to ask about Adebayo I had taken scant notice of my surroundings. I saw now that I was in a narrow passageway, which led in one direction to a small area with performers jostling in various states of readiness, and in the other, via a curtain, to a large arena already filling with people. I drew the curtain aside and looked in. The centre of the tent was dominated by a circular arena marked out with lines of chalk around which sat the audience. A mood of impatience had gripped them and some were calling vociferously for the entertainment to start, banging on the ground and whistling. Joseph shook his head anxiously. I followed his gaze and saw him looking at a large baboon crouched on the edge of the circle. The animal was dressed ridiculously in a man's breeches and waistcoat, and, even more ridiculously, was clutching a violin. Suddenly it put the bow to the strings and struck up a lively air, prancing around the arena in imitation of a dance. The crowd let out a hoot, clapping and urging the animal on, unsure whether it was man or beast. He was by now scampering among the crowd, making little darts into them and amusing the children by his antics, some of whom were sufficiently confused by his ape-like movements to need the reassurance of a parent. On and on he went, becoming ever more daring in his sallies, until with a leap he swung onto one of the ropes which threaded across the interior of the tent. I saw the canvas sag from the force of his leap but he had judged it carefully and was light enough not to endanger the fabric. The crowd gasped and soon began urging him on to new acts of daring. At the top of the tent was a metal frame whose purpose was to serve as a candle-holder for the evening's entertainment. Attached to it was a rope which allowed it to be lowered or raised as required. It quickly became apparent that the frame was Adebayo's destination. It took him only a few seconds to scramble up the rope. Once at the top, however, the frame started to lurch sickeningly from side to side. Those in the audience beneath its swing, pushed and shoved themselves from its path, accompanied by much cursing from the men and squealing from the women. Then, suddenly, Adebayo was on the frame itself, and, to the wonder of all, managed to free his hands and begin playing. There was a chorus of applause from the crowd and cries of 'well done monkey'. What happened next is not entirely clear. Whether Adebayo, overcome with the success of his act became careless, or whether, as Joseph afterwards affirmed someone from the crowd hurled something at him, somehow he missed his footing. There was a gasp from all sides as we saw him slip. He reached out his hand desperately to clutch the frame, but it was swaying too much for him to grasp, and as we watched, helpless, he fell like a stone. The crowd stood still in silent disbelief. For a long moment nothing stirred. Then the air was broken by the sound of an infant wailing. Joseph and I rushed forward, but when we got to Adebayo he was senseless on the ground.

I helped carry him from the arena into the small tent, which was quickly cleared of people. I remember thinking how light he was. Joseph removed the monkey costume and laid him on a makeshift bed of cushions and clothes. His face was deathly pale but he was still breathing. A small trickle of blood was issuing from his right ear and there was a large swelling, horribly discoloured, above his temple. Joseph was distraught. He wanted to remain with Adebayo but knew the crowd, like an impatient child, could not be left for long. They were cowed for the moment, but would soon become restless. They had paid to see the entire entertainment and would not leave without their due. I looked at him and signalled my intention to stay. He and the others could finish the performance. If there was any change I would let him know. He left reluctantly, promising to be back soon, and I saw him talking briefly to his friends before disappearing into the large tent.

Adebayo never became fully conscious again. In that, at least, God was merciful. His injuries were such that it would not have been possible to bear them. He lay contorted, like a doll carelessly discarded, his head flopped to one side and several of his limbs poked through the flesh. I could not believe he had been reduced to this. Adebayo, who had seemed almost invincible. I felt a surge of anger at his fate. Justice had most certainly not been done him. I thought how frail the body was, how easily it could be destroyed. Perhaps my master was right, justice was only to be found in the next life. But, looking at Adebayo, it did not seem enough.

It took him two hours to die. I thought at times he was stirring. His eyes would flicker briefly like a candle and his lips moved feverishly as though muttering some secret incantation. But whatever world he was in there was no pathway into it from mine. I did what I could for him. I cradled his head and moistened his lips with a little water, talking softly to him. Towards the end there was a sound in his throat, like pebbles stirred by the tide, and he became agitated, as though disturbed by some unwelcome thought. I took his hand and began to sing to him. It was a song from my childhood, taught to me by Mama Du, which I had forgotten until then. But it sufficed to quieten him, and after a few minutes, he drifted off into a deep slumber. When Joseph returned he found me still singing and Adebayo dead in my arms.

What followed seems now like a dream. I have a dim sense of the room filling with people and of much weeping, and much anger at the manner of Adebayo's death. Joseph was especially bitter at what had occurred, and convinced he had been killed by someone in the crowd. He was for carrying his body before a justice and swearing out a warrant. But a warrant had to name someone, which in the present state of knowledge was impossible. As for myself, I could not think or determine anything clearly. Common sense told me I could perform no useful service by remaining, and that Betsy would be extremely worried by my continued absence. But I had no will to leave. I was disappointed by Adebayo's sudden death. There was no pretending otherwise. My only real hope of discovering who I was had been snatched from me, as though part of myself had died, and I was ill-disposed to attempt anything sensible. Nevertheless, I got to my feet, despondently. As I did so, however, I felt a restraining hand on my arm.

'He oft'n talk 'bout yo,' said Joseph.

I turned and looked at him.

'Me?' I replied in surprise.

He nodded.

'Say yo like yo mudder.'

My heart began to pound. Why was he saying this now? Did he intend to mock me? Joseph was not one whom I would have counted a friend. He knew why I had come, of course. Perhaps he blamed me for Adebayo's death. I had brought bad luck, like the evening they were thrown out of the Benbow.

'Are you in earnest?' I said.

'Adebayo wan' yo to know.'

'Know what?'

'Dat yo mudder good.'

'Adebayo knew my mother?'

'Yeah, lon' time ago.'

'How? Where?'

He did not answer directly, but what he said next exploded in my head like cannon shot.

'He luv her pretty good. Wan' she be his wife.'

I felt the tent begin to swim around me and heard myself breathing hard. Was this the explanation I had been pursuing so fervently? My voice shook but I pressed remorselessly on.

'Joseph. Are you telling me that Adebayo was my father?'

He shook his head.

'No. But he wanna be.'

I cannot be sure whether I was saddened or relieved at this information. The possibility that I had a father was dangled before me only to be cruelly withdrawn. And yet to know I had nursed him, ignorant of who he was, would have been insupportable. Fate, it seemed, still wished to sport with me.

I stayed with Joseph for a further hour during which he told me all he knew about my mother. Adebayo had confided in him completely, perhaps in case of such an eventuality as this. He told me that my mother's name was Ehuomo. She had been born in the same village in Africa as Adebayo and was renowned for her beauty. When the slavers came to the village they seized her and sold her to a merchant on the coast who kept her to satisfy his own immoderate passions. He brought her to England, pretending to his fellows she was a housemaid. Eventually he tired of her and sold her to a brothel keeper. One day she ran away and was fortunate in meeting Adebayo who persuaded her to join his troupe. Joseph said she was a skilled dancer and could accompany Adebayo on the fiddle. She stayed for some time but then left very suddenly without explanation. Two years later she returned heavy with child. She said she had fallen in love with a gentleman who had taken her to Bristol. But he had deserted her when she said she was bearing his child. I asked Joseph who this gentleman might be. He shook his head and said she wouldn't say. Shortly afterwards she disappeared again and Adebayo heard that friends of the gentleman had arranged her transportation to Jamaica. Some time later he was told she had died on the journey giving birth to a child. I asked whether he had heard Adebayo mention the name 'Bathurst' but he shook his heard.

I thanked him for what he had told me. He said 'it was owed to Adebayo'. Before I left he took me to one side and showed me a small, highly decorated box which he opened reverently. Inside was a finely wrought chain. I recognised it instantly as the fellow to my own. Joseph picked it up gently and gave it to me.

'It bilong yo now,' he said.

I took the chain and left the tent, my heart too full to say anything. Once outside I stopped and leant against a stall displaying nosegays. I picked one up and buried my face in its wilting petals. There was little fragrance left after the heat of the day but I caught the hint of it, like over-ripe fruit. I threw it down in disgust and hurried on. Overhead came the first rumble of thunder. In my anxiety to be gone I had not noticed how dark it had become. It was late afternoon already. Hours had passed since I had left Betsy. I shuddered to think how many. But I could think of little else save the scene that had passed in the tent. It was my first real encounter with death. I had seen dead people before. It wasn't possible to live in London without doing so. But this was different. To see life ebb out of a man. To see the warmth, vitality, extinguished, not just for a few moments, but forever. I thought of my own death, of Betsy's, of my master's. How would it find us? My master lived in nightly terror of death, as of a superior adversary. But I fancied when it came, he might welcome it, for all that. As for Adebayo, life had been cruelly wrenched from him, but perhaps his death had not been comfortless. I had sung to him as I supposed his mother had. He had ended life as he had started it. There was something complete about that. I liked to think so anyway.

So consumed was I with these thoughts that I reached the centre of the fair without realising it. My first sense of where I was came when I heard the roar of the crowd from the boxing ring. It seemed yet another youth had been persuaded to try his fortune. I glanced idly over as I passed by. Despite myself I was curious to see who it might be. Although the crowd was very dense there was a small gap through which I could glimpse a corner of the ring. To begin with I could make out very little, then, as the fight moved in my direction, I had full view of the challenger. To my amazement, I saw that he was black, but, to my utter astonishment, I saw it was Famistan. My first instinct was to call out to him to leave the ring before he was hurt, but this would not have endeared me to the crowd, who were plainly enjoying the fight. Besides, it appeared that Famistan, despite being inferior in size, was giving a good account of himself. He was lighter on his feet and danced around his opponent, evading his lumbering blows, any one of which would surely have felled him. The crowd had begun to sense he might emerge the victor from the contest and urged him on loudly. Too many fights had ended in an easy victory for the giant and they were eager to see him worsted. But he was not about to give in easily. What he lacked in skill he made up for in cunning. Just as Famistan was gaining the upper hand someone from the crowd called out his name. He turned instinctively to look. It was enough for his opponent, who threw a vicious punch at the side of his head. Fortunately for Famistan, he swayed back just in time to miss the full force of the blow, but it was enough to send him sprawling on the ground. This provoked an outburst of booing from the crowd, convinced the call had come from a confederate and angry at being denied the victory they had anticipated. For his part the giant protested his innocence, and feigned sufficient modesty at his victory to go the aid of his defeated opponent. Famistan, however, showed remarkable powers of recovery and was soon sitting up and declaring his intention of continuing the fight. This delighted the crowd who were eager to see more. But I had by now managed to get to the edge of the ring, and was close enough to see the ugly wound which had been inflicted below Famistan's ear. To continue was unthinkable. I reached out and touched his arm. He looked at me almost with indifference. His eyes were hollow and I saw with a profound shock that he no longer cared whether he left the ring alive or not. I got hold of him round the waist and called to those nearest to help me lift him out. They were at first reluctant and told me to let him alone, the blackamoor had guts they said and wanted to fight. But their mood changed when I told them I was his brother, and two men, who had themselves been beaten earlier on, eventually came forward. Even so, it was no easy task. Famistan was not Adebayo. After much heaving, however, we got him clear of the crowd and set him down on the ground. He had lost a lot of blood from his wound, and was too faint to stand, but the flow had stanched now and he was beginning to revive. I was at a loss to understand what could have driven him to such foolishness. Famistan, who prided himself on being a man of fashion, to be reduced to brawling in the dirt of a common fair. It was inconceivable. He looked at me, the ghost of a smile on his lips, as if he could read my thoughts.

'What idiocy is this?' I asked. 'He could have killed you.'

'Or I him, Frank,' he replied. 'If it had not been for his decoy it would have ended differently.'

'Do you think the Earl would care to hear his servant had been brawling in public. What were you thinking of?'

His face darkened and his mouth became ugly.

'The Earl is no longer my master. I have done with him.'

I stared in amazement at him.

'What foolishness have you been guilty of? It cannot be because of Lizzy?'

He shook his head.

'What then?' I went on. 'Surely it can be mended?'

'My life is over Frank. Everything is finished.'

I did not trust myself to reply to this. Famistan had never been a favourite of mine. I had liked him because of his youth and high spirits but I could not deny that he was vain and shallow. He had behaved atrociously to Lizzy. She could say, with more truth than him, that her life was over, and it was in my mind to tell him so. Yet the look of anguish on his face forestalled me. Whatever had occurred to lose him his place I pitied him for it.

'Things cannot be so bad,' I said. 'You were not your master's favourite for nothing.'

He laughed bitterly at this.

'Do you know why I was his favourite? Why he let me wear his clothes, bathe in his room?'

'Because he liked your company Famistan and because you flattered him. We all knew that.'

He shook his head again.

'It was not my company he wished for.'

I looked at him in bewilderment.

'He served me as men serve women.'

His lips moved and I heard the words but they meant nothing to me.

'He forced me, Frank, like one of his whores.'

I put my hands to my ears and tried to resist what he was telling me. Such bestiality was not to be thought of. It was like foulness in my mouth. And even as the idea formed I felt my stomach rise. I turned to answer him and vomited violently on the ground.

It was then I saw Betsy, making her way, almost running towards me. When she saw me, my clothes fouled, and Famistan bruised and bleeding on the ground she stopped, confused, and, so I thought, angry. I waited for the first outburst, expecting her to berate me for deserting her. But she stood there, silently, for what seemed like forever, and then suddenly I felt her arms thrown round me and her wet, sobbing face, on mine. As she held me, the skies opened, and the rain, which had been threatening all day descended in torrents.

7

London

1752

February 15. Most cold and miserable in my 'dictionary room' today. Shiels no better. Insists on continuing despite a racking cough. I said 'Robert, if you wish to add the contents of your lungs to the dictionary be so good as to put them in an appendix.' Poor fellow. I fear this work will kill us all. Dodsley has had his pound of flesh. Five years and less than half done. Dear God. Chaffed everyone with my definition of 'oats'. 'A grain which in England is generally given to horses, but in Scotland supports the people.' Stewart retorted it was well known that in England horses were better treated than the populace. The man is an inveterate Scot.

Spent an hour with Tetty. Complained bitterly of the noise in the house.

'Must your clerks shout all the time, Sam?' she started. 'I cannot sleep for the clamour. They have such loud voices. Why must you employ Scotsmen?'

'I am sorry, my love,' I replied. 'I shall speak to them. Do not distress yourself.'

'That is all very well, but the house is no better than an alehouse. People coming and going. I dare not entertain here. Mrs Fitzroy called to enquire after me and I had to refuse myself to her. What must she think?'

'I am pleased to hear Mrs Fitzroy can think,' I said. 'The world is of a different opinion I fancy.'

'Very witty Sir. You have taken to insulting women to amuse yourself now. That dictionary has turned you to stone. You show no feeling to me. I am neglected and left alone all day. I shall never accustom myself to living here.

London will be the death of me. Cities are not fit places for ladies. They were created for men.'

Took advantage of her observation to turn the conversation into a more general vein and we talked for a while of other topics. Such is the pattern of our meetings since her last attack. She keeps to her room and rarely leaves her bed. Levet says her condition is not helped by strong drink and I have endeavoured to intercept her supply, but to little avail. She has the cunning of many men.

Away at eleven to my room and spent the time until dawn composing the next number of *The Rambler*. The subject of sleep occurring, considered how much time we pass in oblivion. Mankind never so pleased as when sunk in forgetfulness of itself.

February 20. Shiels announced his intention of writing the life of Sam Boyse. Told him he could call on me for information. He asked me if it was true that Boyse pawned his clothes to buy food. I said he had been driven to many extremities by necessity, that it was his practice when writing to pawn the first few pages of his book and then redeem them with the next, and so on, till the work was completed. No one knew poverty like Boyse. Yet he knew how to live. He would refuse roast beef unless accompanied by mushrooms and truffles. Told him I was more affected at his death than by any other, save that of Savage.

Talked at length with Anna about Tetty's drinking. She declared herself innocent of supplying her.

'She has asked Sam, but I would not indulge her,' she said.

'I am glad of it ma'am. Tetty is not given to moderation in such things.'

'I have thought it proper though to allow her cordials. I know by report they can be beneficial in relieving anxiety. Tetty's constitution is excessively nervous and they serve to quieten her.'

'What is the nature of this preparation?'

'A remedy advertised in *The Daily Courier*: "Dr Solomon's sovereign remedy against the spleen". Several ladies take it. I am sure it is harmless.'

Much concerned at Anna's reply. I desired some of the mixture from her and took it to Levet for his opinion. He sniffed the bottle and turned away in disgust.

'Opium Sam,' he said. 'If she is taking this she will be insensible in a month and probably dead in three.'

Conducted a search of Tetty's room. Found three bottles. One under the bedclothes, one under a pile of stays, and one in the commode. This last being most unpleasant to retrieve. Tetty in great agitation.

'Am I to be ransacked as well? Do you intend to search my person?'

'No, of course not.' I replied, though the thought had occurred to me.

'This is monstrous Sam. I am not to have any medicine at all. You would see me suffer without any relief.'

'It is not medicine Tetty. Levet assures me it is an opiate and will kill you.'

'Nonsense. Levet is a quack. He purchased his knowledge of treatments from whores and mountebanks. Why you allow him to stay is a mystery.'

Much provoked by this and determined to reply in kind.

'I took him in my dear when you decided to decamp to Hampstead and leave me. He has since provided me with the company I had hoped from a wife.'

Tetty distressed at my outburst. Began to weep.

'I have not been the wife you wished for, I know it,' she said.

'Nay, do not take on so Tetty. You are my life. It is all for you.'

Consoled her as best I could and withdrew quickly. Such episodes are common. She knows my disappointment and uses it against me. I have not succeeded in accustoming her to the city. Excepting her rooms, the house remains meanly furnished. She has taxed me with this on more than one occasion. What is there to say? She has spent the money from Dodsley and the dictionary has become a millstone.

February 24. The day totally ruined. Returned home early evening from seeing Dodsley to find the Macbeans helpless on the floor with Peyton and Maitland supporting each other and attempting to piss into the pot. Shiels and Stewart mopping up a foul smelling puddle. In short, all my clerks drunk. Worse to follow, however. Not content with rendering themselves senseless the blockheads carried on working and spoilt a week's work. Whole sheets written on both sides, which the printers never will accept. It will cost £20 to put right. Incensed and close to despair. But for the disturbance I would have thrashed the lot.

In great dread of Tetty's humour but found her sleeping soundly. Anna says she was distressed about noon by a visit from Jervis. Mightily surprised at this. He has not visited since our marriage. Called to enquire after her but went away on learning she was sick. The puppy. To treat his mother like a common acquaintance. Deserves to be horse-whipped. He thinks because he has money and a position he can scorn us. Poor Tetty.

Worked till dawn on my *Rambler* essay but much distracted by thoughts of Tetty. To have so little happiness from each other. Thought again of the early years. Our defiance of friends and family. That it should come to this. Her misery is like a poison. It has no cure. Levet thinks me foolish. 'Tetty is not ill,' he assures me, 'she is idle. And idleness breeds fancies. Let her stir herself.' But it is too late for that. She has taken to her bed and will not be persuaded from it. It is my punishment. And the crime, for which I suffer daily, is to wish her dead. God forgive me. I cannot deny it. I see her and feel nothing. Nothing except pity. If she died tonight I would be free. But for what? There's the rub.

February 25. Away to see Richard. Embraced me warmly. Offered me some tea and we passed the time in pleasant conversation. He looks but poorly, however, and I scolded him for neglecting himself.

'You are not eating sir,' I said. 'You are no true friend of mine if you allow yourself to become ill.'

He smiled cordially at me. Nothing disturbs his sanguine nature.

'I bow to you on the subject of eating Sam. But as to physic, you must give way to me. I am the physician here.'

'Then 'physician heal thyself'. I replied.

'I am perfectly well Sam. I am practising a little economy, that is all.'

'And what of your profession Dick, are you practising that too?'

'You have been listening to my father Sam. He is convinced I am not trying sufficiently. But the world is stuffed with physicians. I earn scarce enough to keep body and soul alive.'

I sensed my opportunity.

'I can help you to another patient then.'

He looked at me as if I was not in earnest.

'Who?' he asked. 'If it is your cat again Sam, remember I treat only humans.'

'My wife,' I replied. 'I fear she is beyond any help of Levet's for whom she has developed a loathing.'

'He is too much an advocate of bleeding. Besides the man is not of a sympathetic nature.'

'Nevertheless I am fond of the rogue. He leaves one alone at breakfast. A rare virtue.'

'How is Mrs Johnson Sam?'

'Much enfeebled. She returned to Gough Square from Hampstead after a seizure and has not stirred from her bed since. She has no love for the house and is determined to return to the country as soon as she can. It seems my wife can only live with me when she is ill.'

'I am sorry to hear that.'

'You would be performing a service to me if you would attend on her. She is agitated in her mind and trusts too much to soporifics.'

'I will do what I can Sam.'

He paused for moment as if giving the idea fresh consideration. Then he said,

'I have something to ask of you in return.'

I waited for him to continue.

'It concerns Frank.'

He paused again. But I said nothing.

'My father feels his presence in Lincoln Close is difficult.'

'Difficult?'

'His neighbours know of his hatred of the trade and mock him mercilessly that he has a black boy. They say the child is his.'

He looked away from me. I can refuse him nothing. He knows that.

'Is Frank well?' I asked.

'Yes. He has just returned from Yorkshire where my father put him to school.'

'Could he not return him thither again?'

He shook his head.

'The master is a brute and beat Frank mercilessly,' he said. 'He cannot go back. My father knows not what to do with him. He will not part with him to strangers but can no longer keep him in the house.'

'The colonel has discharged his duty honourably. It is for others to see what can be done for the boy now,' I replied.

Took my leave and hurried away in much consternation. What is to be done? Tetty will not bear Frank at Gough Square, but he cannot be abandoned. His look, when I saw him on the dock attempting to hide his face in Bathurst's coat. Fear and defiance. Like hers. Like the one she gave me when she returned from Bristol. Ehuoma, daughter of the sun. Large antelope eyes, mouth spitting fury.

'Your fren', he no fren' of mine. He do dis to me,' she says, stroking her belly.

I gaze at her, bewildered. She stands confronting me at my doorway.

'Ehuoma. You should not have come here. My wife will soon return,' I say.

'He do dis to me,' she continues, 'Den he turn me away.'

Savage dead but a week. If she is to be believed this has been his final work. She will not sit down or be comforted.

'I glad he dead. He say he take care of me. Den he tell me go.'

'He died in a debtor's prison Ehuoma,' I reply. 'He could not even take care of himself'

'He liar. He say he love me.'

Her distress spills out of her like hot lava. How could I begin to explain Savage to her? I tried to warn her about him. 'Depending on Richard Savage is like depending on a child. He does not mean to harm you but he will'. Straws in the wind.

Tetty's face when she discovers us. Ehuoma's head on my shoulder.

'So Sam, you have taken to entertaining your whores and their bastards at home now. I hope sir you do not intend that I should take tea with your harem.'

I could not convince her. She believes the child mine.

February 27. Most disturbed night. Awake till dawn thinking of Frank. His mother sent to her death. I see it in Bathurst's eyes. 'She will be well in Jamaica. My father will take her into his household' he said. The voyage was too arduous. We should have waited till the child was born. But I cannot bring him into the house. She blames him for the divorce between us. Besides, I have not the means.

Up late and not at the dictionary till noon. Shiels in great distress. The poor fellow has begun spitting blood. Told him to go home and sent for Bathurst to attend him. Anna in some consternation about Tetty. She is refusing to eat without the use of her cordial and is constantly agitated by strange fancies. Professes to believe that I mean to kill her. Instructed Anna to allow her a few drops in a solution of water. There can be but little joy for Anna in this. She has become Tetty's nursemaid now and tends her like a child. But I fear her eyesight is worsening. This morning she missed the stair and fell, though without injury. Chaffed her about this.

'You and I must cling together Anna. We have but one good eye between us.'

Mightily surprised to see her cheeks redden. Enquired about Zachariah by way of diversion. She replied that her father was poorly but still in hopes of winning the prize for the longitude.

'The Admiralty will not part with their money easily Anna. Any assistance I can render him by my scribbling I will gladly do', I said.

More reddening. I fear she is unused to such attention. Pray God her father uses her better than Tetty. Passed an hour with Tetty. Amused her by talking about Mrs Lennox's new book, which she had taken notice of. We conversed like the early days.

'Charlotte Lennox has taken the city by storm, my dear,' I said. 'She has laid siege to it better than any general. *The Female Quixote* is superior to any battering ram.'

'I am pleased for her, but it should not surprise you that a woman has written well Sam. The novel is a woman's territory. Let men keep to histories and moral essays. What do they know of the heart?'

I fancied this shaft was aimed in part at me, my *Rambler* essays being much talked about of late. I replied roundly.

'They know enough for Cervantes to have written the original on which Mrs Lennox's novel is founded. She would not deny her debt to him I believe.'

'Why should she? But come sir, you must agree that more novels are written in our present age by female authors.'

'And more nonsense too ma'am. They are nothing more than romances, the absurdities of which do more harm than a whole fleet of sailors.'

She laughed at the extravagance of my expression.

'You must not play the bully with me Sam. You were not always so averse to reading romances.'

'When I was young perhaps. But a man does not care for the same things in maturity that he did in his youth.'

I saw my mistake too late. Tetty's face clouded, and her voice when she answered sounded small and resigned.

'It was my misfortune to be ignorant of that.'

'Tetty, do not take my words amiss. I meant nothing by them.'

'No, it is true. Let us acknowledge it. My friends and family warned me. I was too old. Twenty years is too much.'

'I do not believe that.'

'You have never wanted to, but you have thought it, and so have I. Now leave me Sam I am weary.'

This is how matters are. There is no safe ground. Nothing that will not lead us into recrimination. Yet she exhibited more spirit than in many nights. There is hope in that.

Worked until dawn on the dictionary. It has become my taskmaster. Occupied with 'N'. Thought of an entry on 'novel' pace Tetty: 'A small tale generally of love'. Determined to add 'a harmless drudge' to the entry for 'lexicographer'.

March 1. Bathurst called to see Tetty. Spoke to me afterwards, choosing his words as a man picks his way across a muddy field.

'She has no disease, at least of a physical nature. There are signs of a stroke some weeks ago which has left her weak on the right side. With moderate exercise she should recover the use of those limbs.'

'She resists persuasion Richard,' I replied.

'You must try harder Sam. Otherwise she will sustain another.'

I thanked him and took his arm, but he stayed back.

'There is more Sam. She complains of strange fantasies and delusions which she believes real. She claims her food is being poisoned.'

'Anna has told me of such things but she has not said them to me.'

'It is an effect of addiction. Her pupils are dilated and her countenance hectic.'

'Levet thinks she should be bled.'

'Let us try what diet and abstinence from opiates and all fermented liquors will accomplish first.'

Afterwards to publishers. Millar not happy with my progress. Refused further advance. A plague on him. Away to Cave. Offered to review *The Female Quixote* for the Magazine, which he eagerly accepted of. Passed a beggar in the street and thought of Boyse, dead of starvation with a pen in his hand. Heaven preserve me from such a fate. Back to the garret about ten in the evening. Heartened by the entries pasted in. My crew are good workers when sober. Sent milk, bread and cheese to Shiels. Worked till dawn.

March 3. Began new regimen with Tetty. Anna not hopeful of success. Tetty fretful and peevish. Her food is to be fresh and wholesome. No sweetmeats, pastries, or rich meats. She is to sit out of bed in the afternoon and walk twice around the garden. A few drops of cordial a day to be reduced as she improves.

Away to the colonel's by invitation. Walked for a while in Lincoln's Inn Fields, it being a bright but cold day. A number of families taking the morning air. Admired the gardens and statues. Nature's smiling face, as the poets have it. Bathurst's dwelling is within the square, genteel but modest, in the style of the last century. A periwigged servant opened the door and ushered me into a drawing room. Some minutes later the colonel appeared. A man of erect bearing, frail but hardy, leaning on a stick. I had not seen him since the dockside, two years before. With him was a black child, dressed in breeches and small frock coat, with buckles on his shoes. Bathurst bowed stiffly.

'You are welcome sir,' he said. 'As you see I am accompanied by a small gentleman.'

'Indeed sir. He is mightily well attired.'

He laid his hand on the boy's shoulder.

'Do you remember this gentleman Frank?' he said.

Frank cast an anxious look in my direction, followed by a shake of the head.

'Is he a school master?' he asked.

We both smiled at this.

'I fancy he has your measure already sir,' said the colonel.

'I believe he has. Though I should not like to think my appearance such as to strike terror into small boys.'

'This is Dr Johnson, Frank. He is not a schoolmaster. He is a friend.'

The colonel turned to me. 'He has a mortal fear of schoolmasters since his unfortunate experience in Yorkshire.'

'I heard something of it from your son sir.' I replied. 'He has informed me of the situation you find yourself in.'

He nodded and took his hand from the boy's shoulder.

'Please to take Jack into the garden, Frank. It is time for his walk.' Frank's face brightened.

'Yes, master,' he replied, and ran out of the room. A few seconds later there was the sound of joyful barking.

'He has his mother's vivacity,' I said.

'So I have heard,' replied the colonel. 'A sorry tale. My son tells me you knew her.'

I looked quickly at him but could discern no hint of irony, though his old-fashioned courtesy was sufficient cover for any such. But I reckoned that Richard had probably been discreet enough in this respect.

'Yes, I was acquainted with her,' I said cautiously. 'Your son was acting on my behalf in sending her abroad. She had little happiness here I fancy but I did wrong. The passage was too much.'

The colonel poured himself a measure of brandy from a decanter on a small table and offered me some, but I declined.

'The ship was delayed by a violent storm,' he said. Otherwise she would have arrived safely. You could not have known.'

'It is kind of you to say so. But it has sat heavily on me these past years.'

'As to that,' he said, draining his glass. 'It is well you have not lived on the plantations. The sights I have witnessed will follow me to my grave.'

'But you have shown compassion to Frank sir, for which I am heartily obliged.'

'It was not a hard task. The boy is gentle and affectionate. I have trained him as a servant but he has been more like a son.'

'Yet Richard says you wish to part with him.'

He sat down wearily in a faded armchair by the fire and motioned me to its fellow.

'I am not a rich man,' he began. 'What you see around you is the last of my wealth.' He held up his hand anticipating my reply. 'It is true I had money once, but I have no stomach for slavery and I could not bend sufficiently to its practices to see my stock advance as others have done. When I returned two years ago I purposed to live out my days with what little capital remained to me. Even so, this house is mortgaged and I have many debts. At my death, which I fear cannot be long now, Frank will be cast adrift. I have stipulated in my will that he shall be free but he will have little else from me, and nor will my son, Richard.'

He paused in his narrative and wiped his eyes, though whether from the effects of emotion or smoke from the fire I could not tell.

'Frank is restless here. I am an old man and can provide little enough for him by way of useful occupation which will be of service. My neighbours ridicule me for the care I show him and have taken privately to calling him Frank Bathurst. I thought to divert such unwelcome attention by sending him to Yorkshire to be schooled. But I was grossly deceived in the headmaster and have had to send for him again. Frank is too young to be apprenticed to a trade and has no one of his own age and situation with whom he may consort. He needs a protector sir and I have asked Richard to cast around among his friends and acquaintances.'

The old man spoke with remarkable vigour. I fancied him no fool, and surmised he knew enough of my situation to avoid a more direct appeal. Still the import of his account was clear.

'I am indebted to you for your frankness,' I replied. 'It is a virtue found too infrequently.' He waved his hand dismissively. 'You have behaved handsomely to Frank,' I went on. 'If you are content to be patient a little longer I shall see how he may be provided for.'

'There is no hurry sir. I wish merely to make all necessary arrangements while I am in reasonable health.'

'Of course. I take it Frank knows nothing of this.'

'No. As you saw he took you for another taskmaster.'

'What does he know of his mother and how he came to be in your household?'

The old man fixed me with a meaningful look. His voice when he spoke had the cold authority which must have served him well when he had the command of men.

'As to that. He believes his mother was shipped from Africa and died on board the slaveship. I leave it to you and your conscience sir what you choose to tell him yourself.'

Left the colonel's mightily displeased with myself. What his son has not told him he has guessed for himself. *Mea maxima culpa*. Away to Shiels. Discovered him propped up in bed dictating the life of Boyse to his wife. He is resolved to return tomorrow poor fellow. Told him how Boyse would have his wife report him on the verge of death and appeal for funds for his funeral expenses. I never knew a man more able to survive on nothing. Shiels pitifully grateful for the story. All his hopes rest on the 'Life'. Amused him by saying he would make more from writing it than Boyse did from living it. He said his wish was not to leave his wife destitute. I replied that Scotsmen had the stoutest constitutions and was in no doubt he would outlast us all. I said once Boyse's 'Life' was finished he should write more and I would assist him, the public appetite for such things being at present considerable. Shiels much cheered by the proposition. Pressed a shilling into his wife's hand on leaving.

To Richard's in the afternoon. Unusually despondent about his prospects and contemplating joining the Navy as a surgeon. Told him to put aside such desperate thoughts, that no honest man ever made his fortune at sea.

'That is all very well Sam, but a man must live.'

'Sailors drink, whore, gamble and die. They do not live sir, not as you and I understand it.'

'But I have very little alternative. You talked to my father. You know I have no prospect of advancement through him.'

'Do not abandon the town so soon Richard. The public will learn of your talents. Your attendance on Tetty has given me hopes of a recovery.'

He smiled at me.

'You must not hope for too much in either direction. Have you said anything to Tetty of Frank?'

I shook my head.

'Not yet. I intend to wait till she is stronger and in better spirits. I believe the colonel is not in haste to settle Frank.'

'You may be right Sam, but my father is not a patient man. He will expect action.'

Thanked him for his warning and hurried away to Gough Square. Encountered Anna on the stairs in great consternation. It seems Tetty has fallen foul of Levet yet again. She has complained at the noxious smell caused in the preparation of his potions. Levet, as ever, in no mood to humour her, said if she did not care for it she could always remove herself to Hampstead again. This set Tetty off, and she called him a beggarly upstart, content to live off the charity of his betters. He replied roundly to this calling her 'a painted poppet full of airs and graces' who nobody cared for.

'She is very distressed Sam.' Anna said. 'She sent me away and locked the door. She refuses to open it.'

I went upstairs and knocked on her door. The smell from Levet's room still lingered on the landing. There was no answer.

'Tetty,' I called out. 'Open the door to me.'

I heard a movement within and then all went quiet again.

'Tetty. In heaven's name open the door. It's Sam.'

I knocked more loudly and presently there was the sound of shuffling followed by the bolt being drawn back. Tetty stood there in her night gown, red-eyed, her hair dishevelled, like an inmate of Bedlam. I called Anna and we quickly got her back to bed. For some moments she would not speak to me and then it began.

'I have been grossly insulted Sam. Levet is a brute.'

'He shall apologise for it my dear,' I replied. 'He should not have spoken to you in that manner.'

'Apologise! A fig for that. You must throw him out. I cannot live under the same roof.'

'I cannot do that Tetty. He has lived here for eight years. It is his home.'

'And mine too. If you cared anything for me you would not let me suffer like this. But perhaps Levet is right, you care nothing for me.'

'Nonsense my dear. Do not listen to Levet. He has no notion of what he says.'

'The man's a barbarian. You allow him too much freedom. It is monstrous.'

She continued her tirade for a full hour so that I wondered at her energy, which was not sufficient it seemed that she could leave the room. Eventually she fell to weeping and ended by pleading for a draught of her cordial to 'soothe her nerves'. She had already consumed her dose for the day, but being insistent I at last relented. A few minutes later the sound of her snoring announced she had fallen into a heavy sleep.

Levet not a whit penitent on his return in the evening.

'You are too soft with her,' he said. 'The woman needs a kick in the rump.'

'She is ill Levet,' I replied.

'Ill my arse. I have seen three women today. Two sick of consumption and the third with a cancer in her leg the size of her head. That is ill!'

'Nevertheless, she is my wife and must be treated with respect. This is not well done of you Robert. You know how things stand in the house. I expect your support sir not your opposition.'

This took effect and he apologised in his own crabbed way for the disturbance. I believe the renegade loves me though he never will Tetty. He apologises to her tomorrow, though it will do little good I fear. She will not be swayed. We are set on a course which must end as it will.

Set to work on the dictionary but to no avail. Everything dark and cheerless. I can work no longer. All things conspire against me.

March 8. A black day. Tetty miserable and difficult. As I feared, she has not kept to her regimen. She has fallen prey to strange fantasies and is convinced Levet means to murder her. Alarmed this morning by sounds of screaming from her room. Hastened there and found her upright in bed holding a poker and striking at the air. Calmed her with Anna's help and soothed her back to sleep. Pray God it was a nightmare. Called Richard again to her. He says we must cure her addiction. But how? Asked Anna to sleep in Tetty's room until she improves. She, poor thing, agreed, but is of the opinion that Tetty should return to Hampstead.

'She is sinking here Sam,' she said. 'The house is too noisy and turbulent. She needs rest and quiet. The country air may revive her.'

I fear she is right but it is not to be thought of. I can scarce maintain one establishment. Hampstead would put me in the Marshalsea. Received a communication from Richard in the afternoon and proceeded to his lodgings. He greeted me sombrely.

'My father has had a fall Sam,' he said. 'It is not serious but he must remain in bed for several weeks.'

'I am sorry for him,' I replied. 'But he is fortunate in having a physician for a son. You could not have been of service to him in the navy.'

'I will not dispute that Sam. But the situation has made him anxious to arrange his affairs now.'

'This concerns Frank?'

'Yes, it does. He wishes Frank to be settled as soon as possible.'

He smiled bleakly at me.

'I warned you this might occur. I would have the boy here myself but I am hardly in a position to house him.'

'No,' I protested. 'It is not to be thought of. He is my responsibility and I must do what is necessary. It has simply come sooner than I expected, that is all.'

'Thank you,' he replied. 'I know you fear his reception by Mrs Johnson but the issue may not be so unfavourable. The boy has a pleasing disposition and can be usefully employed in the household.'

Left in some agitation. The path of duty is clear, but I cannot expect Tetty to see it as I do. That period of our lives was most painful. Decided to confide in Anna. She was startled by my proposal and inclined to think me over-scrupulous.

'I am amazed Sam that you are contemplating distressing Tetty further,' she said. 'You exaggerate your obligation to this child. You must tell the colonel to provide for him some other way.'

Attempted to put the situation in a more advantageous light but with little success. If I am to do this it will be without her blessing.

March 9. A turbulent night. Dreamt of Natty again. Came to me with the cheery smirk of boyhood. He said I was to hurry because mother had guests and wished me to 'perform'. Awoke, my palms sweating, as I was about to recite. I can delay no longer. It must be today. The colonel has sent again to remind me about Frank.

Went into Tetty about noon. She has slept better of late and seemed less fretful. She greeted me with a touch of her old humour.

'What brings you here at this hour sir? Should you not be attending your mistress?'

I gave her a puzzled look.

'The dictionary, you slowcoach,' she said. 'You must not neglect her. Not for your wife.'

Unnerved by Tetty's manner and began more solemnly than I had intended.

'I have something of importance to tell you Tetty,' I said.

Her gaiety vanished and her face became blank.

'What is it?' she said apprehensively. 'Has Levet packed his bags?'

'No, my dear it is nothing to do with Levet.'

'Then it is to do with me. Be quick and tell me.'

I proceeded to tell her in as few words as I could about the colonel and Frank. She looked at me in silence for a while, and I thought I had miscalculated. But she was simply gathering her forces together. Her face heightened in colour till it outdid the paint she had put on.

'No, no, no,' she began. 'A thousand times no. I will not have it. You shall not insult me again. I will not suffer that child here.'

'I have a duty, Tetty.' I replied.

'Stuff and nonsense. You have a duty to me. To your wife.'

'The colonel is ill my dear and might die. I fear what may happen to the boy if he is abandoned.'

'What is that to me? Let him be sent back to the plantations. That is where he belongs.'

Much angered by this.

'The plantations are among the most miserable and desperate places on earth,' I said. 'No one belongs there.'

'Then he will learn a valuable lesson. What is life but misery and desperation? That is what mine has become, though you care nothing for that.'

'You are unjust Tetty. I pray daily for your happiness.'

'You may pray Sam, but you do nothing. If you wish for my happiness then do as I ask and refuse the boy.'

'I cannot. I have promised the colonel.'

She breathed heavily and her voice, when she spoke shook slightly. 'Very well sir,' she said. 'You have made your decision, and I have made mine. I do not intend to remain here and become a mockery. You will please arrange for me to remove into the country.'

'We cannot afford the expense my dear. It is not possible.'

She looked scornfully at me.

'Then you must make it possible or I will shame you sir. The world shall know to whom the bastard really belongs.'

March 10. The house has become a hell. Tetty is obdurate and will not speak to me. Her time is spent weeping and complaining to Anna. Richard attended on her yesterday. He fears she will bring on another stroke. Anna is of the same opinion.

'You must find other lodgings for her,' she said. 'She cannot remain here.'

'Hampstead is out of the question Anna. It would ruin me,' I replied.

'Then somewhere cheaper. Away from the city. But soon Sam, please.'

Away to Strahan's to beg. Found him in the print shop with Manning. His eyes searched me quickly as though scanning the pages of a book.

'Empty-handed again Sam,' he said. 'Poor Manning here has had nothing new to set up for weeks.'

Replied with some heat, despite my errand.

'A dictionary cannot be compiled in haste sir. If you wish to print a mere list of words say so and be done with it. Nothing of this kind has been ventured before. It will bring fame on us all.'

'That will be small comfort in the grave Sam, for I fear we shall be carried there before it appears.'

'That is why I am here sir. To prevent such an eventuality.'

'If you have a proposal which would lengthen my life I should be glad to hear it,' he said smiling.

Took advantage of this change in mood to press my case.

'Had I the ear of Providence it would be my first task to make you immortal William,' I replied. 'However, if you are willing assist me I can assure you of an outcome of almost equal merit.'

'We are still talking of the dictionary I fancy,' said Strahan.

I nodded.

'Yes. You ask why I have nothing for you. My reply is simple. I have scarcely been able to write a line since Tetty's return. Her illness commands my entire attention. I believe she must go into the country for all our sakes. 50 guineas would settle the matter. I could defray the sum from the sale of the Dictionary, which would then be completed more expeditiously.'

Strahan scratched his head and thought for a moment while Manning grinned.

'You have a more curious way of soliciting money than any man I know,' he said at last. 'But, very well, you shall have it. Let it not be said that the progress of learning was impeded for the sake of 50 guineas.'

Gave him a thousand thanks for his liberality and hurried away. This is better than I hoped for. Afterwards wrote to Hawkesworth and asked him if he could procure some rooms for Anna and Tetty south of the river, near Bromley. Told Tetty of the arrangements. Much struck by her calm demeanour. Like being present at a death.

'So, Sam, it seems we cannot live peaceably together. I must go away again,' she said.

'Dear Tetty,' I began, but she held up her hand.

'No Sam, we are past all that.'

March 11. On this day Tetty removed with her effects to Bromley. Most melancholy occasion. All but Levet in tears. Tetty parcelled onto the wagon in blankets. The driver and his boy struggled to lift her onto the seat. Horses restless and threatening to deposit their load into the ditch. At last we were all ready, Tetty, her maid, Anna, and me. As I was about to mount behind, Tetty said there was no need of me. But I shook my head and announced my determination to accompany them.

A raw but bright day. Our breath spiralling into the air like smoke. The wagon proceeded at a good speed down Fleet Street and across London Bridge. How different from my arrival 15 years ago, penniless and footsore. I could have laughed aloud to think of it. Such dreams, such ambitions. Tetty, waiting eagerly in Lichfield for me. And now, this sorrowful procession. It had the bitter taste of failure, however I viewed it. It was four hours before we reached the outskirts of Bromley. Fields and woods had long since replaced the city's sprawling ribbon. Perhaps here, away from the turbulence of the town and the pandemonium of Gough Square, Tetty may recover her health again. We stopped in front of a modest cottage, set back from the high road. Downstairs was covered in sheets and evidently unoccupied. Upstairs lay Tetty's rooms. A coarse, brute of a man appeared and showed us up. Tetty complained to him about the staircase, which was in poor condition and missing much of its plaster. The blockhead had the temerity to laugh.

'That's nothing but the knocks of the coffins of them as died here,' he said.

I told him to hold his tongue and mind his manners for he had a lady as his tenant. He muttered something incomprehensible but the villain was complaisant enough after that. The rooms themselves were spacious and airy and fires were burning in all. They were soon settled and I came away assured in my mind of their comfort.

Arrived home late. Straight to bed.

March 14. Exceedingly cold these past days. We shall have snow. Returned to work on the dictionary with a vengeance. Sleeping and eating in the garret. Definitions now for most of 'N', and quotations pasted in. Levet came and surveyed my empire this morning after breakfast.

'You are prodigal of paper Sam,' he said. 'So many leaves could serve as spills for a hundred paupers.'

'That will undoubtedly be their fate,' I replied. 'It is part of the economy of society that nothing is wasted.'

Set to thinking by Levet. Nothing in nature which cannot be re-used. Even our carcasses. Dust to dust. Subject for an essay.

In the evening to the King's Head. Salter there, talking his nonsensical stuff and Mcghie. Another damned Scot, but I love the fellow. Company good, and felt myself in fine form, tossing and goring several. Hawkins sanctimonious and mean. Refused to pay his share of dinner because he had not eaten. I called him a 'most unclubbable man', which set the table roaring.

Home in the early hours. Arrived to find the house in a stir. Desperate message from Anna. The cottage has proved uninhabitable. High winds have blown in several of the windows and the roof is leaking badly. Tetty is in great distress. She must return immediately. That rogue of a landlord will pay for this. Hurried over to Strahan's and though the hour was late found him just returned from dinner with the Earl of Sandwich. Begged him to allow me the use of his coach and four. He behaved most handsomely and said they would be at my service within the hour. I thanked him earnestly and he said he would do anything to oblige me. Shed tears at his kindness.

Away just before dawn at a good pace, across Tower Bridge and south, through Bermondsey and New Cross. Passed the time berating my foolishness in sending Tetty out of town so late. I should not have entrusted Hawkesworth with the task. I have been too careless of Tetty. Arrived at the cottage about breakfast time and went swiftly upstairs. Met at the top by Anna who took me aside into the drawing room. Inside was Hawkesworth's physician. The fellow had sent him on hearing of Tetty's distress. He greeted me warmly and said my wife's condition was stable, and I should not be alarmed, but for her own good she should return to Gough Square. I replied that I had come with that intention. Went into Tetty's room. Found her propped up, amidst a sea of pillows, in a pitiable state. The floor littered with bowls and jugs variously filled with water and the windows covered but poorly with cloth.

'You have not abandoned me Sam?' she said taking my hand.

'Of course not my dear. You must never think that. We shall have you home to Gough Square this very morning. I was very wrong to send you here.'

'You must not blame yourself. I was anxious to leave.'

'When you are sufficiently strong you shall return to Hampstead if you wish.'

'Thank you Sam.'

After a brief meal of bread and soup, we boarded the coach. Tetty borne by the coachman and me. As we were leaving, the sky darkened and the wind freshened from the north. Observed the coachman scan the clouds apprehensively. At the edge of Blackheath Common the first few flakes of snow fell. The horses whipped into a faster pace. By Shooter's Hill it began in earnest. The coachman in great trepidation at descending the hill. Everyone fearful of highwaymen. Half way down the wheels slipped. Tetty and Anna in great distress. Got down to lighten the load and steady the horses. After half an hour we reached the bottom. All much relieved, though we had only travelled five miles. Progress through Greenwich fearfully slow, thick snow, some drifting. Mid afternoon before we reached the city. Threaded our way cautiously like a caterpillar past abandoned carts and wagons, drivers huddled in great coats. Tetty very poorly, suffering greatly from the cold. Arrived home around early evening and straightway conveyed Tetty to bed.

Sent for Bathurst to attend on her. He came within the quarter hour.

'She has survived the rigours of the journey remarkably Sam. But her heartbeat is irregular and I fear the onset of fever. She will need constant care for the next few days.'

I am in dread of her dying.

March 16. Day piercingly cold. Fresh falls of snow. Tetty's room like a furnace. She lying helpless, while Anna fusses round. Towards evening Anna came to me in great agitation.

'You must send for Dr Bathurst Sam. Tetty is in pain and I cannot asist her.'

'Is it the fever. Is it reaching a crisis?'

She shook her head.

'I fear it is another seizure.'

Bathurst came in haste. The poor fellow was on his way to an engagement with his father. His look when he came from her room struck terror through me.

'Tetty has suffered a stroke Sam. It has paralysed her left side.'

'Dear God. Is she in pain?'

'No. She is comfortable now. She has the power of speech, though her voice is faint.' He paused. 'I do not wish to alarm you Sam. But you should prepare yourself. She may not last the night.'

'Then I must go to her immediately.'

Entered the bedroom and found Tetty her face cruelly disfigured, as though bent out of shape by a madman. Her eyes stared upwards and I thought for a moment she could not see me. But as I approached there was a small movement of her head.

'Sam,' she whispered. Her right hand fluttered towards me on the blanket.

I knelt down at the bedside and clasped it in mine. Her fingers were cold despite the oppressive warmth of the room.

'Forgive me.' She spoke slowly and with effort.

I shook my head.

'It is I who need forgiveness,' I said.

She gestured towards a table at the side of the bed on which stood a glass of water. I picked it up and bent her head forwards. She took a few sips and I seized her hand again.

'I may not have long,' she said.

'Nonsense. You will soon be better.'

'Bathurst told me Sam. I know how things are.'

She paused for breath. Taking the air as though sucking on a straw.

'We must part friends,' she said.

'We have always been that,' I replied She moved her head slightly.

'No Sam. I have not been kind.'

I protested loudly at this but she was determined to continue.

'You should not have married me.'

'You have been the best of wives Tetty.'

'In the beginning perhaps.'

I felt her fingers tighten on mine.

'Forgive me Sam,' she repeated.

'Don't be foolish Tetty,' I replied.

'Say the words Sam. Say the words.'

She would not be satisfied until I uttered them. Afterwards she sank back on her pillows.

'Thank you,' she said. 'Pray with me now.'

We prayed together, beseeching God to have mercy on her, and committing her soul into his keeping. Tetty much comforted. About nine o'clock she fell into a slumber. Anna came to sit with us and I drifted off to sleep.

March 17. The darkest of days. My darling Tetty died this morning shortly before dawn. I was alone with her, Anna having retired at my insistence to bed. An hour beforehand she rallied slightly, and it seemed for a moment the doctor was mistaken. Her eyes opened full on me and her mouth twitched.

'Are you in pain, my dear?' I asked.

'No,' she said.

'Do you wish Anna to come?'

She breathed hard, her lips edged with spittle.

'Tell me,' she said. 'While there's time.'

'What, my dear?'

'Frank. Is he your child?'

My face must have betrayed me. Even in her enfeebled state she could discern my bewilderment. I knew not how to answer her.

'I thought it was so,' she said.

'No, you mistake me my dear. I do not know.'

'Be good to him. Anna too. Promise me,' she said.

I nodded.

'Forgive me Tetty. I have wronged you,' I said.

The hint of a smile crossed her face. Then she gestured towards the table. I picked up the water.

'My cordial too.' She said, her hand fiddling with her pillow.

I reached behind and pulled out a bottle nestling underneath.

'No Tetty,' I said. 'It's bad for you.'

'One good turn….' She murmured with a touch of her old humour.

I began to protest again but she turned her face expectantly to me. 'You cannot deny me this,' she said.

I hesitated and then removed the cork. What followed haunts me still. I shook a few drops into the glass and raised it to her lips. She sipped eagerly at it, some running down her chin, till the glass was empty.

'Thank you,' she whispered and sank back. 'You have repaid your debt.'

A short while after she sank into a heavy sleep and an hour later she was dead. Sent for John Taylor to sit with me, Bathurst being away from the city.

March 18. In torment. Awoke in horror about four in the morning. Hands clammy, body hot and shaking. Tetty is gone. My dearest wife. Immediately nauseous and began retching over the side of the bed, though I had eaten nothing for above a day. God forgive me. What have I done? Took off my nightshirt and knelt down in prayer. What words can absolve me? Anna wakened by my movements called to me. Hastily covered myself and allowed her in. She poor thing in tears and shaking her head.

'Sam, Sam,' she said simply, embracing me.

'I have lost her Anna,' I said. 'She is gone. I shall not find her equal.'

She drew my head on her shoulder and we wept together. Afterwards, went into Tetty's room and looked at her, lying quietly in the awful solemnity of death. Thought how composed and indifferent the dead seem.

'Nothing can touch her now, Sam,' Anna said.

I nodded, too full to answer. Went over to Tetty and kissed her. Her cheek cold and hard.

'God bless you Tetty,' I said. Knelt down with Anna at the bedside and prayed fervently that God would receive her into his kingdom and that we should be re-united one day. Begged God's forgiveness on my sins and asked for grace that I should hereafter lead a more worthy life.

Bathurst arrived at mid-day full of apology. One look at his solicitous face and I could hold back no longer. I poured my soul out to him, after which he took me by the hand and spoke kindly to me.

'You are not at fault here Sam,' he said. 'Tetty was more ill than we thought. It is certain she could not have survived.'

'But I failed her Richard,' I said. 'I administered the opiate. Without that she might have lived.'

'For a few hours perhaps. But no more. She was dying. Your action but eased her passage. It is more commonly done than you think. I have myself performed the same act when it is certain the patient has no further hope of life.'

'You are merciful Richard but I cannot forget the occasions when I have wished for this. Fate has granted it and I am bound upon a wheel of fire.'

'You censure yourself too harshly my dear sir. Tetty was not the easiest of patients. You would not be human if you did not think sometimes what life would be like without the burden of her care. You should consider that everything you did was for her comfort.'

Towards evening John Hawkesworth arrived. In great consternation over Bromley and blaming himself for Tetty's death. I told him the fault was entirely mine. That I had been too much occupied with my own affairs to see to the matter in person as I should have done. He had performed the office of a friend for which I was grateful. He, poor fellow, in tears. I said I was much concerned where Tetty should be laid to rest. I should like her by me but I could not imagine her at peace in the city. He bid me not to distress myself, Tetty should lie in Bromley churchyard and he would see to the arrangements himself.

'My own dear wife lies there,' he said. 'She will value the company sir I assure you.'

He is a fanciful fellow but good-hearted.

March 31. Two weeks since Tetty died, and one since she was laid in the ground. I think on that day with fear and trembling. The trappings of death are terrible. What anguish when her coffin entered the ground. Taylor says she has gone from this world into a better. Pray God it is so and that I shall one day follow her there. But I fear my sins are many. Thought much lately about Richard's words. He is a good man and wishes to shield me, but it is not true that I did everything for Tetty's comfort. I did not give her love. All else is but 'sounding brass and tinkling cymbal'. She has left me and the world is desolate and empty.

This day Frank came into my house. Bathurst delivered him around two in the afternoon. The boy looks well. My heart smote me on seeing him again. Much moved by Tetty's last words to me. That she should think kindly of him at the end. He asked why everything in the house was draped in black and when I explained said he feared his master would die soon too. I said the colonel was not injured badly and should recover, but he was not to be worried because I was his master now. He said he should like that and, noticing the cat, asked if he might stroke him. I replied that if he gave him an oyster he would be his friend for ever.

But I fear Anna and Frank will not agree. She thinks him responsible for Tetty's death. She will have it that my insistence on adopting Frank, so she put it, broke Tetty's heart.

'She gave up after that Sam. She wanted to die. I saw it in her face. I wonder that you can suffer that child in your home,' she said.

'Whatever you may think Anna,' I replied, 'Tetty, at the end, made me promise to provide a home for him.'

She shook her head.

'Poor Tetty,' she said. 'Who can say what the distress of her illness may have driven her to say.'

Much angered at this and of a mind to tell her of my promise to provide for her also, but reflected that she spoke from grief and love of Tetty, not from malice. In time perhaps Frank may win her over and she may learn to love him. As for me, when I see Frank I see his mother. I see her standing on the quayside waiting to embark. She is cradling her belly. Her last words echo in my head like the last trump.

'Dis is yours Sam,' she says. 'I lie 'bout Savage.'

I stare at her in disbelief, looking for her smile. But she is serious. Why is she saying this?

'You mean the child you are carrying is mine, not Savage's?'

She nods.

'I do not believe you,' I say. 'You are lying.'

'No. I no lie.'

'If it is true why did you not say so before?'

'You mebbe help me if you tink it your fren's child. Not turn me away, like he do.'

I shake my head. Her words do not make sense.

'But why go to Savage at all?' I ask. 'Why did you not come to me?'

'You got wife. You no wan' Ehuoma. Savage wan' me till he see me like dis. Den he tell me go.'

I take hold of her arm, a little roughly. She winces slightly and pulls away.

'Ehuoma,' I say. 'Why should I believe you? How do I know you are not still lying?'

She shrugs her shoulders.

'No reason lie now. I gain nuthin.'

What she says is true. There can be no advantage in lying now. But her next words put all in doubt again.

'I tell you,' she say, 'case one day the chil' need help. 'Case I die.'

We are interrupted by a bell which clangs from the boat. It is time for passengers to board. She has waited till now to tell me this. To tell me I am not childless. I am in turmoil. She has given me the pieces of the puzzle but the pattern is missing. Like all mothers Ehuoma cares only for her baby. She will lie, cheat, anything, to protect him. It occurs to me that I am witnessing the most perfect and the most corrupt love, earth has to offer.

She takes my hand and places it on her belly. Something kicks from inside. I look at Ehuoma. She is smiling now.

8

'You will spoil her Frank. Put her down and finish your meal,' said Betsy. I made a face at Elizabeth and she gurgled with delight. Then I moved her from my lap and placed her on the floor, where she sat and howled. There was an answering whimper from the corner of the room.

'See,' said Betsy putting down her sewing, 'Now she has woken Samuel.'

I curled my hands in front of me like lion paws and made the growling noise Elizabeth loved and the howling stopped. After a few moments so did the whimpering.

'I can do nothing with her these days,' said Betsy. 'You and Doctor Johnson are equally at fault.'

'Master says she makes him laugh which is a more valuable service than all the tribe of physicians put together,' I replied.

'He does not have to deal with her tantrums Frank. She is too easily excited.'

I moved the plate aside and assembled the pieces of a jigsaw in front of me on the table. Elizabeth scrambled up again and surveyed the wooden shapes eagerly. She never tired of the puzzle though she had done it many times before. Since her birth three years before, she had become mistress of Bolt Court, which we moved into soon after master had abandoned the close confinement of Johnson's Court. My master had been fond of her from the first.

'Elizabeth is a pretty name,' he said. 'It was my wife's, as well as Betsy's.'

'Yes, master,' I answered. '

A detail you are already acquainted with. Forgive me Frank.'

He had of late become more tender and affectionate in his notice of me. I remarked on this to Betsy who observed that we were the closest he had to family. And in truth, to see him smiling while Elizabeth played with his coarse stubby fingers, would be sufficient to confound his critics who have since rejoiced in terming him severe. Such would not have been possible while the shrew was alive. She hated me to the last. She had withered away in her final illness like a piece of old gossip.

'Anna and Levet have left me Frank,' he said. 'Such society as I had with them I am not like to have again.'

I tried to imagine a heaven which contained the shrew and Dr.Levet, but my mind misgave me. It would be a strange place indeed which could accommodate them both. But then it was ever my belief that she was destined for a more equatorial zone. For my master, however, death cancelled all offences. It had removed her beyond criticism. He had forgotten the rancour which was in the house, and which had forced Mrs Desmoulins, who had finally managed to move into Bolt Court with her daughter, to shake the dust off her feet and depart after a particularly bitter set to with the shrew. He pitied the dead, like fallen warriors. The great enemy had levelled them, good and bad alike. And the greatest of the fallen was his wife. I would hear him often in his room, weeping as he read his diaries and uttering her name aloud in great anguish. At such time, I feared our continued presence in the house might annoy him. I said as much to Betsy.

'He is troubled in spirit,' I said. 'And he is not well. I am greatly concerned the children will disturb him.'

This was not an idle concern. Samuel was not yet one year old and exceedingly fretful. For the first few weeks of existence he had hovered between life and death, and now seemed exhausted by the effort to survive. Most nights he would cry, a weak penetrating noise, like the wail of a departed spirit. I was fearful lest this should disturb my master. He had ever been a poor sleeper and, since the worsening of his dropsy, even poorer. The fluid on his chest forced him to sleep upright in bed, but the cramps and discomforts this occasioned in his lower limbs made him continually restless. He could not be left alone for fear of injury. Jonas, who sat each night with him, lived in mortal terror that he would capsize the bed, which drew much scorn from my master.

'The fellow's as sleepy as a dormouse. I pay him half a crown a night to snore,' he complained.

Betsy, however, made light of my fears.

'Your master is not ignorant of the ways of children Frank,' she replied. 'Nor is he fond of quiet and solitude. He will welcome the distraction they will bring.'

And so it proved. Master asked continually about them and was not above advising Betsy on their management which, on the whole, she took in good part, though he could have spared his vehemence against wet nursing. A practice she equally abhorred.

'I am glad to hear it Betsy,' he said, when she informed him of it. 'My wet nurse left me more dead than alive. She was a poor wretch, exhausted and ill from nursing her own brood. I would gladly see the practice outlawed by act of parliament.'

But Elizabeth was his favourite. He introduced her with great solemnity to the cat, of which she was at first in awe, by reason of his green eyes and huge mound of fur.

'Shake paws with master Humphrey, Elizabeth,' he said, taking hold of her hand. 'You and he must become better acquainted.'

She let her hand be placed over the paw of the cat, lying docilely in front of the fire, whilst both were shaken together.

'Now you are friends for life, and may stroke him whenever you wish. But you must never pull his tail' he said.

She nodded seriously and bent down to stroke him. From thence arose a close alliance between all three, though, in my master's case, one which was rarely acknowledged openly, at least to visitors. To Mr Burke, or Sir John Hawkins, he would maintain his usual air of being imposed upon, and would not interject if Sir John inveighed, as he was wont to do, against the house being overrun by brats. But as death approached he seemed like some great animal at bay. By day he shambled round the house, his breathing ever more laborious. One morning I found him on the stairs clutching the banister, his head bowed over as if in silent prayer. I went to assist him but he shook me off. 'I will be conquered,' he wheezed. 'I will not capitulate'. By night, as the shadows lengthened, he would glare into them defiantly and call me to him to read from the Bible, and sometimes pray. Fierce, passionate outbursts repenting of his sins and beseeching God for his mercy. I asked Mr. Boswell before his return to Scotland what ailed my master that he should be in such torment.

'He stands in terror of damnation, Frank,' he said.

'What sin has he committed that he should fear that?' I asked.

He shrugged his shoulders in the easy well-bred manner I had become accustomed to.

'Doctor Johnson is the most devout man I know,' he replied. 'But there is one article of faith which is a stumbling block to him. He cannot believe in the forgiveness of God. Not for himself.'

'Then he is in hell already.'

'I fear so Frank.'

I pitied my master in those days more fervently than ever. In former times he would have sought consolation from Mrs Thrale, but that door had been closed by her remarriage. The news had left him desolate. He shut himself up for days on hearing it, refusing food, and raging against her 'perfidy'.

'It is not enough that I should lose Henry Thrale', I heard him say to Sir John Hawkins. 'But this unseemly haste. And to an Italian, dancing master.'

When I relayed this to Betsy she said,

'It is time enough. Mr Thrale has been dead these three years.'

She wrinkled her nose knowingly.

'Doctor Johnson had hopes in that direction himself. It is the green-eyed monster Frank, mark my words.'

That my master should harbour such feelings for a lady, above thirty years his junior seemed scarce credible. I was more inclined to think he missed the services and offices she could perform, which would now be forbidden him. Henry Thrale had been his ally. My master had been appalled by his passing and had never truly recovered his spirits. It had begun the sad decline which left him increasingly prey to the black dog.

'That a man should kill himself by over-eating,' he said to Dr Levet 'It is little better than suicide. That house is closed to me forever. I am afraid of thinking what I have lost.'

This occupied him much. I encountered him often, brooding over letters he had exchanged with the Thrales and shaking his head in sorrow.

'Mrs Thrale could not abide my habits Frank,' he said to me one day as I was clearing his plate away. 'I was always a messy eater. I devoured her roast beef and plum pudden too dirtily for her to endure. Do not fall into the same error with Betsy.'

'No master,' I replied, wondering if he would recall the time his wig became dislodged and fell onto the plate.

For my part, since the advent of my children, I could no longer wait upon him with the same assiduity as before. The current of my life had settled into a different pattern. A fact of which Betsy never tired of reminding me when the need arose.

'You cannot be at Dr Johnson's beck and call Frank. You have a family to consider now.'

So it was that my attendance grew less. I went to bed early and rose early. I took my meals with Betsy and nursed the children. Family life enclosed me till it seemed I had never lived any other. My hot pursuit of Adebayo, the compulsion to discover my parentage, all appeared now like the tale of someone else's life. And of what consequence was it after all? My mother had been a poor black girl in London, and my father an impoverished gentleman. It was scarcely an illustrious history, nor one of which I cared to boast. And the intervening years had seen it all drop away. Betsy had been right. I had my own life now. The past was dead to me. A veil had been drawn over it and I was content that it should be so.

Elizabeth took her time completing the jigsaw. She had divined very early that there was no advantage in finishing it quickly since this only hastened her bed-time. On this occasion she was pretending to have forgotten the picture, a game which pleased her mightily, but which did not amuse my wife.

'Make haste Elizabeth,' I said. 'You have but two minutes to finish the puzzle.'

She pouted at me, then seeing Humphrey wander into the room she got down and scooped him up in her arms. Betsy looked at me enquiringly. 'What do you intend doing now?' her eyes said. As fate would have it I was not required to provide an answer, for at that moment a maid entered the room bearing a note.

'It's for you,' she said, giving it to me. 'A boy delivered it a few moments ago. He said it was urgent.'

I took it from her and opened it. The paper was rough like that used for wrapping things and smelt of meat. But there was no doubting the handwriting. I recognised it instantly as Costano's. I stared at in surprise. I had neither seen nor heard from him for many years. Since my marriage I had written to him occasionally, receiving only terse notes in reply. But to my suggestion that we should meet again he was silent. The message was brief and had evidently been written in a hurry. 'Come to me quickly,' it said. 'My life depends upon it. Say nothing.' At the bottom was his name and an address in Whitechapel.

'What is it Frank?' said Betsy.

'It is from Costano. He is in trouble,' I replied, handing her the note. 'He needs my assistance.'

She ran her eyes quickly over it and when she spoke there was fear in her voice.

'You cannot go to Whitechapel. It is a place for cut-throats and thieves. What business has he there?'

'I don't know. But I must go to him.'

She took me anxiously by the arm.

'The note speaks of danger Frank. It would be foolish to go.'

'He was my friend. I cannot desert him.'

'Then you must not go alone.'

I nodded.

'Very well. I will call on Obadiah tomorrow. He shall accompany me.'

Next morning Betsy let me go with much reluctance. She clung to me tenderly on leaving and bid me return before it was dark. I gave her my promise, kissed the children quickly and departed. I walked briskly to Obadiah's shop in the Strand, rehearsing in my mind what I should say to him. Obadiah was a sober, industrious man, for whom the misdemeanours of Soubise and Famistan were a source of scandal. Such foolishness, he considered, brought disgrace on all blacks. His own case, of course, was one of exceptional good fortune, as Costano had never tired of reminding him. His master had converted to Quakerism late in life, had freed him, and set him up in trade, much to the surprise and envy of his fellow blacks. But he had an eye for business and had succeeded where others would not have done.

'We are like Jews', he said to me on one occasion. 'We must work twice as hard before people trust us.'

With prosperity had come respectability. It had settled on him as naturally as a bird on a perch. He joined a merchant's guild, attended dinners in the city, and talked of acquiring his own coach. He was fast approaching the wealth and status of his old master. What he would think of Costano's present plight I could not but guess. Like the rest of us he had been, at one time, in awe of him. Costano's manner and princely rank were enough to assure that. But he had never understood his bitterness, his hatred of servitude.

'What gain is there in anger?' he would argue. 'It is wasted energy. Men will despise us more. Strive to please your master Costano and improve yourself. That is the way.'

But I trusted to his instincts. He could not but know of the indignities still visited on us. The hostility to our Fraternity had been sufficient notice of that if such were needed. And although the threat had receded, the press gave evidence daily of the continued harrassment of negroes. I did not doubt that he would accompany me once he was aware of the urgency of Costano's note.

Obadiah was engaged in dealing with a footman as I entered his shop. He looked up and smiled.

'What's this Frank,' he said. 'Has your master discovered that he cannot better my fruit?'

I shook my head.

'No. But I have been praising your wares since the death of your antagonist and do not doubt of my success.'

I had forgotten in my haste that he would interpret my visit as the latest salvo in his war with the shrew. My master had been purchasing fruit from Obadiah for years, but shortly before her death the shrew had been involved in a violent altercation with him about the price of a casket of pears, as a consequence of which she had cancelled the account.

'I have come on a more pressing matter Obadiah,' I said. 'If you could spare me a few moments of your time it would oblige me exceedingly.'

He seemed a little surprised by the formality of my address and glanced at my hand, still clutching the note.

'You had better step inside,' he said and directed me to a door at the back of the shop. 'I will be with you shortly.'

The door led into a warehouse in which all manner of vegetables and fruit were stacked. The air was ripe with their scent as they sweated in the windowless interior. Several men, stripped to the waist, despite the chill air, were engaged in making up orders which they gave to runners for delivery. Obadiah boasted that he delivered further than any other grocer in London. I noticed that most of the runners were black. Ten minutes passed before Obadiah joined me, looking well pleased with himself.

'I am favoured by the nobility Frank. That footman belongs to the Duke of Westminster. He is to give a large dinner party and wishes to patronise my establishment,' he said.

'But does he also wish to pay? My master says the nobility are freer with their patronage than their money.'

His brow furrowed slightly.

'We have come to an arrangement,' he said. 'It will create considerable custom for me. That is the way of business nowadays.'

He loosened his necktie and began mopping his forehead with a large kerchief.

'I am pleased to hear it,' I said. 'But I fear my business is of a different nature. I received this note from Costano yesterday.'

I handed it across to him and watched while he read it. He stood still for a few seconds absorbing its contents then snorted briefly and handed it back to me.

'So Costano has got himself into a scrape. I thought better of him than that,' he said.

I looked at him in surprise.

'There is no knowing what has happened,' I replied. 'But he is in need of assistance. That much is evident.'

'You are not thinking of going to him Frank? It would be foolish in the extreme. What would your master think? If Costano requires help why does he not come forward openly and ask for it, like any honest man, instead of skulking in Whitechapel?'

'You know the answer to that Obadiah. Is your memory so short that you have forgotten what we endured at the hands of honest men at the Dog and Partridge some years ago?'

His gaze faltered. I could see that he remembered all too well, and that he was not anxious to be reminded of it.

'That was the fault of those blockheads, Soubise and Famistan,' he said. 'Their prancing and fopperies enraged people. If they had conducted themselves in a seemly manner it would not have occurred.'

'It was an act of malice. It was meant to punish our presumption. You read the letters in *The Morning Post*.'

'But that was years ago. It would not happen today. I do not deny that injustices remain Frank. But there is still the law. If Costano has been the victim of injustice let him seek its protection.'

'The law is one thing, enforcing it another. Costano is in need of our help. He would not write such a note lightly. I mean to go to him. You were his friend once. If that means anything you will accompany me.'

He spread his hands in a gesture of helplessness.

'I am sorry Frank. What you ask is not possible. Look around you. Have you any idea how long it has taken me to build all this up? I cannot.

'Then you can go to the devil!'

He attempted to take my arm, but I brushed him away and left the shop precipitately. My first sensation, once the feeling of anger had subsided, was one of shock. I had not expected Obadiah to be so brutal about Costano. I had always esteemed him. Even Soubise and Famistan, though they might mock him, regarded him as worthy of respect. That he should refuse so obvious a plea for help was inconceivable. He could not be so far beyond common humanity that Costano's fate would be a matter of such indifference. Such was my turmoil that I had reached the outskirts of the city before I could take stock of my situation. I was now on my own; that much was clear. Also clear to me was that I should go to Costano, even though it meant going alone. But I wondered what danger it might be which could threaten his life. He was not a man who would frighten easily, yet there was a reckless vein in his nature which might lead him to court danger that others would avoid. Obadiah had suggested as much and, angry as I was at his coldness, I feared he was right. Some hidden sense warned me that I should be careful in what I promised Costano. There were Betsy and the children to consider. But no sooner had I admitted that thought than my conscience smote me. How could I be so ungenerous after what I had said to Obadiah? Costano would come to my aid. I was sure of it.

As I turned into the lanes at Whitechapel the clock of St Mary's struck two. I fancied it would take me another hour to find the address Costano had given me which would leave at most an hour if I was to arrive back before dark. I entered an inn to ask the way and was met by the hard stares of several drinkers at the bar, one of whom spat on the floor as I passed. It crossed my mind that I should have dressed less conspicuously. But they seemed content to air their scorn in mutterings and laughter, and I was let go by, except for a short heavily-built man talking to the landlord, who took a keen interest in me as I approached. He was wearing a heavily stained coat and breeches and smoking a pipe from which smoke coiled effortlessly to the ceiling. At his feet lay a dog, the image of his master, with a thick neck and short powerful limbs. I fancied that once he took hold he would not let go quickly. The landlord eyed me and asked me what I wanted. I was on the point of asking for directions when a warning note sounded in my head.

'A pint of ale,' I said and threw some coins on the bar.

The landlord drew the pint. I thanked him and took the tankard to the far end of the tap-room. I sat down and caught the gaze of the man at the bar. His face creased slightly in what gave the appearance of being a smile. Then he winked at me and turned his attention again to the landlord. I finished my drink as soon as I could and left. Outside, I stopped for a few moments and breathed deeply. Then I plunged down a lane to the right of the inn. After about a hundred yards I stopped and waited until I was certain no-one was following me. Then I continued, alternately turning left and right to shake any would-be pursuer off. In my anxiety to help Costano it had not occurred to me that others might be seeking him too. I thought again of the man at the bar and told myself I was probably being foolish. But at all events I had tacked and veered so many times that no-one could have possibly kept up with me. I had also, in the process, become completely lost. I looked up at the sky. The sun was sinking lower. In an hour it would be dusk. I got Costano's note out again and looked at the address. 'The Pie Shop, Midden Lane, Whitechapel'. That explained the smell of meat. I remembered him telling me once he had a relative who kept a shop in Whitechapel, though in his pride he had not said of what kind. I looked about me. The lane was empty save for a boy playing with a cat in a doorway. As I approached, the cat sprang out of the child's arms and sped away. He was about to follow suit when I hailed him and held up a shiny coin. The boy stopped and waited for me to come up. He held out his hand expectantly.

'If you can tell me where the pie shop is you can have this,' I said and flourished the coin. He said nothing but raised his arm over my shoulder. I turned round and saw a grimy sign half-way down the lane. In my eagerness to avoid pursuit I had passed by it completely.

'Thank you,' I said.

He snatched the coin from my fingers and raced off. I looked around to make sure I was not observed, then made my way down to a small wooden triangle depicting a pie with steam rising from it, though so obscured that a passer-by could be excused for thinking it a hat on fire. The shop itself was boarded up and looked deserted. I began to think I had been mistaken. Could there be another pie shop? To one side of the doorway was an alley. It was narrow and dark, and smelt bad. Despite the uninviting prospect I determined to try it. I ventured down, picking my way carefully through the litter of discarded wrappings and old food. Half way along I came to a door set into the wall. I tried the handle and it opened noisily. If anyone was within they would be alerted to my presence now. In front of me as I stepped inside was a steep flight of stairs. Abandoning any idea of caution I mounted them calling out Costano's name loudly. As I reached the top, a door opened and a head appeared. To my relief it was Costano's. He recognised me instantly, and coming forward fell upon me with evident pleasure. His face touched mine briefly, and with surprise I noticed that his cheek was moist.

He drew me quickly inside the room. It was bare of any furniture save for a bed and a chair with three legs leaning against a wall. The window, which gave onto the street, was boarded like the rest of the house, the gaps in the boards serving as the only source of light, as well as a means of observing the street. Costano was leaner than I remembered him and his clothes hung about him woefully. There were holes in his breeches through which I could see signs of blood, and his right eye was swollen. He was agitated and nervous in the extreme.

'Thank God you have come. Were you followed?' he said.

'No. I don't think so.'

He went to the window and peered through the boards.

'I thought there was a man observing the house yesterday,' he said.

'A burly fellow with a dog?'

He turned to me in alarm.

'Yes,' he replied. 'Have you seen him.'

'He was at an inn I stopped at nearby.'

'Did he see you?'

'Yes, but he could not have followed me. Who is he?'

'One of my master's lackeys. It was he who gave me this.'

He pointed to his eye.

'I am in great danger Frank. I fear I shall be taken soon.'

I grasped him by the arm.

'Whatever your situation you must not despair. You have friends. Tell me frankly what has happened. I shall do all I can to assist you.'

He motioned me to the bed but would not sit himself, preferring to stay by the window.

'The matter is very simple. My master has sold me,' he said.

'Sold you?' I repeated. 'But he cannot. You are not his to sell.'

'That will not prevent him. He has been persuaded by others that he is within his rights. Besides he stands in need of money.'

'But he has the reputation of great wealth.'

Costano snorted.

'The reputation, yes, but not the wealth. He has squandered it in gambling.'

I looked at him incredulously.

'You have been sold to pay a gambling debt?'

He nodded.

'Yes. He informed me several days ago. He said he was parting company with me to a gentleman with an estate in the Carolinas. I answered him that I did not wish to go, to which he replied that it was of no consequence what I wished, I belonged to him and he could do with me as he desired.'

'But that is monstrous. You are not his property.'

'You and I know that Frank. But there are many who believe as he does. To be truthful, it has been on his mind to dispose of me for a good while. Some years ago I angered him greatly by contradicting him in company when he chanced to utter just such an opinion. Ever since then it needed but the right opportunity. Last month he lost heavily at cards to the Earl of Northampton. The Earl gave him two weeks to settle the account or he would have him declared a bankrupt.'

'So you are to be sacrificed to your master's vanity and avarice?'

'Fortunately he did not consider that I would take matters into my own hands and attempt an escape. It is ever the way with powerful men Frank. They do not think that those beneath them have minds of their own and can use them. As soon as it grew dark I collected my belongings together and climbed out of my bedroom window.'

'And came straight here?'

'No. That would have been the sensible course, but I was uneasy at imposing on my kinsman in such circumstances. I decided instead to hide for some nights on my master's estate till the hue and cry had died down. But I reckoned without the gamekeeper. I believe it to be him who you saw at the inn. His dog sniffed me out in a thicket where I was hiding. I tried to run but the vicious brute sank his teeth into my leg. His owner then laid violent hands on me and was for returning me straightaway to my master. But I persuaded him that if he waited a few days my master would surely publish a reward which he could justly claim as his. Happily the villain was greedy enough to see the wisdom of what I said. I spent the next few days locked in his cottage until I could take advantage of one of his nightly stupors to give him the slip. His dog barked fit to wake the dead as I left, but he slept on. Since then he has been seeking me to gain the reward of which he was cheated.'

I listened carefully to Costano's story. I did not doubt that he had been grievously wronged. With every word he uttered I found my anger rising, and with it, my resolve.

'The situation is clear,' I said. 'You must deliver yourself up to the magistrate and defy your master. He must be shamed before the law for his cruelty. I will help you.'

To my amazement Costano smiled.

'You mean well Frank and I am grateful for your offer. I shall never forget it. But that is not why I called you here. I do not intend to fight my master. He has too much influence, and I have not the money to plead my case in the courts.'

'But you have the law on your side. You must do this, for yourself and for others too. Otherwise you are acquiescing in injustice.'

He was surprised by my passion and I could see him become less certain. I pressed home my argument.

'What alternative do you have?' I continued. 'Do you intend to spend the rest of your life in hiding, never knowing when you might be taken? Is that how the proud Costano wishes to end his days.'

The smile vanished from his face and I could see I had stung him. The scars on his face twitched and he seemed about to vent his irritation on me. But when he spoke his voice was quiet and sad.

'I wish to end my days with my people. That is what I wish,' he said.

'Then do so openly and with pride Costano. For all our sakes.'

He was about to reply when a look of panic crossed his face. The explanation announced itself a moment later. From outside came the unmistakable sound of the door being opened. We listened in complete silence. After a few seconds I heard the sound of someone cautiously climbing the stairs. Costano picked up the chair and together we crept to either side of the door. Our visitor would have us both to reckon with. I put my hand to my brow. I was sweating profusely. We waited for what seemed like ages. Whoever was there was clearly in no hurry. Then slowly the door began to open. It was the shoulder and arm of the man which first became visible, his hand grasping the handle loosely. This was enough for Costano who tensed himself to deliver a crushing blow with the chair. As he did so I stretched out my arm to intercept it and shouted, 'Wait!' Despite the poor light in the room I had glimpsed enough of the man's hand to see it was black. The force of my cry made him start back. I swung the door wide open and found myself staring at Obadiah. He stood there, defenceless, holding a basket of fruit. The ludicrousness of it struck me so powerfully that I could not forebear laughing.

'For God's sake Obadiah You were like to have your head knocked in. Why did you not call out?' I said.

Costano, with evident relief, put the chair down.

'Come in man. Don't just stand there,' he said.

Obadiah entered awkwardly.

'You're a damnable fellow to find Costano.'

He thrust the basket into Costano's hands.

'It's all I could carry,' he said. 'I guessed Frank would not think to bring you anything.'

He looked at me as if this explained his change of heart. But I was not about to challenge him. Whatever the reason I was glad of it. Costano welcomed him, as he had done me, and bade him rest on the bed, for the basket was large and must have cost him many a weary stop. Then he took an apple, and in-between bites recounted his story briefly to Obadiah. When he had finished we resumed our discussion of what his best course of action was.

'I have been trying to persuade him to go to a magistrate and seek the protection of the law,' I said to Obadiah.

'And I have been explaining to Frank that I have neither the money nor the influence to pursue such a course,' returned Costano.

We both looked at Obadiah, as if his late appearance qualified him as an arbiter in the dispute. He did not answer immediately and I was beginning to find his continued silence irritating, when he suddenly cleared his throat.

'Costano is right Frank' he said. 'To challenge his master would take both money and influence. Neither of which he has.'

'You see. Obadiah agrees with me,' said Costano.

'But we do.' Obadiah went on.

He paused, enjoying the momentary stir this change of tack had caused.

'I have the money. And Frank has the influence. Or rather his master, Dr Johnson does. What is there to stop us providing both?'

He paused again and let his extraordinary offer sink in. I could see Costano thinking of an objection. But there was none. Obadiah's solution was perfect. Why had it not occurred to me to apply to my master? He was an inveterate and fearless opponent of slavery. He rejoiced in relating that when called upon to deliver the toast at Oxford University, he had stood up and said 'Here's to the next insurrection of the negroes in the West Indies.' Besides, he was well-versed in the law and knew anyone of any consequence. That he was in poor health and at a low ebb was undeniable, but an enterprise such as this might be the thing to lift his spirits. If Obadiah would pay for lawyers and other expenses I could not see what possible reason Costano could have for rejecting the idea.

But I reckoned without his pride. The prospect of being indebted to either of us for his freedom was a bitter medicine.

'I cannot accept your generosity,' he said to Obadiah. 'Kind as it is. I could never repay you and that would be a burden almost as heavy as that which my enemies wish to lay on me. As for you Frank, your master is ill and may not have many more days to live. He should not have them shortened by concerning himself in my affairs.'

I was about to protest at his stubborness but Obadiah forestalled me.

'Nonsense,' he burst out. 'You cannot deny your friends the right to help you. That is the act of a dolt not a friend.'

Costano was shaken. He had not expected such a violent reaction. He put up a hand to calm Obadiah but there was no halting him.

'Let me tell you something,' he continued. 'Frank would not, but I will. Before he came here, he visited me and asked me to accompany him. I refused. I told myself I could not afford to involve myself, and anyway it was probably your own fault. But the truth was, I was frightened. If harm could befall you, it could any of us. I didn't want to believe that, but it's true. Either all of us are safe or none of us are. That is why I have come. You must fight this Costano. I will not allow you to do otherwise.'

When he had finished we remained silent for a while. Then letting out a great sigh Costano said, 'Very well. I will do as you say.' I put my arm round his shoulder.

'You will not regret doing so,' I said. 'You have many friends.'

'I have not always performed the service of a friend,' he replied.

I looked at him in surprise.

'How can you say that?' I asked.

'I have often thought it was wrong of me to tell you about Adebayo.'

'Nonsense. It was well done and I was grateful to you for it.'

'It amused me to tell you Frank, to see you pursuing a dream. It was no surprise to me that you discovered so little.'

I saw in his eyes that he was telling me the truth. This was the old Costano, hard and disillusioned. But I saw something else too.

'But why?' I asked. 'What harm did I do you?'

'I have always envied you Frank. Your master has been almost a father to you. Your life has seemed so content, so untroubled. I wanted to disturb it a little.'

'And I am glad that you did. You should have no regrets. I do not. It has made me realise where I belong.'

'And I too. I meant what I said about returning. I must go back to Africa. To my father, if he is still alive.'

'But before that there is work to be done,' broke in Obadiah. He jumped up from the bed, all energy to our inertia.

'Are you safe here?' he asked.

'Not for long,' replied Costano. 'I fear my adversary is closing in. Besides my kinsman will be returning shortly. He has obliged me by going into the country. But this shop is his living.'

'Then we must find you somewhere else,' said Obadiah. 'I will send one of my men to you tomorrow. He will guide you to a safer place. Meanwhile Frank and I will busy ourselves on your behalf.

'I will talk to my master as soon as I return,' I said. 'Take heart. All will be well.'

He thanked us fervently and embraced us both with great warmth. Then after promising him our best endeavours, we departed into the gathering dusk. Outside we looked around carefully before emerging from the alley. The lane was deserted. If someone was observing the house he had taken great pains to conceal himself. But the area was so rabbit-warrened with decayed buildings and alleys that concealment would not have been difficult. A fact which struck me forcibly as I considered which direction to take. Fortunately, Obadiah had some knowledge of the area from his trade and could remember the route he had taken there, with the consequence that after half an hour's brisk walking we found ourselves on familiar territory once more. We parted company at Ludgate and I sped on my way up Fleet Street and was soon embracing Betsy.

I forebore to tell her that I had gone alone to Costano's and kept to a plain unvarnished account of what had happened which I delivered whilst consuming the remains of a cold chicken pie. She was both alarmed and relieved by turns in my narrative. When I told her of our plan to vindicate Costano she was generous in her support, though doubtful that my master was in any condition to be of much assistance.

'He has been in great pain all day from the dropsy Frank,' she said. 'The physician has bled him again but it has done him little good. About noon he called for Elizabeth to amuse him and she played a card game with him for an hour. Jonas is there now but has most likely fallen asleep.'

I considered the time. Nine o'clock. I knew my master's habits. He would be sitting in bed resisting the onset of oblivion.

'I shall go to him directly,' I said. 'I fancy my visit will distract him enough from his discomforts.'

I went to my master's room and found things as Betsy said. Jonas was sitting in the chair by the window his chest rising and falling in a sonorous rhythm. My master was upright in bed, a large bandage stained with blood on his left arm. As I approached he opened one eye and surveyed me calmly.

'Ah Frank,' he wheezed. 'You have returned from your errand of mercy.'

I looked at him in bewilderment and he smiled.

'You must not expect women to keep a secret.'

'Did she tell you all master?'

'Never fear Frank. She said you had gone to help a friend. That is all.'

'I am glad of that for his safety depends upon it.'

His eyes met mine and I saw with pleasure the usual gleam.

'Does it indeed? Then you shall tell me all,' he said.

I motioned towards Jonas.

'Do not concern yourself about the dormouse. He will sleep till the last Judgement, or until the next plate of food appears. Whichever is the sooner.'

I related Costano's story to him briefly and saw indignation and despair cross his countenance in turns. When I had finished he said.

'You did right to persuade your friend. The law is plainly on his side. Some years ago I performed a small service for a countryman of yours who went to law against his master. I believe I have the notes about me still.'

He was for leaving his bed to search for them that minute and it was with great difficulty that I restrained him.

'There is not a moment to be lost Frank,' he said. 'Your friend must declare himself to a magistrate immediately and seek the law's protection.'

'Yes master,' I replied.

'But Costano is in great fear that his master will have more influence with the law than he.'

Feeble though he was he attempted to snap his fingers at this.

'Fiddlesticks,' he said. 'I have the ear of the Lord Chief Justice. Let his master go higher than that, if he can.'

I was pleased to see him talk in such style. I thanked him profusely for his kindness and said if he was willing to exert himself on Costano's behalf he was certain to achieve his liberty. He brushed away my compliments after his usual fashion and I left him with a promise to return the following day to copy a plea on Costano's behalf.

The next morning I went early to Obadiah's. He had taken the precaution of closing his shop for the day to avoid any distraction. He greeted me with great energy, and I could not but wonder at the transformation which had occurred since my last visit.

'I have just the place where our friend can escape prying eyes,' he said.

I waited for him to continue, as I knew he would.

'Here,' he said, with evident satisfaction.

My face must have revealed my doubts too plainly, for he went on.

'It is perfect. I have several black workers who sleep here already. He will not be noticed.

'But will your workers not be curious about him. What is to stop them gossiping?'

'I shall say he is a cousin of mine in need of employment.'

There was sense in Obadiah's suggestion but I could not forebear smiling at the thought of Costano under the employ of Obadiah. I wondered whether this had been in his mind too. I readily agreed and he straightaway sent a note to Costano instructing him to wait until nightfall when someone would come. Meanwhile I returned to Bolt Court where my master was already engaged in consulting various documents and books brought into him by Betsy. She frowned at me as I came up the stairs.

'He's been calling for you all morning Frank,' she said. 'I have not seen him in such a fret for a long while. The physician says if he continues like this he may need to be bled again.'

I entered the room. He was propped up in bed and holding a manuscript so close to his face that I fancied he was about to eat it.

'There you are Frank,' he said, as I came in. 'I have been waiting for you. The legal precedents are clear and unmistakable. The Mansfield Declaration of 1772 establishes that the practice of slavery is not legal within England. The Knight versus Wedderburn case of 1778 establishes the same for Scotland. There can be no argument that your friend is not bound to his master. He cannot be sold. If you will sit down I shall dictate a memorandum on his behalf which he can submit to a magistrate.'

I did as I was bid and took dictation from my master for full half an hour, at the end of which I read the memorandum back to him and he pronounced himself satisfied with it. After completing the task my master sank back. It was evident that the effort had cost him dear. He began wheezing heavily and I feared he would suffer badly for it. However, after a short time his breathing subsided and he became calmer. I sat with him for a further half hour, at the end of which he drifted off into a light slumber. I stayed with him until early evening when Jonas arrived and I was able to withdraw. As I came out of the door there was a commotion at the bottom of the stairs. Someone had entered in a great hurry and seemed intent on rousing the entire house. I leant over the stairs and saw Obadiah waving his arms in the hall.

'Costano has been taken, Frank,' he said breathlessly.

I went quickly down to him.

'Three men seized him,' he continued. 'My man saw them leading him away.'

'Did he follow them?'

'He attempted to but they threw Costano into a coach and drove off.'

'This is his master's doing I have no doubt.'

'All is lost Frank.'

I took him into the parlour and bade him take some tea. The poor fellow was quite distraught and inveighed repeatedly against his foolishness in not taking Costano home with him the previous evening. I said I was as much to blame as him in that respect but that nothing was to be gained now by recrimination. We had to think how best we could help Costano.

'But what can we do Frank? We have no idea where he has been taken and even if we did we can hardly remove him by force.'

'That is true, but consider that his master intends to ship him to the plantations. In all likelihood this will be soon.'

'That does not help Costano.'

'But it does us. Unless he is sent to Bristol to be shipped, which would incur more expense, he must be embarked in London. There cannot be many boats bound for the plantations. Set your men to watch the docks and report on the boats and their times of departure. Meanwhile we will lay the matter before a magistrate and form a posse to effect his release.'

Obadiah was heartened by my words though in truth I expressed myself with more confidence than I felt. There was but a slender chance of rescuing Costano now. He would be watched and guarded well and might already be under sail. However, I had often heard my master say that activity breeds hope. There is something in the nature of it which braces the nerves. If Costano could be saved, Obadiah and I were determined it should be done. It was already dusk by the time we set off for Gray's Inn. The hour was against us and we had no time to lose. Obadiah had already sent word to his men to scour the London docks for information. We crossed Fetter Lane into Chancery Lane and were soon at Holborn. Here we were delayed for several minutes by some wagons which had fallen victim to street subsidence and now lay helpless on their sides like wounded beasts. All around people were swarming in an effort to right them, though I saw more than one make off, his hands laden. We extricated ourselves with difficulty from the scrum and entered Gray's Inn Lane. My master had warned me that at this hour the justices would be found in the Coachman's Arms, hard by the courts, and it was there we made our way. He had directed us to Judge Mortlake. 'The fellow's a rogue,' he said. 'But he will serve our turn well enough'. My apprehensions at these words were increased several-fold when I saw him. He was seated with three other gentlemen all of whom had the florid countenance of intemperance, and was still wearing the robes and wig of his office, though stained and torn in numerous places. He looked up when we entered and immediately took us for waiters.

'Another bottle Sambo,' he said. 'Make haste man.'

I ignored this and advanced towards him.

'I have come on a matter which requires your urgent attention sir,' I said.

He was momentarily taken off guard by my mode of address and surveyed me closely.

The rising tide of understanding showed in his eyes and it began to dawn on him that we were not servants of the landlord. Our interruption was not welcome.

'The devil take you. What d'you mean by accosting me here? Can you not see I am with company?'

I apologised for disturbing him but said it was a matter of life and death.

'Indeed it is. If you continue with your nuisance I shall have great pleasure in seeing you hang.'

He belched loudly and waved me away.

'I do not conduct affairs of the realm whilst I am in my cups.'

Obadiah was for withdrawing but I pressed on with my suit. I took out the memorandum which I had about me and thrust it towards the judge. He flinched as if he thought I was drawing a weapon, and seemed on the point of calling for assistance.

'This is from my master Dr Johnson sir,' I said. 'If you read it, it will make our errand clear.'

The mention of my master's name calmed him sufficiently that he took the document.

'Johnson?' he said. 'I thought he was dead. What does the fellow want?'

I quickly explained the purpose of our visit whilst he scanned the paper I had given him. At length he handed it back to me.

'I can do nothing until the negro comes forward. He must swear out a warrant against his master for assault and false imprisonment,' he said.

'But he cannot do that. He has been seized by his master and we do not know where he is being held,' I replied.

'Then there is no evidence. Did you see him taken yourself?'

'No.'

'Just so. I cannot send officers of the law scouring the country for a missing negro.'

'But you could send us.'

He snorted loudly, and his companions who had been looking on in amusement at the proceedings now roused themselves enough to urge his consent.

'Set a nigger to catch a nigger,' said the largest of the three, a corpulent man who had been steadily emptying the bottle while his companion had been distracted. 'It's a good dodge Mortlake'.

The judge paused for a moment and then seemed to tire of the whole business.

'Very well,' he said. 'If it serves to rid me of you. Give me paper and pen someone.'

Obadiah produced both, for we had come prepared, and the judge hurriedly scribbled a note and then signed it.

'This obliges anyone holding the negro Costano to deliver him into your custody or incur the penalty of the law,' he said. 'Now have the goodness to leave.'

We did as we were bid and left the room. I could not help thinking that we had accomplished the easy part of our mission. By far the hardest part still lay before us.

'Let us hope that neither you nor I fall foul of the law,' said Obadiah. 'I would not care to entrust myself to the mercies of Justice Mortlake.'

Half an hour of swift walking brought us back to the Strand and Obadiah's shop where Obadiah lost no time in sending for his runners. While we waited we had a small meal of bread and cold meat washed down with ale. By the time we had finished, most of his men had returned and we retired into the warehouse to learn their news. Obadiah surveyed his runners like a general surveying his troops. For my part I could not but marvel at this private black army which was at his command. There were about twelve men in all, though Obadiah said each man had relatives and friends we could call on if need be. Knowledge of Costano's plight had spread quickly through the community and, despite my anxiety, I could not suppress a sense of pride in what we were about.

Obadiah's runners were eager to give us their intelligence. They had been along the length and breadth of the docks and enquired in alehouses and pie shops about the boats moored alongside. There were only three that were ocean going. The first, a man'o'war bound for Spain, the second a cargo ship trading lace with Holland, and the third, a sloop shipping whisky from the Scottish Highlands. Obadiah looked at me with disappointment.

'None of these can be our object,' he said.

'No,' I replied. 'But we know at least that they cannot transport him immediately. Time may be our ally.'

Obadiah nodded, but like him I could not but feel discouraged by the lack of information. He was about to send his men home when a late runner appeared, breathless and distinctly under the influence of drink. He excused himself to Obadiah by explaining that he had spent some time at The Fox and Goose at Wapping, listening to the sailors. We were, at first, not inclined to believe him, strong liquor being a weakness of his, according to Obadiah, but he brought fresh intelligence about the sloop. She was called the Kicking Nancy and some of her crew had let their tongues wag under the influence of the landlord's ale. It appeared that she was journeying back to the west coast of Scotland with her hold empty except for a single item of cargo. Furthermore she was to rendezvous off the coast of Somerset in two days' time with a vessel bound from Bristol for Jamaica. This news sent a thrill of expectation through the entire company.

'It must be Costano,' I said. 'There can be no doubt of it.'

Obadiah asked the runner when the sloop was set to depart and was informed it would set sail with the morning tide. We had but a few hours to effect Costano's rescue. I said we should muster as many men as we could at the dockside but conceal them so as not to alarm the captain of the Kicking Nancy. Obadiah and I would go on board and present him with the injunction. If he was not willing to release Costano we would summon our men and demand his return. Confronted with such a superior force the captain would have no alternative but to concede.

Emboldened by our plan we set about putting it into effect. Obadiah instructed his runners to assemble as many able-bodied of their kin as they could and join us outside the Fox and Goose at two o'clock in the morning. The alehouse would by then be closed. From there we would proceed under the cover of darkness to the sloop. He impressed on them the need for complete silence. If the alarm was raised the captain would not be above calling out the militia and making good his escape. The men departed and, left to ourselves, Obadiah and I reviewed our situation.

'This enterprise is not without its danger,' said Obadiah. 'In seeking to secure Costano's liberty we may put our own in jeopardy.'

'And those of the men who accompany us,' I replied.

'I have no great confidence in the scrap of paper given us by the judge. What is to stop the captain destroying it?'

'Nothing at all, but at least we can say we are proceeding according to the law. If the captain chooses to put himself outside it then the consequences are on his own head.'

'Some of the men are very angry Frank. They will come armed.'

'Let us hope it does not come to that.'

At about midnight we set off together to Wapping. The air was crisp and chill and we wrapped our greatcoats tightly round us. I observed a bulge in the side pocket of Obadiah's which from time to time he would pat like a friendly dog. We made our way down Ludgate street past St Paul's and along Eastcheap. The streets were empty save for late night revellers and an occasional member of the watch. We walked quickly and kept to the wall, avoiding lighted areas, and after about an hour reached Tower Bridge. There we descended to the river and followed its course past moored ships until we reached Wapping. The path was well trodden but treacherously muddy and we were glad to arrive at the Fox and Goose without mishap shortly before two o'clock. Our band was already assembled and I was amazed, and not a little concerned, to see that its size had swelled four-fold. There must have been above fifty blacks, standing expectantly, some quietly smoking, and most nursing a weapon of some kind. I looked at Obadiah and saw the same anxiety in his face. We could not risk a pitched battle. I spoke to the men and said our purpose was not to cause a disturbance and that if the captain would surrender Costano peacefully we would retire without further ado. To that end Obadiah and I would talk with the captain alone first. There was some murmuring at this, but Obadiah added his voice to mine and we eventually prevailed with them so far that they agreed to follow our commands. We then made our way quietly to within a hundred yards of where the Kicking Nancy was moored. I signalled to the men to remain there until Obadiah and I were aboard. If we did not return within a quarter of an hour they were to board the vessel.

I turned to Obadiah and we walked the remaining distance to the gangplank as silently as we could. Fortunately, the captain had not mounted a lookout, no doubt judging an unladen ship not worth guarding. As for the crew, I had hopes that having consumed a quantity of ale, they would be past caring about anything but the pleasure afforded by their hammocks. We were highly pleased, therefore, to get aboard the Kicking Nancy undetected. Once on board it occurred to me, that having achieved this much, we might hope to ascertain for ourselves the whereabouts of Costano and possibly even effect his release. I whispered to Obadiah and we crept aft towards where we supposed the hold of the vessel was. The boat was old and creaky which made our traverse hazardous. I fancied that the timbers were protesting against our presence. But still no one stirred, and we reached the rear deck with no sign of any of the crew. Set into the deck was a trapdoor with a large metal ring attached to it. I bent down to feel its weight and as I did so heard the snap of a pistol being cocked. We were not, as I had thought, alone. My mouth went suddenly dry and my heart turned to stone. For a moment I was certain I was going to be shot. I waited for the ball to enter my body and the pain to start. Then a voice broke the silence.

'Welcome aboard gentlemen. You have ten seconds to convince me why I should not shoot you.'

We turned round and found ourselves facing two pistols held out at arm's length towards us. The bearer was a smartly dressed man in his middle years, clean shaven except for a carefully trimmed beard around his lip, which gave him the appearance of a Frenchman. I could not suppress my surprise. I had fancied the captain of such a vessel to be a ruffian, not the obvious gentleman who now stood confronting us. He, for his part, seemed equally surprised. He raised his eyebrows in amusement.

'A brace of niggers,' he said. 'What the devil do you mean by boarding my ship?'

'We have come for Costano,' said Obadiah roughly.

The captain's gaze did not falter.

'Speak the King's English man. I'll have no nigger babble here.'

'We have a warrant from Judge Mortlake to secure the person of Costano who has been forcibly taken for transportation to the plantations. We have intelligence he is aboard the Kicking Nancy,' I said.

I thrust the warrant towards the captain.

'Do you now?' said the captain unperturbed.

'You are fine fellows indeed to trespass on my ship and threaten me with the law. We shall see how fine you are after a flogging.'

'We have not come alone,' I said. 'Look on the shore. We shall take Costano by force if we have to.'

The captain leaned over the side of the ship. What he saw brought about a marked change in his demeanour.

'Devil take it. What is the meaning of this?' he said in ill-concealed alarm.

'It is simply a precaution,' I replied.

'Piracy is a hanging offence. You'll swing for this.'

'We intend no harm to your vessel. Let us have Costano and we will depart.'

He lowered his pistols.

'If that is indeed your purpose you have wasted your time. There is no-one of that name aboard my ship. Whatever intelligence you have received is mistaken.'

'I fancy not,' said Obadiah, who had recovered his composure with the change in our fortunes. 'You have a cargo to be transferred to a ship out of Bristol bound for Jamaica.'

The captain gave a grim smile.

'That is true. Though how the devil you came to learn of it I don't know. The governor's wife has a liking for Dutch lace. A quantity arrived yesterday on a ship from Holland. She is impatient to receive a barrel and I have offered to accommodate her. The lady is my sister.'

I looked at Obadiah and saw the same thought enter his mind. The captain's story sounded uncomfortably likely. A Dutch ship was in port. The runners had reported as much. We had never considered the possibility of the cargo being anything other than Costano.

'Nevertheless, we should like to see for ourselves,' I said.

'Very well,' he replied. 'We shall need candles. I will ask the mate to fetch some. You will then have the goodness to leave my ship and take the rest of your army with you.'

'I have a flint and some tapers. They will do well enough,' said Obadiah.

The captain nodded and thrusting his pistols into his waistband bent down to pull on the metal ring. The trap door opened easily and we motioned to him to lead the way. The hold was bigger than I had thought and the descent into the pitch black below seemed like the descent into oblivion. I had the strange conviction that the ladder was too short and that we would fall off the end into a bottomless pit. But before I reached the floor, the darkness was dispelled by a flickering light, held aloft by Obadiah. The air inside the hold was heavy with the smell of tar and hemp. Coils of rope lay everywhere and I fancied that I was inside some huge intestine. The captain pointed to a barrel which lay over the far side. I signalled to Obadiah that I would go and look at it, but even before reaching it I could see that the captain's story was correct. The barrel bore Dutch markings on it and had a label confirming the quantity inside. I prised open the lid and found some of the finest lace I had ever set eyes upon. I could well imagine the impatience of the Governor's wife to receive it. I replaced the lid and gestured my disappointment to Obadiah. Plainly, in our eagerness to believe Costano was aboard we had over-looked a simpler explanation. We started up the ladder again rehearsing what we would tell the men. The captain had already reached the top and I was on the first rung when I heard a low moan coming from an area just beyond the barrel. It was covered with a tarpaulin and concealed, so I thought, yet more coils of rope. I took the light from Obadiah and went over to it. The moan came again, and this time I saw the edge of the tarpaulin move. I bent down quickly and threw it aside. Underneath were indeed coils of rope, but enmeshed in them, his eyes white with fear, was Costano. I spoke to him hurriedly in a whisper and bade him not be afraid for we had come to release him. He seemed to understand but he had been badly beaten and looked as though he had been starved. His legs were shackled in irons fixed into the hull by large bolts. An animal could not have been worse treated. I was about to do what I could to ease his discomfort when I heard the captain behind me.

'Leave him', he said. 'While he is on this ship he is my property and you and your accomplice will do as you are told.'

'Our men have orders to board the ship if we do not return within the quarter. Let Costano go with us and there will be no disturbance.'

I felt a stinging blow to the side of my head and the cold barrel of a pistol thrust in my ear.

'You think to come aboard my ship and threaten me. A jumped-up nigger boy. Listen to me and do exactly what I say. Go back on deck and tell your men to disperse immediately.'

'They won't leave without Costano.'

He pushed the pistol deeper into my ear and cocked it. The sound was like a mill-wheel turning in my head.

'I said listen to me you whoreson nigger. Tell them you made a mistake. He is not aboard. Play me false and I'll blow his brains out and your friend's here too. Once they've gone we'll drop down the river and I'll let you ashore.'

He waved Obadiah over to Costano and drew his other pistol.

'Go on,' he said. 'And no nigger tricks.'

I climbed the ladder, trembling mercilessly, the feel of the cold steel still in my ear. My whole body was in rebellion. It took twice as long to ascend as it had to descend. Every rung seemed like ten. When eventually I reached the top, I sat on the deck and tried to take stock of things. It did not bear thinking about. I had not reckoned on the captain being so desperate. He was plainly prepared to gamble his life rather than give in to our demands. I could not let Costano and Obadiah die. To do so would be to defeat the very purpose of the venture. There was nothing for it but to go along with the captain's orders and hope to obtain Costano's release some other way. At the very least we knew where he was and, as yet, he had not been transported. I stumbled to the gangplank and braced myself for the task ahead. It was by no means certain the men would leave peaceably. I had just begun to address them when the sound of a loud gunshot pierced the air. I turned back to the ship fearful that the captain had carried out his threat to kill Costano. In my mind I was waiting for a second shot. But none came. Meantime the men had decided to take matters into their own hands. They swarmed up the gangplank yelling and waving their arms. I just had time to race ahead of them onto the boat before they came aboard. The noise roused the crew who rushed on deck, some naked and others dressed only in their drawers. When they saw the force of the army bearing down on them they immediately lost heart, some jumping overboard and others retreating below decks and battening down the hatches as well as they could. Within minutes we had taken possession of the ship. I made my way aft as quickly as I could, expecting the worst. As I reached the mouth of the hold a face appeared. It was stricken with pain and tears were coursing down it, but I recognised it as Obadiah's. I helped him out and lay him on the deck. He was bleeding from a wound in his shoulder but otherwise unharmed.

'It is over Frank,' he gasped. 'He's dead.'

'Costano?' I said.

He shook his head.

'No. He is safe.'

'Thank God.'

When he had regained his breath he told me briefly what had happened. He had waited until I had clambered up the ladder before deciding to act. As he informed me later, the captain's arrogance and brutality were sufficient to determine him on his course of action. I had correctly surmised the presence of a pistol concealed in his great coat. He needed but the opportunity to reach it. Costano was still moaning, but under the cover of this he began talking to Obadiah in his African tongue. The captain, who was sufficiently ignorant that he considered Costano to be babbling, attempted to quieten him by kicking him, and in so doing stepped within the coils of rope. At a signal from Obadiah Costano pulled on the ropes. In the same instant Obadiah dropped his taper plunging them into darkness and reached for his pistol. The explosion I had heard had been the sound of three guns firing almost as one.

Costano was overcome with joy when we eventually brought him up. Apart from some bruises he had sustained no real injury and would soon be well again. The captain's body was also brought up and covered with the tarpaulin against the night air. Obadiah's shot had pierced the temple and must have killed him instantly.

'I have not fired that pistol in thirty years,' Obadiah said.

'I am glad to have been in ignorance of that,' replied Costano. Then pointing to the captain's body he said,

'Do you recognise him, Frank?'

I shook my head.

'No. Not at all.'

'Imagine him without the beard and ten or so years younger.'

I did as he bid me. There was something familiar about his face but I could not place it.

'Do you recall the lieutenant of the press gang?' he asked.

I looked again. Now I saw it. I exchanged glances with Obadiah and Costano. The irony of the situation was clear to us all.

The remainder of that night was obscured by sensations of excessive weariness. For most of it I was close to tears. We had been victorious but it still felt like a defeat. Blood had been shed and a man killed. Obadiah and Costano were both unable to walk and were carried home by Obadiah's men, where a physician was called out to attend on them. The body of the captain, wrapped in the tarpaulin was conveyed to Obadiah's warehouse. By this time it was about six in the morning. I took leave of my friends and hurried home. Over the past six hours I had given little thought to Betsy and my family. But suddenly my mind was flooded with tender recollections of them and despite my tiredness I ran the last mile to Bolt Court.

Betsy met me at the door, her face full of apprehension. She had spent the night imagining the worst and came to the door in expectation of hearing it confirmed. I was immediately struck with remorse that I had not sent word earlier of my safety. We embraced and I comforted her as best I could. We went upstairs and whilst breakfasting on ham and bread I related to her the events of the night. She followed my narrative closely and was greatly concerned at the death of the captain.

'His friends and family may bring a prosecution against Obadiah for murder,' she said.

'The weight of evidence is with us,' I replied. 'Obadiah's action was in self-defence and occurred during the enforcement of a warrant signed by a magistrate.'

'I hope it is as you say. But you have made enemies Frank by this night's work.'

I continued to make light of Betsy's fears, but her words echoed what was in my mind too, and I heartily wished we had been able to accomplish our mission without bloodshed. But my own adventure had not been the only event of significance during the night. Betsy informed me that my master's condition had worsened. The dropsy had spread from his breast to his feet and he was in great distress. Dr. Brocklesby had visited him in the early hours and told him plainly that he was past all hopes of recovery. This was cheerless news. Despite his illness I had not believed it possible he should die. Of all men the thought of his passing was most dreadful. I feared even to look upon him, and if it had been possible, would have avoided his chamber.

'You will have to attend on him Frank. It is you he desires to see,' Betsy said at last.

'I know. I shall go to him directly.'

But not until he had enquired several times did I find the courage to go to his room. I found him sitting swathed in bandages, from where the surgeon had tried to relieve the pressure of water, and surrounded with papers. His breathing was like the sound of gravel.

'You must help me with this Frank,' he said.

'I have a deal of stuff to burn.'

'Yes, master. But might the papers not assist Mr. Boswell?'

'They might assist his curiosity, but little else. He knows enough of my life to weary the nation with his narrative, which I have no doubt he will do after my death.'

It was clear from this that my master was in no mood to countenance opposition. The prospect of death appeared to have inspired him with a wish to destroy any memorial of himself. I did as he bade me and picked up a bundle of papers and carried them over to the grate. As I bent down to place them on the fire one fell out.

'What is that Frank?' he said. I picked it up.

'A letter from your mother, master.'

He gestured feebly to me and I took it over to him. I watched whilst he held it against his face. Then he thrust it into my hand.

'Read it to me,' he said.

The letter was brief, not more than two paragraphs long, composed shortly before her death. It was begging her son to visit her one last time before she died. I read it through to him, and when I looked up his head was sunk on his chest.

'I never went. Not till it was too late. Burn it Frank.'

Over the next three hours I laid on the fire some hundreds of letters. Occasionally his eye would light on one, and he would ask me to read it to him, which I did, while he listened in silence. Afterwards, he asked me to pray with him, and I knelt down at his bedside whilst he prayed fervently for God's mercy. He was sufficiently comforted by this to ask me how my friend Costano did. I told him that he was now safe and that his memorandum had been of singular service. He took my hand and, looking earnestly at me, said he was glad for he feared he had not been a good master to me. I demurred strongly and said no man could have wished for a better. He shed tears at this and thanked me, but when I left him he was still stricken by doubts and I knew not how to console him.

'He has some private matter on his mind,' I said to Betsy later. 'He is not at peace and I know not how to assist him.'

'If there is, it is between God and him.'

'But I know he wishes to speak of it. He has been burning letters and papers all day but it is still there.'

'Then there is only one course of action left Frank. You must ask him.'

I slept fitfully that night despite my weariness. I tried to imagine myself doing as Betsy advised but the scenes I painted always ended in disaster. Either he became angry at my impudence or more tormented. There was a boundary between servant and master which I had never transgressed and I feared to do so now. The morning discovered me still undecided what to do and but little rested. I went early into his room and was thrown into immediate confusion by the sight before me. My master lay contorted on the bed like some monstrous foetus, his sheets and nightshirt soaked in blood. By his side lay a pair of scissors. I called for Betsy and went over to him to see what he had done. There was a large gash in his left leg from which blood was still seeping. I tore his sheet and bandaged it as well as I could. When Betsy came in she put her hand to her mouth in horror.

'Whatever has he done Frank?'

'I fear he has been attempting some surgery. He complained yesterday that Cruikshank had not cut deep enough to drain the fluid from his legs. Help me get him back into bed and we shall send to have his wound dressed.'

My master was by now in a state of delirium and muttering incoherently. He scarce seemed to recognise me and thought at first I had come to do him harm. But after a while he was sufficiently in command of his senses to understand what I was about. Once we had lifted him into bed I sent the maid for the surgeon. He came without delay and shook his head when he saw the sorry condition of my master.

'He should not have been left alone Frank,' he said.

'Yes sir. Jonas must have gone early this morning. He cannot have done it long.'

'Thank God for that. Otherwise we should have had a corpse to deal with. How ever did he manage it?'

'There is a pair of scissors in the cabinet. He must have waited till he was alone.'

'The man is amazing. I would not have thought he had sufficient strength for it.'

He dressed my master's wound and left instructions for it to be changed again in two days time. As he leant over him to take his pulse he stirred and opened his eyes.

'Can you minister to a mind diseased?' he asked.

'Therein the patient must minister to himself,' Cruikshank replied. My master smiled and bade him good day. I stayed with him throughout the morning and afternoon as he drifted in and out of consciousness. Towards evening he became agitated and called me over to the bedside. He took me by the hand and whispered to me.

'I have something for you Frank. I should have given it to you long ago but I lacked the courage.'

'What is it master?'

'Unlock the draw of my desk and bring me the contents.'

I did as he asked and saw inside two small volumes which had been heavily written in. I took them over to him.

'These are a narrative of my early life,' he said.

'You wish me to give them to Mr Boswell?'

'No. You alone are to read them, and then you must destroy them.'

I looked at him. He seemed to be waiting for something from me.

'Do they have details about me master?'

'Yes, Frank. Come closer.'

I went to the edge of his bed and he clasped my hand again.

'I have not been honest with you Frank.'

'Master?'

'You once asked me if I knew anything of your parents and I said that I did not.'

'Yes master.'

'That was not true.'

Suddenly I saw in his eyes what he was going to say.

'You knew my mother didn't you?'

'Yes. But I dared not own it. Forgive me Frank.'

I cannot fully describe the tumult which his words set loose in me. I expected to feel anger, but he was beyond any anger I might have felt. A broken old man, forced to humble himself at the last. And in truth I was not surprised. I knew now the question I must ask.'

'Do you know who my father was?'

He did not answer straightaway, and I thought for a moment he had not heard me. Then struggling for breath he said,

'Read the journals Frank. They will tell you all that I know.'

I took his other hand in mine and bade him say no more. He nodded and rested his eyes on mine. A few minutes later he slipped into unconsciousness. My master lingered the rest of that day and most of the next. Once or twice his eyes opened, but he said no more and died about seven o'clock in the evening.

The quay was alive with people and goods. At first I could not make out Costano. Then I saw him standing with his arms crossed, a trunk at his feet. He was leaner than of old and the scars on his cheek were more prominent. I waved to him and received an answering wave back.

'Thank you Frank,' he said as I came up to him. 'I could not have left without bidding you farewell.'

'You are determined then?'

'Yes. England and I have had enough of each other I fancy.'

I nodded.

'You know that Obadiah has said you could live with him,' I said.

'It is kind of him, but I wish to return to my people. We stood silent for a moment. I knew I would never see him again.

'What will you do there?' I said.

'I mean to start a school. Education is the thing Frank. It is the only way to change anything. And what of you? You have money now I hear.'

'My master has been generous to me. But I cannot think what to do. I have been a servant for as long as I can remember.'

'Use it wisely. Make a fresh start.'

'Yes.'

I was pleased to see he had recovered his spirit finally, in spite of everything. The ship's bell sounded and people began to call to him to go aboard. We embraced each other for a long minute, and then he picked up his trunk and walked down the gangplank. The last I saw of him was his head bobbing among the sailors and then he disappeared.

Later that morning as I reached home, Betsy greeted me.

'Obadiah has been taken before a magistrate,' she said. 'He is to be tried for murder.'

9

F rank you have a visitor,' called Betsy. 'Mr. Boswell is here to see you.'
I put down the spade and came into the house. He was standing by the
mantlepiece in his old relaxed pose. My heart smote me to see him
again. He was the same except for his countenance which was much thickened
and florid. I had heard of his drinking exploits from friends in London. He
greeted me warmly and I bade him sit down.

'I have been admiring your wife's ring,' he said.

'Yes sir. It was the Doctor's wedding ring. We had much ado to get it sized
for her.'

'Sam's fingers were never dainty. It looks well enough on her,
nevertheless.'

He brought out some papers from an inside pocket and smoothed them
on his lap. I surmised this was a hint that his visit was not entirely social.

'I am in the area gathering materials,' he said. 'Though God knows I have
enough to fill ten volumes already.'

'Betsy and I are eagerly awaiting it,' I said dutifully.

He looked keenly at me. It was well known that he had been collecting
material now for almost six years.

'So is the whole world Frank. But it is the devil's own job. There can scarce
be a person in the country who has not an anecdote to contribute. Most of
them are worthless thank God, but they must be considered. I intend this to
be a true record of Dr.Johnson. Unlike those scurrilous productions by
Hawkins and Mrs Thrale.'

'I am glad to hear it sir. Betsy and I were dreadfully slandered by Sir John.'

'The man's a buffoon. He could not abide you inheriting Sam's estate.'

Betsy came in with some tea and I offered a cup to him. He looked at it
with thinly disguised distaste.

'No offence Frank, but I could wish for something stronger.'

I spread my hands in apology.

'Never mind. It is too early an hour anyway,' he said. And then as if to explain himself, added, 'I fear the Life will be as long in the publication as the Dictionary. You may have to complete it my dear Frank.'

We laughed heartily at this but I could see from his manner that this was no idle speculation.

'You are after all eminently qualified to do so,' he went on.

'I do not understand you. I cannot be more qualified than you.'

'Did not the Doctor entrust to your keeping two volumes of his early life before he died?'

'Yes, but he gave them me to burn?'

'And did you?'

'Yes.'

He kept his gaze on me.

'That is a great pity Frank. They would have been an invaluable resource.'

'No doubt sir, but the Doctor's instructions were quite clear.'

'Of course. And you did not read them before destroying them?'

'No.'

'I see,' he said, getting out of his chair. 'Well, if you should come across anything, a harassed biographer would be in your debt.'

I showed him to the door and he gripped my hand firmly in departing.

'I sometimes think we were both like sons to him Frank. Do you not think so?'

'He was as good as a father to me in his way.'

'Just so. Farewell, and remember me if you find anything at all. Such things are not without value Frank.'

After he had gone I returned to my garden. I had been glad to see Mr. Boswell, but the naked importunity of his visit reminded me why Betsy and I had retired to Lichfield. The aftermath of my master's passing had been like the wake of a huge ship. There was scarce time to mourn before biographers and writers of memoirs sprang up as if from nowhere. I was besieged night and day as was Betsy. What they could not divine for themselves they were not above inventing. London had been so long our home that we could not immediately imagine living elsewhere but it soon became intolerable. In our innocence we thought the storm of interest would blow over but, after two years, it showed no sign of abating.

Worst of all had been the malice of those who either envied me because of my good fortune, or scorned me because of my association with Obadiah. This last was the most hard to bear. Betsy had been right about the captain. His friends proved inveterate and deadly. They pursued Obadiah with great ferocity and whilst they could not triumph they succeeded so far as to hound the poor fellow to his grave. He came to see me just before he died. The case against him had finally collapsed but he was anything but jubilant.

'They have ruined me Frank,' he said. 'I have nothing.'

'You have your friends. They will not desert you. I have money now. You can start again.'

He wrung my hand pathetically.

'It is too late. I am not a young man. And they will seek me out again. My enemies will not be satisfied until I am dead. If you try and help me they may turn on you too.'

I knew then that he was a broken man. Nothing I could say to him was of any avail and after a while he went away. A week later I heard that he was dead.

'This is my fault,' I said to Betsy. 'I am to blame for his death. I should not have persuaded him to help Costano. He warned me that he might lose everything but I did not listen.'

'Obadiah knew what he was undertaking,' she replied. 'He knew that some things are worth more than life. He came to see you to warn you, not to cast blame. We should heed his warning and leave London.'

Three months later we packed our belongings and left Bolt Court for the last time. A week before we did so Costano's master was taken up for debt and killed himself in the Fleet prison

'What did you tell him,' Betsy asked me later.

'Simply that I could not be of any help to him,' I replied.

She picked up Anne, our youngest, who was playing on the floor.

'He does not look well,' she said.

'He is much concerned about his book. It is all he lives for now.'

'And he is drinking too heavily.'

'That too.'

'Did he believe you?'

'I don't know.'

'Did he offer you money?'

'Yes.'

Betsy said nothing. Since coming to Lichfield we had drawn heavily on my inheritance. We now had three children to provide for and I had been unable to work for the past two years. My old infirmity of the lungs which I had suffered from childhood had seen fit to return. My wife maintained that I had never fully recovered from the bout I underwent after visiting Lizzy in the Fleet. Whatever the case, the congestion was such that I had been obliged to have two operations in the infirmary which had left me no better but significantly poorer.

'You do not owe Dr. Johnson anything,' she said, returning, as I knew she would, to her theme. 'What does his reputation matter now he is dead?'

'It would be a betrayal.'

'You are such an innocent. Where's the harm? The world will learn he wasn't a saint, that is all.'

'I cannot do it Betsy.'

'We need the money Frank.'

It always came down to this. The plain material need. I could not deny that she was right. It was selfish of me to plead my scruples and see my family suffer. If I was unable to help them through the labour of my own hands then I owed them what little I could provide.

'Very well,' I said to her. 'I will consider it.'

I was rewarded by seeing her face brighten immediately.

'Thank you Frank,' she said.

I smiled at her, but felt empty at heart.

At that moment Elizabeth came in from school. She was breathless from running, her little bag of books chasing along at her side like a puppy.

'Mother, father,' she said. 'There's a fair on the common. I've seen them. Can we go? Please say we can.'

Betsy and I looked at each other. The same thought had occurred to both of us. The last fair we had attended was the one at Blackheath just after we were married. The outing had not been a success and the memory of it, though dulled by time, was still painful. Nevertheless, we had not been out with the children for a long time. It was Betsy who spoke first.

'I suppose it would do no harm. It would be a day out for us. What do you think Frank?'

'Yes, my love. We have not had an outing for a long while. It will do us good.'

All that night I lay awake thinking of the fair. I could not explain my agitation. It had all been so long ago. What did any of it matter now? Yet the prospect of the new day filled me with anxiety. Betsy turned and put her hand on my cheek.

'It is not likely to be the same one Frank,' she said. 'I believe this is a travelling fair from the north.'

'I am being foolish, I know. What difference would it make anyway? They are all probably dead.'

Despite this I began the day in a high state of expectancy. The morning was bright and fair. A fine summer's day with only a hint of Autumn. Probably the whole of Lichfield would take advantage of the weather as we planned to do. We roused the children early and got them dressed. Then, after a quick breakfast of porridge we set off. It was a short walk of about two miles to the common, which lay on the outskirts of the town. As we approached, I noticed several handbills posted on trees and gateposts. I studied them as we passed, but could see no mention of Joseph or his companions.

The fair was smaller than the one in Blackheath and I was immediately disappointed. The children, however, were enamoured of everything. To them it was Pandora's box and they were intent on sampling as much as possible. From the beginning I had noticed a large tent at the far side of the fair which was drawing the attention of a goodly crowd. Betsy had seen it too.

'If it is a freak show I do not wish the children to go,' she said. 'It will give them nightmares. You go if you wish. I will take them to see the magicians.'

The children sent up a wail of complaint at this but Betsy remained firm. I debated what to do and decided a quick look simply to see could do no harm.

I walked over to the tent. As soon as I got there I saw that Betsy's fears were not groundless. From the list of grotesques on display inside, this was plainly not a show for the tender minded and I was relieved to see that none of them was familiar to me. I turned to go back when I felt a light touch on my arm. I looked behind me, thinking it was someone in the press of people. A tall, handsome black stood smiling at me. He was expensively dressed and sported a pearl topped cane.

'Hello Frank,' he said. 'It's good to see you.'

I stared in amazement.

'Famistan, in God's name. Is it really you?'

He laughed evidently pleased at the effect he had created.

'What are you doing here?' I asked.

'I'm working,' he said.

I pointed to his coat and knee breeches which were made of silk.

'It looks like it,' I said. 'Those must have cost a small fortune.'

'They are my costume Frank. And by the bye I no longer call myself Famistan. I am Gentleman Jack now. I earn my way with these.'

He held up his fists.

'Dear God. You are a prizefighter?'

He nodded.

'And a famous one too,' he said.

'I thought you had gone back to the Earl's service.'

His smile vanished.

'I am in no man's service, least of all his.'

'He was a brute,' I said. 'It is well you left him.'

'He did me a favour,' replied Famistan, his smile returned. 'If it had not been for him I should never have discovered my talent. I have a bout later today. You should stay and watch.'

'Thank you no. I am here with my family.'

'Yes, of course, Betsy. I heard your master died. You have also become famous. Doctor Johnson's heir, no less.'

There was a suggestion of mockery in the well bred manner but I chose to ignore it. Beneath the showy exterior he was still the same.

'And the others, Costano and Soubise? What became of them?' he asked.

I briefly narrated Costano's story and his face grew sombre as I told him about Obadiah's death.

'There is only one way to get respect in this life Frank,' he said bitterly. 'I broke the jaw of the last man who laughed at me. And what of Soubise?'

'He is dead too. He fell off a horse in India.'

He burst out laughing.

'Poor old Soubise. A clown to the end.'

We talked a little longer but it soon became clear we had exhausted the topics we had in common. I attempted to tell him of my life in Lichfield, but he paid only scant attention. Finally, he took advantage of a distant bell to take his leave.

'I must go and prepare,' he said. 'My public awaits.'

He took my hand on leaving and I thought for a moment he was about to say something else, but he brushed it off, and the last I saw of him he was striding confidently away through the throng. I rejoined my family, and the rest of the day passed uneventfully enough, for which I was glad. We returned home in the evening weary but happy. After dinner I went out into the garden again. The meeting with Famistan was still fresh in my mind. I thought how different our fortunes had been. I wondered what figure I would cut in Mr Boswell's narrative and those of other biographers. It was within my power to play a more significant part if I wished. Was it not a debt owed to me as well as to my children? I went inside and up to the bedroom. Betsy had stepped next door to take some of our left-over dinner to a neighbour who was poorly. I unlocked a cabinet at the side of the bed and took out two small well-thumbed volumes. Then I took them out into the garden again. It was growing dark but there was just enough light for me to read. If I surrendered them to Mr.Boswell our financial difficulties would be eased. But the world would not thank me for it. I knew enough from my master to know that people do not wish their heroes to have feet of clay. People would say I was bitter and envious. That I was not content with being his heir and wished to traduce his memory. Had not Betsy and I left London to escape all that?

I went to the bottom of the garden and gathered some twigs together. Then I struck a flint and the whole caught fire. When it was ablaze I took each of the volumes in turn and fed the pages one by one onto the fire. As the smoke ascended into the sky I finally said goodbye to my master and to my mother too. I finally felt that I knew her and her fierce love for me. Who my real father was no longer mattered. My master had cared enough for her to take me in and had been all the parent I needed. I watched while the last of the paper vanished and said for the final time the word 'father'.

Later, as I came back into the house, I found Betsy, returned from our neighbours.

'What have you been burning Frank?' she asked.

'The past,' I replied.

HISTORICAL NOTE: with the exception of Famistan, Costano and Obadiah, who are fictional, the major characters in Sam's Boy are historical. Of the lesser characters, Adebayo and his black troupe, the servants in the Thrale household, Ehuomo and Miss Sophy Gordon are also fictional.

Printed in Poland
by Amazon Fulfillment
Poland Sp. z o.o., Wrocław

51960041R00146